THE YEAR OF THE LION

The Year
of The Lion

A NOVEL BY

Gerald Hanley

THE REPRINT SOCIETY
LONDON

FIRST PUBLISHED 1953
THIS EDITION PUBLISHED BY THE REPRINT SOCIETY LTD.
BY ARRANGEMENT WITH WM. COLLINS SONS & CO. LTD.
1955

The Year of the Lion
is a novel, and all the characters
and scenes that appear in it are
entirely fictitious

PRINTED IN GREAT BRITAIN BY
WILLIAM CLOWES AND SONS, LIMITED, LONDON AND BECCLES

Chapter I

THE store was there, just as Major Fawn-Cochley had said in his letter. "A long grey stone thing at the end of the Guzu main thoroughfare." What a curiously old-fashioned expression to use, thought Jervis, holding Major Fawn-Cochley's letter in his hand. He was a tall, fair youth with pale blue eyes, and seeing his uncertainty, his obvious newness, Abdul Hafiz came to the doorway of the store and said: "Sahib, are you the new gentleman going to Major Fawn-Cochley's farm?"

"That's right," Jervis said. "How do you know that?"

The Indian examined the Englishman's face, instinctively feeling for the meaning of those words, savouring their sound and finding no resentment there; he smiled and said:

"I guessed, sir. I have instructions from the Major Sahib about supplies he wants you to take with you."

"Oh, good. So have I. I have a six-page letter here full of instructions from him too. Between us we ought to be able to work out exactly what he wants, eh?"

The Indian's face was grave again. How long would this pleasant young man stay like this, keep the frank kindliness? He had seen it before in young Englishmen taking people as they found them in their first months abroad, until the advice of their elders and a deep-rooted Western dislike of un-Western things, almost as great as Eastern suspicion, would fuse into the first hardness of eye when one day he spoke to an Indian angrily. Some survived and kept their good manners and their kindliness, but not many, and they were careful.

They went into the store, and it was cool after the glare

and the long journey. Jervis, his senses still fresh in the new land, smelt Indian spices cooking. He sniffed and said: "That's curry, isn't it?" Abdul smiled and nodded. "Would you like a glass of beer, sir?"

"I'd give anything for one," said Jervis. Oh, such enthusiasm, such freshness of the fair young Englishman undestroyed. Abdul, his back to Jervis, as he reached up to a shelf for a bottle of beer, rolled his eyes, striving not to like this young stranger who in a few months would be curt with him.

Jervis heard a deep bubbling sound from the corner of the store, and turning, he saw an old bearded man wearing a white turban lying stretched on his side on a string bed. The *hukka* bubbled again as the old man sucked at the cane tube and a puff of blue smoke shot from the corner of his mouth. While Jervis stared at this picture of withered bliss, drinking in everything with his twenty-year-old eyes, Abdul kept one eye on him, a half smile of affection on his lips while his hands opened the bottle of beer.

"That's my father, sir," he told Jervis. "And that's a *hukka* he's smoking."

"That's it," said Jervis, "a *hukka*. I remember the word from books I've read. But I thought they had long flexible tubes instead of just that sort of short cane pipe."

"Ah, yes. In Lucknow in India you'll find those, but usually they're like *that*." Against his will, Abdul was becoming friendly. "Enough," he said to himself. "It must be business only from now on." There were so many unsuspected snares, so many delicate webs.

The beer foamed in the long German glass. He could tell by the way Jervis looked at him that the young man was wondering if he, Abdul, would not drink with him. He was about to explain but cut himself short, saying instead: "I'll just get out Major Fawn-Cochley's instructions, sir. Oh, and the car has come too. It's waiting at the Buffalo Hotel. The Major's driver, Wangi, is with the car and is coming in for instructions at two o'clock, but I can send for him if you like, sir."

"No, it's all right," Jervis told him, happy with his beer. "Let him come at two. How many miles is it to the farm?"

"Seventy-five, sir."

"Seventy-five. Good lord." Seventy, a hundred, two hundred miles, still seemed a long way to him. The three-hundred-mile journey he had covered in the last two days was still a great experience, and yet he had only, he knew, covered a few paces in Africa's vastness. England was a toy country growing dim already.

"I admire the English. I respect them. But I can't like them," Abdul was thinking. "I can't like them after they have eaten the air of India or Africa for a year. After that they become Brahmins. Angry Brahmins." He sighed as he sorted the papers in search of Major Fawn-Cochley's letter.

Abdul was thirty-seven. He was tall and broad, clean shaven, with a Moslem face, that lean, hollow Perso-Arabic face which had spread itself across India and now was filtering into East Africa. It was more a Moslem look than a face, this dark-eyed, hollow solemnness which Islam has stamped on to so many of its children's faces. His skin was darker than ivory and he had flat, black, secret eyes which could smile when he was touched. He had an air of regret, too, as though, like his favourite poet, Ghalib, he thought: "Oh, God, it is not the sins I have committed that I regret, but those which I have had no opportunity to commit." He wore a long, thin muslin *kurta* which hung outside of his khaki trousers. The neck of the *kurta* was fastened with four gold studs given him by his uncle in celebration of the last *Id* festival.

Jervis studied the languorous old man lying on the *charpai*.

Soothed by the long steady bubbling of the *hukka*, Jervis sipped his beer. At last he felt at home in this strange Africa. He watched Abdul covertly, admiring his long lean fingers, his straight, slightly hooked nose and his sympathetic gravity.

"Have you been long here?" he asked.

"Oh, yes, sir. My father came as a soldier in the old days and stayed here when his service was done. He became a trader in Abyssinia and then he came here."

"Were you born here?"

"No. In India, sir. But now I have made my home here." There was more he wanted to say but he thought no, a word too much could be like the devil's finger meddling; *Shaitan ki ungli*. He felt at home with this good-looking blond Englishman. Ah, how much that was not of race separated all men. He found the letter. "Here it is, sir. Shall I start packing the things?"

"I'll get my letter out too. There's ammunition, a lamp, oil, rice, a sack of sulphur and a whole crowd of things. Oh, and he said I've got to get proper shorts. Aren't these I've got on all right?" He stood up, embarrassing Abdul, who had to examine him and give judgment, something no Englishman had ever asked him to do in his life. He hoped that Jervis would not one day regret this and bear him anger for it.

The shorts were brownish-khaki, narrow in the leg, and not at all like those as worn by Englishmen in East Africa.

"They're not quite the same, sir, as the usual kind," he said gravely. "If you have them wider in the leg they're cooler. Most new Englishmen arrive wearing the kind you've got."

"I thought they weren't quite the thing myself," Jervis told him, both of them slowly caught up in Abdul's thoughtful, nodding solemnity. "Now what do you say I should do about it?"

"I'll arrange for you to be measured, sir." He called out an order in Urdu and a small, clean Indian boy came running.

"Bring the tailor," Abdul told him, and the boy ran off. Jervis sat down again. "It's very kind, all this trouble you're taking over me," he said.

"Oh, no, sir. It is my job. I am here to arrange things." They laughed. This was the first Indian Jervis had ever spoken to and his interest was awakening. This gentle and understanding will to help was drawing him, relaxing him after the long bewildering journey during which he had seen brown women wearing leaf skirts and nothing else, a sight that had stirred him and worried him. He had seen reddish painted tribesmen carrying spears behind humped cattle and smelled their sharp flesh-scent in the bright heat of yesterday's journey.

"Major Fawn-Cochley has dealt with this store for many years, sir," said Abdul. "He is very particular about everything."

"Is he?"

"You don't know him at all, sir?"

"No. I'm a pupil. I've come to learn farming from him."

"I hope you will be very happy, sir."

Particular was not the word for Major Fawn-Cochley, if the letter he had written Jervis was anything to judge from. "Do not engage any African servant. I have made all arrangements here. See that Wangi, my driver, does not drive at more than twenty-five miles an hour. If yourself can drive a car, kindly refrain from doing so as far as my car is concerned until I have weighed up your driving abilities. There is a rifle in the car with Wangi which I have told him to leave with Abdul Hafiz until the return journey. Do not use it unless you meet rhino or lion—I cannot bear indiscriminate slaughter of game for pleasure." And so on. This letter had been awaiting him at the Indian garage when the truck carrying him and his luggage arrived at Guyu. After reading it he had pictured the Major as an old white-haired and irascible person. "They get cracked living alone, you know," someone had told him on the ship. "The loneliness brings out all the ego after a while." The letter had depressed him. He wondered miserably how he would get on with the writer of such a letter. But this was Africa, the land he had longed to see, and his senses, sharpening every moment, carried him quickly away from his foreboding.

While he poured out the rest of the beer a big heavy man came into the store. "Hey," he cried to Abdul. "What about that damned tin of cattle dip you said you'd send out for me? A damn fine thing, I must say. There I am out in the blue with no dip for the cattle, and here are you sitting comfortably on your bum after promising you'd send it." He mopped his sweating face irritably, his eyes on Abdul.

"I'm sorry, Captain Wills. I tried my best but there was no transport going out your way at all. I have it here." Abdul was flustered and Jervis looked away until the big man said: "Hallo, who are you? New face, isn't it?"

"My name's Jervis."

"Oh, I know who you are. You're the feller that's going to sweat your guts out for the Prawn-Cocktail, aren't you?"

"Prawn-Cocktail? Oh, is that a nickname?"

"That's right, Prawn-Cocktail. Mad as a bloody hatter. Doesn't like me. Doesn't like anyone. I tell you he's mad. Stay away. Don't go. He's had about a dozen pupils in the last ten years, and they come in here one after the other after a few months, nearly as mad as the Prawn-Cocktail himself. None of them stay long. Can't stand it, I tell you.

He's mad and he's as mean as a starving Jew in Scotland.
You wait and see." Then he turned to Abdul and in that
different voice, that coldly neutral and hectoring key, said:
"And how's Gandhi these days?" Abdul smiled and said:
"I haven't heard lately, sir."

"*He's* mad too," said Captain Wills. "Mad as a bloody
hatter, I tell you. Well, put the dip in my car." He switched
to the other voice and said to Jervis: "Well, the best of luck
to you. Take a strait-jacket out with you for the Prawn-
Cocktail." Then he turned on his heel and left the store.

So it was true. People in this country were said to be
mad, and the big man walking out of the door seemed mad
enough.

"Is Captain Wills living near here?" Jervis asked Abdul,
in an effort to forget the Englishman's attitude to the Indian.
Abdul smiled again and said: "No, he lives a long way up
the mountain. He is a very kind man, Captain Wills. He
makes jokes always."

"Does he always ask you how Gandhi is?"

"Yes, always, sir."

Jervis did not know whether to laugh or not, for he felt
that Gandhi was in some way a holy man for Indians.
Abdul, his sensitive eyes reading the Englishman's face,
said: "He does not mean harm, sir. It is only his fun."

"Do you think a great deal of Gandhi?" Jervis asked as
casually as he could.

"Oh, yes, sir. But he is mad, as Captain Wills says. I want
industrialisation in India. I believe in the West, but
Gandhiji doesn't." There was so very, very much to explain.
He sighed again.

"What's the *ji* for? What does Gandhi*ji* mean?"

"It's respect, sir. *Ji* at the end of a name means respect or
affection."

"I see."

"Have you ever been to India, sir?"

"No, never."

"Of course not," thought Abdul. He drove away the liking which this young man was forcing on him. He could sit here all day in his pleasant easy-going way and he, Abdul, would like it, but it had to stop.

"I've got the list ready, sir. It's twelve o'clock now and you've got two hours before the Major's driver comes with the car. You can get lunch at the Buffalo Hotel. When you get back I'll have everything ready for you, sir. Would you like to be measured for the shorts now, or after your lunch?"

"Can't I just stay here?" said Jervis. "I don't need any lunch, really. I like sitting in your store. It's very peaceful, isn't it?" He drank some more beer. Abdul was perplexed. Yes, it *was* peaceful, but it was hardly the place to sit if the young man could have lunch with his own kind at the Buffalo, Guyu's only hotel.

"Can I get you something, then, sir?" suggested Abdul.

"How do you mean?"

"Food. I could get you some sandwiches sent over from the hotel." This Englishman was going to break all the rules if he was not guided.

"That's kind of you, but as a matter of fact I'd rather like some of that curry that I can smell cooking in there." The store was rich now with the hot, golden and reddish scents of Indian cooking, the *masalas* and the chillies married in the most appetising odours which seemed to cling to the palate. Jervis smiled and Abdul looked at him thoughtfully. He had never thought of an Englishman as a guest and he brushed the thought from him at once. It was impossible. It would cause nothing but trouble for both of them, and yet what was he to do? The ease with which Jervis took everything was like a weapon. He felt he would like to say:

"Listen, sir. You can't talk to me like this. English people do not approve of Indians in this country and you'll only get into trouble if you forget it. Also, you'll make it awkward for me, because the English people will say I'm getting above myself and there'll be trouble. You should just *use* me. I keep a store and I know my place. No other Englishman wants to eat my curry or chat with me and I'm not used to it and don't know what to do about it." Instead, he said:

"I don't know what Major Fawn-Cochley will say if he hears you've been eating curry, my curry, sir." He could hear himself simpering and he hated himself and all Englishmen for a moment.

"To hell with what the Major thinks," said Jervis brusquely, and then, seeing the swift, dark flutter of the Indian's eyes, he smiled and said: "I don't want to worry you, you know, and you mustn't worry so much about people and what they think. I know all about it. I've heard about it. But whoever's cooking that curry is a wonderful cook, and if you can't give me a little of it it's quite all right." Miserably, he knew that Abdul could be wounded by misunderstanding what he had said. The first racial depression fell across him, the sense of despair, the mess, the dark pitfalls of empire and skin and untruth. Abdul's flat eyes watched him while he sipped the beer and he broke the reverie which his thoughts had woven. He almost laughed aloud.

"I'll get you some *samosas*, sir, some curry and some *chapattis*. Do you know what a *chapatti* is?"

"No."

"I'll show you. But, sir, there is one thing. I don't think you should eat it here. If anyone sees you—I mean——"

"It'll make things awkward, I know, I know." Jervis sighed. He felt angry, wanting to call the whole thing off.

It was all so sad and tedious and irritating, but no, he would go on until the end.

"Where'll I have it then?" He looked so young and eager when he said that, and Abdul was touched so that he almost took his hand and pressed it, thinking: "Oh, sir, what a cruel, stupid world it is and how cowardly we make it."

"There's a little room at the back here where I keep the ammunition supplies, sir. You can have it there. And would you like a bottle of beer with it?"

"Definitely." Jervis laughed and Abdul laughed too, only a little apprehensive, a little thoughtful of the snares which this young man threw about him right and left. "I was a fool to think he did not know," Abdul thought as he went to see his wife. "He knows all about it and yet does not care. And can this last, this goodness which makes me like him against my will?" He was at once angry and pleased, worried and puzzled.

Jervis wondered what a *samosa* could be. He liked the name and was saying it aloud when Abdul returned.

"What's a *samosa*?" he asked him before Abdul could speak.

"It's a kind of—it's a——" Abdul was in difficulties.

"Is it a kind of vegetable?"

"No, sir, it's like a small pie with thin crust all round, and it has meat in it and chillies and potatoes and peas."

"God, that's wonderful." Jervis got quickly to his feet. "You've made my mouth water now. Lead me to the *samosa*." He watched Abdul's nervous smile, his uncertainty, and was sorry for him and for the whole bloody world of Indians and Englishmen wound up in a trap of misunderstandings, hate, respect, love, rage, humiliation.

"I'm going wrong, I know I am," thought Jervis as he followed Abdul. "All this will lead me wrong because I like it. I should stop now and withdraw, but I won't. I like this chap and I like curry and to hell with the other sahibs."

Abdul left him sitting before a small table on which was a small bowl of meat in red curry gravy, a saucer with sliced tomato and onion, both sprinkled with small fresh green rings of cut chillies, and on another plate were three *samosas* and two hot *chapattis*. "Those, sir, are the *chapattis*," Abdul explained before he left the room. "You can use them to eat with or you can use the knife and fork."

"No, I'll use the *chapattis*," said Jervis, looking up at the tall Indian who stood near his chair. "How do they work?"

"You tear a piece off, sir, and scoop the food up with it. I'm afraid you won't like it." "He thinks I think it's primitive," thought Jervis.

"If you can eat with the *chapatti*, sir, you'll want to wash your hands, won't you?" Abdul suggested in a soft voice, a voice which he could hear was careful and right, containing no hint, no instruction concerning custom and cleanliness.

"Oh, yes," said Jervis, awkward for a moment (and for the first time, noted Abdul, thrown off his balance). "I should have known," added Jervis, his honesty recovering him in Abdul's amused eyes.

A boy brought a brass basin and a white metal ewer shaped like a lidless teapot. He washed his hands and dried them, and then Abdul left him, saying: "I'll bring you some more *chapattis*, sir, and some fruit." He felt happy serving Jervis, yet mistrusted this happiness which came when you served a friend in your house.

"By God, they live well," Jervis was thinking, as he popped a piece of *chapatti* and meat into his mouth. "Everything seems to come so easy to them, and the food, God, it's delicious." The chillies, cooked cunningly and expertly into the *ghee* by Abdul's wife, excited his appetite. It tasted like the best food in the world after years of cauliflower, roast meat, potatoes, bread, soup, kipper. In his youth and his hungry pleasure, Jervis dismissed the world he had left in England. "Marvellous," he mumbled as he chewed the *samosa*, "absolutely marvellous." Watching him through a crack in the plank wall, Abdul laughed softly and affectionately. It was the first time he had made an Englishman happy, and it was strange. It was very worrying too.

Abdul brought him a large mango. It was firm and green and gave off a sharp and aromatic scent.

"Do you know what Englishmen say about the mango, sir?" said Abdul.

"No. Tell me."

"They say you should eat it in the bath."

"Is that because it's so juicy?"

"Yes, sir." Because eating his first mango was a serious matter, Jervis forgot to laugh at Abdul's story. He cut open the green fruit and saw the soft, orange plush of its pulp, smelled its fresh odour of paraffin and flowers. When he had eaten it, his hands were covered with yellow juice, and his mouth and chin were stained.

"I see what the Englishmen mean," he told Abdul in that curious grave way he had when he said these dry things, and Abdul laughed, almost too hard, he reminded himself quickly: "Oh, God, what is the matter with me?"

"Now, I've got to get him on to the purchases for the Major Sahib," Abdul was thinking. "I've got to be firm with him, yet polite. He'll never do a thing unless I make him. The Major Sahib is not going to like him at all more the way he goes on. So casual, but so determined, too."

"You've been most kind to me, you know," Jervis told him while he washed his hands.

"Oh, no, sir. I'm glad you enjoy Indian food."

"But you have, you know," Jervis said dreamily as he dried his hands.

"Look sir, what about all the stores for the Major Sahib? Should we not do them now? First, I'll get the ammunition." Abdul opened a heavy iron chest and began taking from it yellow cardboard packets. "It's mostly softnose, sir. The Major says he has plenty of solids—as it is."

"Softnose? What's softnose?"

"It's the opposite to solid, sir. It's a bullet with a lead nose."

"Oh, I see." He picked up one of the packets and read "Mauser, 7·9 softnose. Cellulose." "How much is this stuff?" he asked.

"That calibre right down to ·256 is forty-five shillings a hundred rounds."

"H'mm. And how much is this stuff? It's a bit bigger." He showed Abdul a packet of ·318.

"That's seventy-five shillings a hundred, sir. It's special ammunition."

"Does Major Fawn-Cochley do a lot of shooting?"

"Oh, a lot, sir. He kills lions and a lot of buffalo and rhino." During his twelve years in Africa Abdul had not seen one of these wild beasts, and yet twenty miles from his store they abounded. He had no desire to see them, regarding them as relics of a savage age of which the world had no need. He liked comfort and peace and certainty.

"Are there lots of lions out at the Major's place?"

"Lots, sir. It's one of their favourite hunting-grounds."

"Oh, dear, what a pity." Jervis lit a cigarette and squinted at Abdul through the smoke.

"Don't you like shooting, sir?" He had never known an Englishman who did not like shooting.

"Not particularly, though I won't mind having a go. I don't know if I could shoot a lion, though." He grew thoughtful and was about to sit down again when Abdul moved smoothly and quickly to the door leading to the store and said: "This way, sir." It worked. Jervis seemed to be absorbed by the varied goods which were for sale there. Cooking pots, *karais*, mattocks, veterinary drugs of all kinds, fishing tackle, beer, whisky, wine, cigarettes, tinned and bottled foods, writing materials, even tinned hops awaiting a shy African buyer. Abdul sat down behind the counter and fretted. Then, when Jervis had wandered and gazed his fill, he came to Abdul and hurried him through the lists of the Major's requirements without consulting a single note. It was all done in five minutes and Jervis said: "You see, you've been worrying yourself for hours about this, and now it's all done in five minutes. A stitch in time cannot take the camel through the eye of the needle," he added thoughtfully.

"No, sir," said Abdul as he packed the goods for the Major. "But the Major is terribly particular and I always take extra care."

"You never forget to send *his* cattle dip, do you?"

"Oh, no, sir."

"Tell me something. Is it true that he's mad? Is it true what Captain Whatdyoucallit said to-day about all his pupils leaving him?"

Abdul thought for a moment and then said: "Most of his pupils wanted other work, sir. Are you going to buy a farm, too, sir, when you've finished being a pupil?"

"Me? Oh, no. I haven't got any money, you see. I'll get a job on somebody's farm when my training is over. But it's strange, isn't it, that the Major never keeps his pupils in a country like this?"

Abdul stroked his nose until he found another answer. "The Major," he said, "is a very strong-willed man, sir, and he has his own ideas." He was disappointed that Jervis had no money. It seemed wrong. He was shocked.

"Strong-willed?"

"Yes, sir." He could see that blank look appearing again on Jervis's face, the look which preceded one of his strange remarks.

"You don't mean that he has a bad temper, do you?" By Abdul's silence and lowered eyes he knew that the answer was yes.

"Ah, well," he told Abdul, "I suppose it's the climate," and Abdul changed the subject by reminding him that the car would be here any time now.

The driver gave Jervis an exaggerated salute and then swayed slightly back and forth, his small dark eyes peering into Jervis's. He was a short, squat man with dark reddish brown skin. "He is an ex-soldier, sir," said Abdul in a low voice as though describing the cause of an illness. The African leered at the Indian, despising him.

"He's drunk too," said Jervis as he gazed back into the driver's eyes, which were striving to focus properly on him.

"*Jambo, sana, Bwana M'Kubwa,*" mumbled the driver. He then gave up the struggle with his eyes and let them wander about aimlessly while he tried to stand to attention. "What does all that mean?" Jervis asked Abdul. "He is greeting you as the Big Master, sir," Abdul replied.

"I see. I suppose he thinks that will please me." He thought: "By the sound of the Major I might take to drink myself in the end."

"Will you tell him," he asked Abdul, "that I'm going to drive?" When this was conveyed to the driver he appeared to be stunned.

"But the Bwana Major," he said to Abdul. "The Bwana Major will be very angry with me. He told me not to let the Bwana drive."

"*Bwana na sema wewe na lewa,*" said Abdul in his own form of Ki'Swahili, and at his words the driver became indignant, for while he looked up to the white man, he looked down on the Indians. Some of them cheated so much when they sold grain and rice to the Africans, men said. Denying Abdul's accusation, the driver said: "I am not drunk. I am a Klistian like the Bwana."

"He says that he's a Christian and is not drunk, sir," said Abdul.

"Oh, good," said Jervis. "What is his name?"

"Wangi, sir."

"Well, could you tell Wangi that it doesn't matter if he's a Christian and is drunk or not, but *I'm* driving."

When Wangi was told this and coupled it with the Bwana's determined mouth and eyes, he smiled sadly and said: "As the Bwana says. I cannot refuse."

"Good," Jervis told him.

"The word for good is '*M'zuri*'," said Abdul.

"*M'zuri*, Wangi," Jervis said to the African, using Ki'-Swahili for the first time, and Wangi's smile of appreciation dissolved the slight tension that had grown between them.

While the Box Body Model T Ford was being loaded with stores and Wangi could be heard shouting unnecessarily at Abdul's African assistant, Abdul gave Jervis the Major's rifle which he had held for him. Jervis had never used a rifle in his life and he was attracted by its gleaming dark blue lines and its slender walnut stock and the cunningly-made butt. It had a sling of soft animal hide on which the yellowish hairs still sprouted in patches, and he slung the rifle across his right shoulder, conscious of a hint of change in his character, aware that already he wished to use the rifle, to kill with it. He experienced a pleasure, almost a pride, as he felt the weight of the rifle and the grip of the sling in his right hand. "Africa," he was thinking, "Africa, Africa, Africa," repeating it until it was a word of magic again as it had been in boyhood such a few years before. Without the rifle it had not been quite Africa.

They drove through ravines laced with thick jungle, and the roar of water among the trees, and the flooding yellow sunlight began to break the last links with home. Africa was becoming before his eyes a stirring vastness, a smell of sap and sun-warmed black flesh; Africa, Africa, Africa. He forgot Major Fawn-Cochley and his own apprehension, and when they left the ravines and entered a great rolling grassy plain he heard a soft, uneven thundering, and there on his left a herd of animals was galloping, moving like a brown, tossing, glinting wave towards the horizon where blue hills flowed away into the sun-mist.

"What's that?" he called to Wangi. "What are they?" He pointed with his left hand to the herd of game. Wangi, sitting among the stores in the back of the car, said: "*Nyama, Bwana,*" "Meat," for basically that was what it all was to men. Jervis nodded, pleased, repeating the name to himself, thinking he had seen a herd of large antelope called *nyama.* The eland, led by a big bull, had now disappeared in their own yellow dust-cloud which hung swirling in the sunlight. Then he saw zebra spread right across the plain. Like striped toys, they cantered when they heard the car, slowed to a trot, stood and watched him like old, short-sighted men. He wanted to shoot one but changed his mind, thinking it best to meet the Major first. The plains, the distant blue hills, and the sense of freedom they gave him, all moved him to a sort of bliss, so that when Wangi pointed up to the hill where clumps of blue gums all but hid the long tin roof of a house and said: "*Nyumbani huku, Bwana,*" he felt happy, and even anxious to meet Major Fawn-Cochley.

Chapter II

HOW long do you think this new white man will stay with our old one?" Kyonga asked Jeru in the kitchen. The old cook raised his eyes to heaven in mock piety and said: "For as long as the old one can bear him. And what of me? How long can I go on with the old one? This morning he sent for me and questioned me for an hour. It was like the jackal talking with the crow, so clever were we in question and reply. Not until he mentioned my age, my exhaustion and the stimulating drink did I realise that he suspected me of stealing his whisky."

"And what did you say then, old one?" said Kyonga, sharp-eyed.

"I told him I had seen *you* drinking it."

Kyonga became grave and said: "That is not a true word to speak of me, old one."

"You are young and must suffer. You are as shrewd as an old man and you are a liar. You have everything a man needs for outwitting the world. Why then should you not share the storm with me?" The old man thrust his face forward until Kyonga could see into his smoke-reddened eyes. "You are only here, young one, because I put up with you. When you are tired you can go. See to it, then, that I do not grow tired of you first."

Kyonga chewed his lower lip and looked at the floor. "What will be eaten to-night?" he said.

"To-night it is the onion soup and the rissoles and the papaya." They always discussed the Major's meals as their own, which was true, for they ate everything he ate and he knew this but could never prove it.

"Good," said Kyonga.

"You are like all the young," Jeru told him. "A hyena.

If I made a soup from your grandmother's arm you would eat it."

"And what of you, with your grey bristles and your rat-eyes? You would sell your father's heart for a shilling."

"Enough," shouted Jeru. "Go and lay the table." He grumbled under his breath when Kyonga had gone. His sight was failing and he would not confide in anyone. He dreaded blindness and his worry was beginning to affect his work. Forgetting to put salt in a soup, or standing in a strange daze of he knew not what while the meat burned; in a vague way thinking about other days when he was a small boy newly circumcised, when the first white men had come to the lands of his tribe, and that year of the circumcised generation was called "the year of the white men," for the year was remembered by a thing. He wondered whether to go blind here, or to go back to his village half a day's walk away. The Major's land stood on the boundary of his tribal country and sometimes he could smell the smoke of the villages, and on a warm breeze the scent of his tribe's flesh, so much softer than the sharp soapy stink of white men. In his daze, ladle in withered black hand, he heard the Major's sharp voice calling: "Jeru! Jeru! Jeru!" impatiently as usual. He hobbled out of the dark, smoky kitchen and across the patch of clean, beaten earth to the house. "Bwana!" he replied absent-mindedly to each cry of his name.

"So there you are, eh?" said the Major. "I thought you were dead." He threw back his white head and laughed.

"Bwana!" said Jeru. He wiped his hands on a filthy piece of cloth.

"Still at it with your dirty habits, I see," said the Major in English. He always used English when upbraiding Jeru, for it made no difference if he used Ki'Swahili, and he could carry on better in English, for the servants were all he had in the world to love. "Still mucking about after twenty years of civilisation in my house, you dirty old bugger." He was thinking about other things, trying to remember why he had sent for Jeru. "Must get out and have a bit of leave. Getting woolly." He had been too long alone, he was sure. Jeru turned and went back to the kitchen, for he knew the Bwana had forgotten his wish, his plan, his intention. He knew by the way the Bwana slowly beat his hands together and talked to himself. Fondness for the Bwana was a habit now, and later the Bwana always remembered what he wanted.

Kyonga was waiting in the kitchen shining with glee and cruel with youth. "His brain is dying in the skull. I have told you this. See, again he had forgotten what he wants." The old man turned his two reddish eyes on to Kyonga and said: "Do you wish me to tell him who broke the big meat plate?" Kyonga's glee faded and he shook his head. "Do you wish me to have you thrown from your low position without a signature on your *kipandi*?" Again Kyonga shook his head. Jeru said no more and turned back to the cooking dinner and into his daze. How cruel was age and its friend, youth, he mumbled in his mind. How the young waited for the old to become a mockery and a clown, like a drugged and reeling enemy in the laughing village when the wizards had turned him into a buffoon. As though remembering something, Jeru turned to Kyonga and said: "You cannot be cook. You know nothing. I am old but I will be here for years, so do not sneer." He looked broodily into Kyonga's eyes.

"I do not sneer at you, old one," Kyonga told him seriously. "I was only laughing at the Bwana, who is funny when he forgets."

"He has no wife to quarrel with and keep him sharp. But he is still strong. When you are young you feel you have drunk a river and could stab the world, but it is all a lie, a lie. Go now and lay the table and do not nibble things from it slyly like a rat. I have seen you, nibbling quickly like a rat. Go now." "The young," he thought when Kyonga had gone, "they think that even to be alive is to be a warrior."

That nervousness which had increased of late was beginning to affect Major Fawn-Cochley while he waited for the arrival of the new pupil. This nervousness, he noticed, appeared when he had to face a stranger. ("Must get away for a spell. Cooped up here all the time——") It made him walk about, and button and unbutton his shirt, twist his moustache, cough, call for Jeru. "I wonder if I'm going to like the young chap," he thought, sentimental for a moment, and then, striding the length of the veranda: "He'll probably be insufferable like all the rest, bone lazy, a mouth to fill, and useless with the *watu*. The *watu* were all right. It was the white men who bossed them who were the failure. The *watu* knew when they had a real boss to deal with. The *watu* will soon weigh him up. They may be savage but, by Jove, they know a boss when they see one. Not that he's to throw his weight though. There's only one boss round here and that's *Me. Me.*" Reminded of the load of Africa which awaited orders, which lay down on its back when the Bwana was not there, he called "Jeru," and again: "Jeru! Jeru! Jeru!"

"Where is that *toto*, that small boy who is going to be the new Bwana's servant?" he asked suspiciously when Jeru arrived. He always treated Jeru with suspicion. It was the only weapon left to him after twenty years of self-revelation to his aged black man who was like a discreditable elder brother.

"How am I to know where the young are wasting their time——" Jeru began.

"Now don't start that. Don't start that," said the Major. "I've asked you a question and, by God, I expect a sensible answer, a civil reply, a respectful manner when you come here grumbling and giving your damned impudence. By God, you wouldn't have talked like that twenty years ago. Been standing there, trembling, anxious to please. Knew your place then, not like now. Well, what about it?" He had almost forgotten the original question. "What about it, I say, eh?"

"He is cleaning the new Bwana's room, getting it ready, Bwana," Jeru lied quietly.

"Good. That's right. Good." Then keenly: "Did you tell him to do that. Did you?"

"Yes, Bwana."

"H'm. Not bad. Not bad at all. Well, don't stand there scratching your belly like that, like a baboon on a holiday. Off with you. Go on. Wasting my bloody time like this. Go on."

If this young fellow who was so damned late was going to carry on like this *every* day, then where were things going to end? Where? Then he heard the car. About time too. He began shouting to Jeru, to Kyonga, to Nyangi, the *toto* who was going to work for Jervis. "Tea. Come on. Tea. What about the *watu* to unload the car? Where's the tea?" When they began to run aimlessly to and fro, he was satisfied and went down the veranda steps as the car chugged to a halt, some steam escaping from its radiator cap.

"Boiling, by Christ," shouted Major Fawn-Cochley. "Are you Jervis? Then what the devil are you doing driving my car? I gave strict orders. *Strict* orders. And you've boiled her."

Jervis got straight out of the car and ran up the steps past the Major, who turned and followed him into the house. His face was red with exasperation when he found Jervis waiting for him in the dining-room, smiling. He was a tall young man, and smiling into the bargain.

"Are you Major Fawn-Cochley?" he said pleasantly.

"I am," he was told belligerently.

"Well, do you mind not shouting at me like that in front of your servants?" Then the young man took the Major's hand and shook it, saying: "Your driver was drunk so I drove instead." He watched the old man with careful, bright eyes, watched him swallowing, letting him forget the sharp, smiling request he had made.

"I see," said the Major, pulling his moustache. "I see." Then after eyeing the floor for a second or two, he said: "Bit wrought up, you see. Nothing much. Gets on your nerves, this place."

"That's right, I know," Jervis smiled and added: "Good, I'd love a cup of tea."

"Tea?"

"Yes, please."

"Why not a whisky?"

"Thank you."

Deep in thought, the old man went to a cupboard, saying: "Sit down and let's have a talk."

"Got him," thought Jervis. "A windbag with a heart of gold. But I wonder if I can stick him for long."

"I wonder," Major Fawn-Cochley was thinking, "I wonder if we're going to get on, if I ought to knuckle down in the way I did just now. Better look out or he'll boss the show."

Chapter III

THE next morning Jervis sat on the veranda from six
o'clock until nearly ten, waiting for Major Fawn-
Cochley. The breakfast table was laid. There was silence
throughout the house. No servant appeared. He could hear
Nyangi, his small boy, brushing out his bedroom. Then
again there was complete silence, and he watched the sun
swelling as it rose high into the sky from behind some
jagged scrub-covered hills. Immersed in this new Africa
which already was losing that alien hugeness which had at
first disturbed him, he forgot the Major and his anxiety to
make a good showing on his first morning as the new pupil.
But soon he became impatient, and he went on tiptoe to
the Major's bedroom window, which looked out on to the
veranda. Carefully he peered in and saw the old man lying
asleep on a bed which was covered with books. There were
books all over the floor and on the dressing-table and
chairs. Jervis sighed. He was hungry and annoyed. He crept
away and found Nyangi, and pointing to his mouth, he
said : "Food. Grub. Breakfast."

"*Chakula*," said the small boy, his glistening dark-brown
face alive with sympathy and understanding. He had eyes
like a young dog with its first master, trusting, anxious,
watchful. "*Chakula, Bwana*."

"That's right, *Chakula*. Bring it. Hungry as hell." Jervis
decided he was going to like the Africans. What was that
strange touching innocence and trust which they had in
their faces? If they were savages, what was the touching
thing he saw already in their eager eyes?

The Major slept on, tired again after yet another struggle
for the keys of the mystery of death and eternity. Book after
book he read : *Journeys of the Soul*, *The Dark Curtain*, *End or*

Beginning. They had come in parcels from England ever since the balance of forces within him had altered, bringing the realisation that he was entering the shadowed areas where the old sat for hours in idle memory of things past. The feeling of age had come like a message one day when he had quarrelled with one of the *watu*, a big, simple African, who in his innocence had argued with the Bwana.

"It is not as you say," he had cried, like a big boy in an argument. The Major was shocked. "Damn you," he had cried. "Be silent when I speak to you." But this man had turned to his uncomfortable companions and said: "It is not as the Bwana says. I did *not* avoid my proper task. Tell him that that is so." He still thought in his newness that he could be right and the Bwana wrong. Major Fawn-Cochley had known in that instant that he was old. Once he would have stepped forward and struck the African, but now he had hesitated and he knew why. He had had to bluster and shout, to overcome the African by a sustained vocal rage so that the others muttered against their companion who had thus angered the Bwana Major, for to agree with a white man was to please him.

He had begun to think about age and death after that, seeing how vast was the territory he had lost already, and for the first time he knew fear and foreboding. He had killed thousands of animals, for to kill was a necessity for him, a continual reminder to nature that it was the target area for his rifle, his will, his urge to destroy for pleasure, for the meat was secondary to that almost spiritual pleasure when the beast fell in its own blooded dust. Now he felt it harder to kill. He felt lonely and afraid, and he began to read what men could tell him about the body and the soul and about death. He sought assurance that dying was not painful and that the soul lived on, and when he found it the sun seemed warmer, the world more kindly, the heart stronger. He watched himself change from a very active and hearty man into a recluse, a seeker after comfort, as he had felt the slender store of his days diminishing. He felt for the first time the great weight of that anguish of the world which is the companion of speculation.

He led up to it in his first evening with Jervis, seeking his religious views, his beliefs about what he called "survival" after what he had begun to call "Passing on," not death, that cold iron word of darkness.

"I'm a fool," he told himself. "But I can't help it. I'm afraid. I wonder why I am afraid." He felt cut off for ever from youth and hope when Jervis had replied to one of his casually careful questions: "Death? What do I think about it? Well, I never think about it at all. It doesn't worry me."

Of course not. Why should it? The old man reminded him of a bird. He had a small hooked nose, and bright, darting hazel eyes which had grown unused to the calm movements of companionship with other men. They were the eyes of one who had lived too long alone, resting on walls or inanimate things with a sort of glazed fixity while he talked. His talk had no consistency. It moved from farming to death and sickness, from short, almost private monologues to eager questioning which did not await answers. He could be querulous, too, when he asked Jervis to pass the water-jug and it was slow in coming, or he could be vaguely kind—"Are you quite sure you like that Papaya? Is it fresh enough?"—but would not await an answer. Jervis thought he must be nearly seventy. He was still lean and fit. His withering face was sunburned and his white hair still thick on top. About the ears and neck it was cropped down to a short silver stubble. He wore shorts and shirt and thick walking shoes. His brown lean legs were still well shaped and muscled. His movements announced energy and drive, and he was restless in a way that almost flurried Jervis. "Come on. Come on. We're finished eating. Let's sit over there. Come on," or: "Well, you can ride round with me to-morrow and see the farm. No, next day. No, to-morrow's all right. To-morrow." He would always live alone, no matter who lived with him in that house, his mind working along its own lonely channels. His thick moustache was stained with cigarette smoke at one part of its lower edge and his small worn teeth were yellowed and stained.

"Time for bed now," he had told Jervis. "Up early in the morning. Breakfast at seven." He had made up his mind not to read that night, but to rise early and fresh for a day of authority with his pupil, but the books were a drug and he reached for them one by one until they covered the bed. He strained his eyes in the yellow light of the hurricane-lamp, and time, his enemy, fell away, was forgotten as he rushed into the versions of the universe's mystery.

Jervis had lain listening to the first hyenas he had ever heard, their idiot laughter and gurgling moving along the edge of the river he had seen from the veranda at sunset. He could hear Africa moving out there, Africa which had waited for darkness in which to raise its voices. There were rolling hoofbeats like the slow crescendo of drums, zebra panicking across the plain from the smell of some creeping enemy, and once there was a sharp demented screaming from the hyrax, which clutched the tree branches above the house. So sudden and shocking was this screaming that Jervis had sat up, frightened, saying, "God, what's that?" He slept only a little, for his ears were sharpening and curious. Those lions of which Abdul had spoken. He listened for them but they made no sound. Through his window he saw the cold stars sparkling and the branches of a tree moving in the soft wind. "Africa," he had whispered, "Africa, Africa," bewildering, enormous, and fell asleep.

He had his breakfast of maize porridge and milk and two fried eggs with brown coarse bitter bread. Nyangi brought him a glass of cold milk and then stood in the corner of the room with his hands behind his back, watching him, anxious to say something. When he caught Jervis's eye he said in his piping voice: "*Bwana, Simba*," but Jervis could not understand what "*Simba*" meant, and dodging panto-mime, went out on the veranda and sat down in a cane-chair. He grew restless after a time and ordered Nyangi to bring him a horse, having to gallop down the veranda holding imaginary reins before the small staring boy could understand. Then feeling annoyed and foolish, he watched Nyangi run off to get the horse, to tell the others of how the new white man had acted like a child in order to show what he wanted.

"I *must* learn the language," he told himself irritatedly as he climbed into the saddle and rode down past the garden towards the low hills which had drawn him since dawn. Kyonga came running after him with a rifle and ten rounds of ammunition, saying: "*Bwana, bunduki yaku.*" He took them and rode on.

Major Fawn-Cochley woke up in a bad temper. He called Kyonga and said: "Why did you not wake me? Why did you wait until now? Damn you all, all of you." When he was told that the young Bwana had breakfasted and ridden off towards the Sabuga hills he felt deep humiliation. This lying late in bed would have to stop. He wondered how he could explain it to Jervis without appearing to excuse him-self. He could only think of a lie, and after that he gave Kyonga a long telling-off for slackness, angry because he felt the need to lie to his young pupil.

Then Kyonga told him that a lion had twice tried to enter the cattle-boma between Sabuga and the river. The herds-man had arrived at dawn with the news and wished the

Bwana to know that he had driven the lion off before it had had time to kill.

"Damn you, leaving me asleep until now," the Major told Kyonga. "Damn you all, all of you."

Chapter IV

THE lion did not come again during that month. Jervis and Major Fawn-Cochley measured each other, Jervis learning never to refer to the old man's late mornings in bed. He noticed that the avoidance of the subject was almost a mania with the old man, whose energies in other directions were enormous and tireless. He found that the old man was a storehouse of information concerning wild beasts and their habits. He learned never to speak of lions but only of lion, of how to distinguish between the various night sounds in the trees, the ravines and even close to the house. One night he heard a sound like a saw making small cuts in a thick log. This sound had a fierceness in it which kept him awake as it moved from darkness to darkness around the house.

"A leopard looking for a dog," Fawn-Cochley explained, and told him that leopards had a great liking for dog flesh and when really hungry would enter a house silently and walk away with the dog. Leopards had been known to take a dog from a man's heel with a delicacy beyond the powers of any other carnivorous beast. The leopard was fierce, too, and when cornered came in a flat, weaving rush and at great speed. "Tear your face off. Scoop your guts out. Best thing for a charging leopard is a shotgun with a lethal charge in it." He showed Jervis a lethal charge, a shotgun cartridge with a large lump of lead pressed into its mouth.

2

When you had your eye on a moving leopard, you should never take it off him for an instant, for the leopard was fast, cunning and almost indistinguishable from the grass and scrub as he glided along on his belly and his swift, clawed pads. And never trust a leopard as a pet, even if you had brought it up from birth. One day they turned round with that mad yellow look in their eyes and you were torn up like old clothing. They seldom killed one sheep when they got into a flock. They fell into a blood lust unknown in any other creature and killed right and left until satisfied. Then the leopard would move off with one of the dead. The Major had known a leopard to kill over sixty sheep in one short flailing orgy. He had no time for leopards, he told Jervis. "Wipe 'em out," that's all. "They're vermin."

Jervis grew accustomed to the old man's eccentricities, his fierce rages with the Africans, the *watu* whose minds could not keep up with the Major's mercurial moods, or who were found asleep, open-mouthed in the sun beside their forgotten work, like men shot dead. They could see no larger design beyond the strange ways of the white men. The digging of this hole was work unrelated to anything else, for the white man seldom told the *watu* of the hole's part in his plans. If ever men deserved the name "labour" it was the *watu*. "The labour's not up to much to-day," or "Get some of the labour on to that digging near the paddock." To call them the *watu*, the Ki'Swahili plural for men, was the Major's affectionate way during the good moods. He had a genuine affection for them, and, Jervis noted, they trusted him. Once or twice he saw them smile at each other after the Major had thrown himself into one of his rages; but it was the smile of men who understand that there are times when white men have a fire in their bellies. They never, Jervis saw, comprehended the urgency which animated white men, that urgency which demanded speed in work as though it might stave off some fast-approaching catastrophe of which only the white man knew. And their fury, when a thing was done wrong. Jervis saw the signs of this strange fury in himself. It sprang from the half-formed conviction that it was hopeless to try to explain exactly what you wanted the *watu* to do. They stood there beside the botched job, interested but gaping, awaiting the storm of words. They could not picture in their minds the square, the oblong, the abstract picture which white man painted in words. But there were one or two, he began to see, who, through practice, could understand the strangeness of the white man's wishes, and Jervis could see they were strange. He tried to imagine himself a tribesman, young, innocent, straight from the tribal village, listening to a white man say: "I want it done like this, see"—waving of hands, bending down to sketch some fast strangeness in the grass, then up again and saying: "*Nataka, sawa-sawa.* Understand?" There was only one thing to do if you were an African, Jervis could see, and that was to nod vigorously, or even slowly and knowingly as some of them did. He found himself liking them, beginning to understand them, and because of this, excusing them their mistakes. He had a feeling it was better not to understand them if you wanted work from them, for you became involved with their world of little mysterious pictures and curious reasons for this and that. If you drove them, raged, threatened, they worked stubbornly and patiently, pained perhaps, but anxious to please. Jervis felt the beginning of a compassion for them, and Major Fawn-Cochley saw this, and warned him not to be too friendly with the *watu*.

"They're good chaps," he said, "but childish by our standards, and they don't understand reason yet. You just have to be strong with them. They respect that."

Jervis began to pick up some Ki'Swahili and some of the

local dialect. When he is to give orders or use some power, a man is quick to learn the necessary words of a foreign language, and Jervis was quick. He found it had an almost magical effect to use some secretly stored tribal phrase at the right moment. "*Bwana!*" they would say, accenting the final syllable in their admiration, and Jervis found it sweet to say casually: "Come on now. Get on with the work."

As the grazing grew scarce in the plains below the ridge, thousands of zebra moved on to Major Fawn-Cochley's farm, and on to the farms of other Europeans who were scattered along the great ridge above the plains. The zebra became a plague. They grazed voraciously and trampled out what they did not eat. They moved on in unhurried dazzling troops as the sun caught their stripes and varnished them with aching heat. By the thousand they moved across the country, and with them mingled the splendid massive eland and the humped red kongoni with their ugly hammer heads. From a distance, on horseback, Major Fawn-Cochley and Jervis could hear the sound of the zebra's teeth tearing the grass as they ambled slowly across the plains. Stallions moved on the edge of the herds, sometimes lifting their shining black noses and staring at the two motionless men.

"You never see a thin zebra," said the Major bitterly. "They're always fat, even in a drought, save when they get *enga narau*. That's a sickness they get if drought goes on too long. The quick sickness, it's called, and it wipes them out fast. But this is a menace. Look at them."

They were spread right across the plains. One or two playful stallions, happy on the Major's grass, led short gay stampedes between the grazing thousands.

"We'll have to do something about it, that's all," the old man told his pupil. "We'll have to shoot and shoot."

Then pointing to a stallion about two hundred yards away which was gazing at them in the puzzled, patient way of zebra, Major Fawn-Cochley said: "Let's see you hit that brute."

"I've never used a rifle, you know," Jervis told him earnestly. He wanted to shoot the zebra but was held back by a fear of failure. "Then you'd better start now," the old man told him. "Come on, we'll dismount and I'll hold your horse." They dismounted carefully, the stallion still watching them, even more perplexed now, it seemed. "Sit down to it and rest yourself. Take a full sight on the two-hundred-yard leaf." Jervis pressed the sight-leaf up with a soft snap and quietly withdrew the bolt of the ·256 rifle and pressed a round into the breech. His breathing had quickened and there was a small tension growing in his throat. "Go on," the old man told him. "Knock it over." He knew Jervis would probably miss. He slid a round into the breech of his ·375 and waited. Jervis squinted until he had the small ivory bead of the foresight in the vee and he saw it waving slowly across the stallion's body as his breathing deepened in nervousness and excitement. He knew he had pulled the trigger instead of pressing it. He heard the explosion and the short screech of the bullet and saw the stallion jack-knifing up and down, his legs working like scissors. There was a long slow thunderous movement in the herds and they began to race across the plain.

"You've burned him across the belly," said the Major. "Too low." Then Jervis heard the flat concussion of the ·375, and the stallion fell as though struck by lightning. "That's a head shot," said the Major. He worked the bolt of his rifle and the empty cartridge case spun in the sunlight.

"A lovely shot," said Jervis.

"You'll do it yourself soon," the old man said. "You'll

have to practise and you can practise on these fellows."
He pointed to the sea of tossing zebra buttocks which
flashed through the dust from their hoofs. "We've got to
get rid of them," he said, and Jervis saw the zebra now as
their enemy.

"Let's go and take a look at the zebra. You've never seen
one close up, have you?" Jervis said no. He had never seen
a large wild beast lying dead, and when they drew close to
it he smelled the sharp salty heaviness of wild blood for the
first time. The zebra lay on its side, its black muzzle curled to
show the big yellow teeth. In death it still kept its wild, free
look and its tufts of black and grey coarse mane standing
out from between the ears heightened the illusion. There
was a thin red line across the belly where Jervis's bullet had
grazed it. The thick, grey-white belly was stiff with ticks
which made a hard, bluish, shell-like coating to the grey
and red blushing skin between each hind leg and the belly.
Major Fawn-Cochley rasped the muzzle of his rifle across
the field of feeding ticks and said: "Those are the devils
which finish the farmer in Africa. The ticks. Those are the
devils which carry the diseases, and while we like wild
animals, that's what they bring you. Rinderpest, Texas red-
water, and a dozen others. You'll be doing the dipping on
Saturday morning and there'll be plenty of ticks, more than
usual, on the cattle, thanks to the zebra. D'you want the
skin off the forehead and nose? It's the only part of a zebra
you can make any use of. You can make a purse out of it
or a wallet. The rest of the damned creature is quite useless,
dead or alive."

In his best moods Major Fawn-Cochley was a likeable
man, even generous and thoughtful. To keep him that way,
Jervis said he would like the skin from the forehead and
nose, and the old man took a large horn-handled Spanish
knife from his pocket and with the skill of a tailor cut the

mask from the zebra's face and gave it to his pupil. "A present from the zebra community," he cackled with laughter. "It's about all they'll ever give you."

Riding back in the hot, falling sun, Jervis thought that the old man was beginning to like him and he could return this affection, for he did not find eccentrics disturbing. He knew that the old man was a hard worker, despite the lazy mornings so at variance with the rest of his character. He only worried lest he be unable to measure his own energies against those of Major Fawn-Cochley, and fail. "I must try and be more mature," he told himself. While he idly dramatised the new maturity he foresaw, and Major Fawn-Cochley covertly watched his pupil's riding manners, the vultures began to sail down past them in long hissings and to waddle towards the dead zebra. They were the first vultures Jervis had seen and they frightened him. They craned their obscene necks, which were livid and raw as if they had been scalded or burned. They turned their knobby heads this way and that, and the glint of their eyes was hard, steely and keen. They sidled about the corpse in dank brown fluttering soft feathers, resembling ragged ghouls about to rifle a corpse. One big hunched marabou stork sat at some distance off, like a judge awaiting a case. The vultures began to scuffle on the kill, digging with their beaks and then staring about them with their cold, murderous eyes for a second or two.

"Pretty, aren't they?" said Major Fawn-Cochley, watching the young face of his pupil, which reflected a mixture of horror and fascination as he gazed on the struggling heap of vultures, which grew as more and more planed down to the meal. It was hard to remember that not twenty minutes before the zebra stallion had been in his prime, a stranger to the bullet, with Africa's grass before him and his herd.

"They'll finish him off in about half an hour," the Major explained. "But if ever you want to keep a kill intact and safe from vultures and hyenas, if you have no time to skin and have to pass on for a while, there's one sure way. Tie the legs together and stick your handkerchief or a bit of paper between the hoofs, anything white will do, and they'll sit round it for hours, watching it. But they won't touch it. And when you come back to it you can skin at your ease. Come on, let's get back to the house."

They cantered when they reached the level stretch of country leading down to the house. "There's a car there," said Jervis, and he heard the old man swear as he reined in.

"So there is," he said. "Now who the devil can that be?" He began to mutter and fret.

"Why do they come here? I never asked them. No one ever comes here. Everyone knows I like my own company. Damn them. Damn them all."

"It might be a friend," Jervis suggested, depressed to think that while he was a pupil at this farm they must have no visitors.

"No such thing as a friend," the old man said sharply, his eyes on the car which glinted half a mile away in the sun. "I don't have any. They only let you down, use you, suck your blood and your brains. It's probably that bloody missionary man who's always after my *watu's* soul, or maybe it's one of the stiffs who live on the ridge come to cadge some dip or sulphur." He burst out again, choleric, furious: "Why can't they keep away and stew in their own damned juice? *I* never go near them, do I?" He was talking to himself, and Jervis did not reply.

Chapter V

FAWN-COCHLEY had never intended to build a house. When he came first to the land he had bought, he came in an ox-wagon and pitched a tent some miles uphill from the ridge which overlooked the sweltering plains of Aran-jiju. He had built himself a small and comfortable hut of cedar planks sawn by a Sikh carpenter called Hirnean Singh, who would still come from Guyu to do any odd carpentry for the eccentric Major Sahib.

It was out of boredom that the house grew. Fawn-Cochley, with plenty of money, added to the hut over a period of ten years, and gradually a long stone house with a tin roof had grown. The veranda was now thickly hung with pallid roses and small tenacious creepers.

There was a dining-room with a sitting-room at the eastern end. Off this ran two bedrooms, and completely on its own, with no entrance to the house, was Jervis's hut, the original one from which Fawn-Cochley had begun his house. There were three outhouses, one an office and the others stores. It was a comfortable house, cool in the heat, and there was a big grey stone fireplace for the cold of the rainy season. The furniture was simple, from the hands of Hirnean Singh, and the highly polished floors of the dining- and sitting-rooms were covered with the skins of antelope, with one superb lion skin before the fireplace.

Sitting, waiting for Major Fawn-Cochley's arrival, Mrs. Helena Brinden wondered why it was that bachelors in Africa deteriorated, went to pieces, and they all did it in various ways. Take the old man, Fawn-Cochley. Look at the barrenness of the dining- and sitting-rooms, the stark, square, hard chairs and tables, the empty wooden walls, the dust here and there which a man alone never sees, and the cold uncared-for effect of the whole house. The room was a place in which to eat and sit, but it had no comfort. She wondered how the new pupil would like it. A bit hard for a young man to find himself along with a selfish old crackpot like Major Fawn-Cochley, but still, there were worse men, as she knew only too well. A man was a strange animal. Seeing the haphazardly cared-for room of a man, like this one, she felt pity and impatience. If you could not snare them with the body, you could often do it with comfort, with the offer of peace when the man came tired and defeated from the world which he had loved alone, but not with this old crow, Fawn-Cochley. She, unused to feeling fear, almost a stranger to doubt, felt some nervousness as she awaited the arrival of the old man. She had not seen him for nearly a year, not since the time Louie had been found lying in one of his drunken stupors on the old man's boundary line. That was the day that dear, useless Louie had raged at her and shouted: "Then bug you, I say. Go my own way. Ride by myself and bug you. S'my ranch. My horses. My booze." She had not felt shame when Fawn-Cochley had brought her unconscious husband to the house in his car. She had got over that some years ago. She only felt a sort of cold, bitter gladness when she saw him drunk, almost a hatred. She liked to tell him he was incapable when he was drunk. The word incapable seemed to madden and humiliate him. "Careful, darling," she would say in a quick, high voice, her hand raised, as he staggered, "careful. You're incapable." Then she could look with shining eyes at his contorted, angry, shouting mouth. She knew he hated her because she was a slut, but she could not help it. She always noticed dirt and untidiness in other houses, but forgot her own, almost hating the neatness forced on her by the servants. "Without them," Louie had cried at her one day, "without them this house would sink into a pigsty."

"And why not, darling?" she had said in a voice too low for his impatient ear, "What's that?" he flared at her. "I suppose you're right, darling," she said, her eyes shining again.

"I love the bush," she would tell herself when doubt came. "I'm not cut out for this bloody housekeeping nonsense. I love to shoot and ride and live. I'm like a man, save that men keep wanting me and reminding me I'm a woman." That was partly true, but her own dark beauty could hardly rest before an attractive man. It took control and cavorted quietly until the man stared with that special interested male look, the look before his mind was taken off his world and he was stricken. How easy it was in Africa, in a place like Guyu, where the bachelors hardly saw a woman and where the black women, it was said, became whiter every day in the bachelors' eyes.

During her first two years in Africa she had at times longed for her Welsh mountain home. She missed the early, blowy mornings, those mornings just before dawn when the wind came from grey skies, a soft wind, heavy with rain, soft and cool on the cheek, and the warm breeze, tender after the blustering, gave background to the warblings of birds and the far bleating of sheep on the mountains. In Africa there were no hawthorn hedges, no dark yews in mountain churchyards a thousand years old where warriors had cut their bows, yet Africa drew her with a different and darker charm, hardly a charm, more like a threat, a threat of blood and sun and darkness. She had seen it in the reddish-brown skins of the tribesmen, and felt it when alone on the ridge looking down on Aranjiju, a feeling as though she were looking down on the cradle of her own secret and savage self. It was a self that had not looked inwards, she thought, until Africa, with its dead rolling wastes, its green

forests, its racing herds of wild animals and its scent of dead
fires, had put its dark hand into her centre. She had never
resolved the struggle this land had caused in her. She felt
a deep affection and pity for the Africans, and to avoid the
burden of it she drove them harder than a man, watching
them, weighing their efforts at labour, their reactions to her
orders as men, for there was no denying they were men.
Not "men" as Englishmen were men, but of the male sex,
yet lost in their swamp of tribalism, and silly with sun.

She had met Louis Brinden at a cattle fair near Shrews-
bury twelve years before. She was buying a heifer with a
cheque her father had given her for her twenty-second
birthday. Her grey Burberry and crumpled green hat had
not hidden her warmth from the short, squat East African
farmer with the deep scar on his forehead. "Shrapnel," he
told her later. The mark of the century, its stamp of frenzied
brotherhood. He was twenty-four and back on leave after
two years as an assistant ranch manager in Africa. There
was only one thing to do when their involvement reached
that indeterminate stage of possession and selfishness, the
prelude to habit, and that was to marry him and go to
Africa with him.

They started their home together in three African huts
he built on the new land he had drawn. He was too much
in love to notice her chaos at first. This chaos sprang from
her complete lack of interest in a house and what he
fondly thought of as the "feminine ability" to create comfort and order. He could not understand it, and after a year
or two he grew sullen and hateful to her. She lived in a
world of her own, a world behind dark eyes and level brows,
and sometimes when she revealed her fantasy he saw that it
had lost its charm for him. His own tendency was to let
things slide and he had imagined that she would cure him
of this, but her slovenliness, her bright, cooing happiness

amidst disorder and dirt, which puzzled him at first, awakened his longing to be alone again. The African bush, the savage background to this multiplying bitterness, drew her more and more. He saw her as a dirty gipsy who had hooked her man, and who knew he was too weak to escape, and he would learn to understand and accept her. Her home was in her body. The house was a number of walls inside which clothing, books, boxes, were stored in disorder. It was her body and the world around her which mattered most. She had watched his face grow sulky, his eyes resentful and his temper touchy. She could not please him and sometimes she pitied herself, in one of those grey moods, ecstatic and quiet, when she stood staring from the window, seeing what he had brought her to. But they never lasted long, these moods, they were private dreams of happy, luxuriant grief, for in them she could imagine how she had wasted herself. She had the ability, unrealised by her, of bringing out his weakness. He drank more often and he talked to her less and less. She had a greater resilience than his and she could forget what had angered him yesterday, and her careless brightness locked him in a mood half of hatred, half of contempt, until pity for her and for himself was all that remained of the ardent and blended desire which nature uses for its urgent purpose. They had cheated that purpose and Brinden was glad of it, for he longed to escape from her but only drew closer to the bottle. She took over the running of the ranch, for it suited her. It was easy to give orders, easier than keeping books and filing papers. He did that for her and it was easier for him. She lived most of her time on horseback, and she got a name in the country for efficiency and drive. They called her a "thruster." She left the running of the house altogether, and Brinden engaged two African houseboys whom Lady Joan Ribbing had recommended to him. They made the house clean and liveable despite her and in the new comfort Brinden enjoyed his drink. He drank too much and became rather a problem for Helena, as people could see. When the zebra poured on to the land in increasing numbers she told him that something would have to be done about it.

"Well, do it," he told her, his grey eyes narrow, catlike with malice. "Do it. You're the man around here." She always called him darling. No one could say she was cold, inconsiderate, stupidly harbouring resentment. She was patient with him. "Now, Louie, darling," she answered, "there's no need to talk like that."

"There's no bloody need to talk at all," he told her. "Get on with your gipsying and leave me to my weakness." He had developed a soft snigger as though he were alone in the room. She knew she was a slut and selfish, but after all he had ruined her life, had dragged her out here and she had made the best of it. Everyone knew that.

"I don't know how you stand it, dear," as some of her girl-friends told her in the Guyu club. That was the time for wistfulness, for playing with her necklace while she gazed into space and said: "One learns to. One has to." And she had come to believe in it all, for she hated problems and self-examination. Let Louie start first.

She loved animals. They were easier to love than humans, they made so few claims and they did not argue. The relationship with an animal was uncomplicated. You could ignore an animal and then love it fiercely for a whole day and there was no comment, no jealous longing, no anguish of possession. You could not do that with a human being. Only with an animal could she give all of herself, and where some women thought the body was all of the self, Helena meant the spirit. She had given the body to several men but not the spirit. That was something precious. She would have given it to Louie, was anxious to at first, but he had not appreciated her, had wanted practical, stupid things like a clean and comfortable home and much other wearisome female slavery, so she stayed locked within herself. Sometimes she could feel his hatred for her like a strong, stone wall between them, but in herself she was stronger than he, and while he drank she got on with her life of deep private sensation and pleasure in beasts and servants, and in nature which she understood as though it were a sister whom she loved and trusted.

"So it's you," said Major Fawn-Cochley, his voice tangled, in surprise and pleasure. He had a soft spot for her but he had no desire to see her in his house. Knowing this, she gave out more and more of herself as she saw his suspicious eye examining her, wondering why she had come. "He thinks I want something," she thought contemptuously while smiling that white almost genuine smile of warmth and goodness for him.

"Yes, it's me, Major," she said. "*Such* a long time since we met." She heard with amusement the honey in her voice, the almost girlish innocence. She had always longed to act. What a dreary waste life was, no matter what all these damned writers and poets said.

Fawn-Cochley began to fuss. When Jervis came into the room Helena drank him in in one quick look. Young, *terribly* good-looking, strong and *not* shy, not at all.

"You must be the new pupil," she said, giving him her small warm hand. Something passed between them, no one can say what it is, that something, not magnetism alone, but like fear and pleasure, fast and vague as in a dream, almost a conspiracy of the forces, the germs, the tumultuous silences of awakened longing.

She tried not to imagine his hard, flat belly, his long, slender, muscular back and his grip. His slightly sunburned cheekbones caused a soft fluxing behind her ribs that felt like a faintness, a weakening of the whole organism which for so long had been controlled, lost in the pleasures of being her own mistress.

"Too long without love," she was thinking. "I'm a fool."

Jervis felt that something too, but he was not sure of its meaning. Never having made a woman unhappy, he did not know what power was. He associated women with what he still thought of as goodness, though he knew an ache of flesh when it came.

They talked idly. How he liked the life, how different it was from home, yes, very different, and he was sure he was going to like the country. She let him grow interested in her, and saw something of an already growing loneliness in him. He had not known he was lonely until now. She appeared so bright, so gay, so good to be with. The room seemed quite different. Major Fawn-Cochley, filling his pipe, saw his pupil's growing interest in the woman, only a hint of it, but it was there. "Have to keep an eye on this," he told himself. "She'll eat him up." For the first time he noticed that Jervis was an attractive person, and there appeared in him flashes of a vitality and humour he had not known were there. She saw that the Major was surly with his pipe, and she turned to him and said: "I've come about the zebra. We're swamped with them and I saw coming over that you are too. I wanted to ask you if we could all join forces and do something about it." She gave Jervis a bright glance from the sides of her dark eyes, as though saying: "Isn't he the *darlingest* old grumpy? But we'll win him over, won't we?"

"It's an idea," admitted the old man, pressing the tobacco down into the bowl of his pipe with a small brown thumb.

"I reckon we have about ten thousand on our place alone, Major," she said. "They swarm like locusts. Why can't we drive them? I'm going to ask the Ganners and the Brownings to join us all in our great drive."

"How's Louis?" the old man asked her, studying his pipe. She knew that this old man saw deeper than some others into her cracked marriage. He had seen her house before the servants relieved her of the burden. She had once seen him weighing it up, the jumbles of books and old papers, dusty furniture, the slow mounting chaos of a lumber-room. He did not often come to her house, only when some common farming problem forced him to consult her.

"He's the same as usual," she told him. "Ill, you know." Her tone annoyed the old man but he said nothing. So Brinden was boozing as hard as ever then. A stiff, but it was not his fault he had married the wrong woman.

"All right," he told her, "I'll join you in the drive. What's your plan?" At once she became the serious and confident farmer, pouring out her observations of the zebra's movements and her plans to drive them back over the ridge and beyond the cedar forests which covered the lower side of the ridge.

"It's very difficult to drive zebra exactly through a break in forest country," he told her. "They're afraid of lions, and while you can gallop them across a plain, it's another matter to push them through a gap in thick forest, you know." She waved his caution aside.

"If we have enough people and we're determined, we can force them through," she said.

"I'm sure *you* can do anything you put your mind to, Helena," he replied, rolling his eyes as though helpless before her forcefulness. From the Major, thought Jervis, that tone and gesture were almost intimate, almost warm and jolly. What a character this woman was, and how attractive too. She was wearing a soft khaki drill skirt and a green short-sleeved shirt. Against his will he examined her, her long golden legs, her breasts, her throat. As she talked to the old man, apparently intent, she watched Jervis from the corners of her eyes, watched his eyes lingering on her here and there, and she fought against the faint excitement this caused in her. He had reached her thick, black, piled hair when she turned and smiled at him, saying: "I'm sure you'll enjoy it too, Mr. Jervis." He felt cut off, chilled by that sudden "Mister", but he said: "I'd love it." Their eyes tangled for a second and then retreated back into the as yet hardly-formed motive among the unrest they had created in each other.

"There's one thing we can do," she said. "It's a tip I got from one of my old herdsmen. He's a Wandarobo and what they don't know about game isn't worth knowing. He said that if you want to drive zebra away from a piece of country then shoot their foals. Where a foal has been killed they don't return for months."

Major Fawn-Cochley looked pained when he heard this. "How damned cruel that is," he said to the wall. "How typical of the *watu* to think of a thing like that."

"Hypocrite," she thought. "What's the difference in killing a foal or a stallion or a mare?" she asked him. "It's hard killing anything, isn't it?"

"That's true," he agreed. "But there's something rotten about killing the foals."

"Then kill the mothers too," she told him. "The point is we can't let them eat us out of grazing like this. And what about the ticks? They'll bring millions with them."

"A million ticks is the same as twenty," the Major said despondently. "But I suppose you're right. We'll have to do it."

"You remember that offer the Government made—a hundred of ·303 ammunition for ten bob specially for shooting zebra? Well, I've got six hundred rounds of it."

"That's the ammunition salvaged from the cruiser sunk off the coast, isn't it? A fat lot of use it'll be after eighteen years in the water."

"No, it's good," she said. "A few duds here and there. I've tried it. Have you got a ·303 rifle?"

"I've got two," he told her. "But if there's one nerve-racking thing, it's laying your sights and getting ready to fire when you know there might only be a click when you press the trigger."

"Well, never mind," she smiled brilliantly. "We can use everything we've got. We'll shoot, drive, everything."

"When?" he asked her.

"As soon as I've fixed it with the Brownings and the Ganners, I'll have it all arranged for some time next week."

"Right," the Major said, and to Jervis: "You're in for some hard riding. You'd better get some shooting practice in. I don't want any browning into the herd. I can't bear that kind of shooting."

"I'm sure you're going to enjoy it," she told Jervis.

"I shall love it," he said. She did not want to leave his presence yet, and the Major knew he would have to offer her tea. It was only civil to do so. He offered it and gave Jervis a sly, sardonic look when he saw the young man's smile of gladness. The woman was charmed and said she would *adore* a cup of tea.

"You remind me so much of Daddy," she said. "You even talk like him."

The old man coughed and said: "H'm, very nice, that. A compliment, I'm sure." He called Kyonga and ordered tea. Through a crack in the door, Kyonga had been watching Jervis examine Brinden Memsahib. Would this young Bwana now pursue the Memsahib until he got her and she felt the weight of him on her? He would speak about it with Jeru, for Jeru knew the white men and their ways as few men did in this age of lust and breakage of custom. Kyonga had been born in The Year of the Mouth Organ, when an Indian had sold some mouth organs in the tribal villages. There was a gulf now between the young and the old about custom. Jeru stood up in argument for the white men when the young ones said that white men did not have these old customs about women and goats and behaviours. Kyonga watched Jervis from under his eyelids as he laid the small tea tables beside each of the white people. Yes, the young Bwana was hungry for the Memsahib. There were thorns in his eyes.

"I have seen that our young Bwana has desire for Brinden Memsahib," he told Jeru, while he waited for the teapot. Jeru sighed and rumbled in his withered throat. "Aye," he said. "It comes to all men, this madness to spend the seed, even in worn soil. Then it is over and a man sits in the sun outside the huts, empty and sad. It is like being full of flame, the madness, and the emptiness is like a broken calabash. Get out now and see that you have done all you should have done. And turn your mind from this thought about the young Bwana. He is clever and he will read you and you will get hurt." One day a white man would strike Kyonga. These young men needed a law when the tribal ways, once so strong, were beginning to crumble like the dried mud of a wall.

Chapter VI

AFTER a week went by Jervis could bear it no longer. He had to see Mrs. Brinden somehow. The old man had hinted that the husband was a chronic drinker and that the wife did all the work. He had tried to question the old man about her in the most casual of voices. The information about her husband, after a couple of days, had helped him to want her company. There was a merging of sorrow for her, and longing. Desire, as always, found its allies, its excuses. He was disturbed when he thought of her. There was an unrest which made him fret and which sought to give a perfunctory character to all his work.

"I'd better go over one of these days and see how Mrs. Brinden's plans are getting on for the zebra drive," he suggested to the old man after a long day castrating and branding calves.

"You might do that," the Major said. He took his pipe out of his mouth and looked at it as though he had never seen it before. He would have to work Jervis even harder than at present, if he got mixed up with Helena Brinden. One other pupil had spent too much time over there, though he was fairly sure "nothing" had happened. Damn this bloody sex business. If only it were possible to tell a young man what a trick the whole thing was in the end, despite the good times it gave. It gave good times, he remembered well enough. Still, there it was.

"Mrs. Brinden has got some queer ideas about the *watu*, you know," the Major warned Jervis, as though warning him against infection. "She's one of these Masai worshippers." Jervis had already heard of the Masai on his journey out from England. Aboard ship he had met a tall, thin Englishman who had talked about the Masai as the "only true and noble savage. Africa's gentlemen." They were brave, handsome, independent and doomed to syphilis and extinction.

"She has a couple of Masai herdsmen and they can do no wrong. She even follows their recipes for quarter evil and a couple of other diseases. She's a bit cracked about the Rendille too. She had a Rendille herdsman. But nearly all of us in this country are a bit gone about something or other." He chuckled. "People say I'm gone too. Do you think I am?" It was a trap question and he squinted over his pipe at the young man whom he had almost discomfited. Jervis decided on the truth.

"I think you spend too much time alone," he said, as soothingly as his experience of men would allow.

"You do, eh? So people do think I'm cracked, do they?"

"Oh, no, no. It's just that you should meet people more often."

"Well, God damn you, *you* think I'm gone, do you?"

Jervis floundered. He could see the old man wanted to hear more but would not be able to stand it.

"Go on, you'd better say it. Say it, go on." His small red-brown face reflected crossness and deep curiosity. He felt his authority loosening too, but he had become fond of Jervis and he hesitated on the border between affection and that neutral correctness he had always affected with his pupils.

"No, I don't think that at all. A couple of people in Guyu told me I'd find you difficult to get on with, but I don't find you anything of the sort. I don't think you're cracked, as you put it."

The old man was delighted against his will. It was something new to be fond of a person and he mistrusted it. Abruptly he said:

"Well, you'd better go over and see Mrs. Brinden and see what she's fixed up about this zebra drive. She'll lend you books too. She's a great book-fiend in her way."

"You are too, aren't you?" said Jervis innocently.

"Am I? How do you know that?" The Major seemed put out and Jervis saw at once that he had trodden in the difficult territory of the old man's sluggishness abed in the mornings.

"I saw a lot of books in your room one morning when I came to see if you were ready for me," Jervis told him lamely. Major Fawn-Cochley snorted and said: "All right. I read late into the night. It's a new habit, blast it, and it's like a disease. There, are you satisfied now?" He hammered his pipe in the stone fireplace.

"There's nothing wrong in reading late, is there?" Jervis was breezy. What a difficult old devil he could be. Full of queer corners.

"I haven't quite made up my mind about that," the Major said in his sharp voice. "Come on, lunch." They were silent throughout the meal. When it was over, the old man said in a surprisingly friendly way: "It's like this, Jervis. I think I've either got religion coming over me, or I'm getting senile, but I'm reading about eternity, whatever the hell it is. And what surprises me is that I haven't thought much about it before now. It's an old man's business, I expect. Not for a young feller like you."

"I often think about it when I'm riding alone in the bush," Jervis assured him. "Somehow, this country makes me think of it."

"Then resist it. Enjoy your life. Don't bother your head about eternity unless you find yourself looking down a lion's throat or running like hell with a rhino behind you."

Jervis thought that at last they were becoming friends. "I might stay on here after my year's pupil training," he was thinking. "Why not?" He would be near Mrs. Brinden then.

Feeling he had gone a little too far with his pupil, Major Fawn-Cochley said in his more usual authoritative tone: "We'll go and mix the doses for the sheep now. We'll finish it to-day and you can leave it at the main *boma* on your way over to Mrs. Brinden's place to-morrow." Jervis's disappointment was great. He had already planned his

arrival at the Brindens' this afternoon. It was eight miles'
ride, and he had planned his entrance, his greeting, the
charm which he would exercise and the slow blossom of
their association.

"Yes," he said, "we should get the doses finished to-day
easily."

"That's the ticket," the Major said, using one of his old-
fashioned descriptions of the right thing.

For four hours they sat mixing Cooper's Dip and sulphur
in the cool dimness of the store. It was a job the old man
would allow no African to do, for the Cooper's Dip was
highly poisonous, and Africa had not yet reached that sense
of care and precision about these things, not even over their
own cattle, as the old man was never tired of telling Jervis.
Jervis was certain he could find Africans reliable enough to
learn the right thing and feel the necessary responsibility for
many things, but he knew it would be many a long day
before he could set out to prove it. He had seen in one or
two of the *watu* that gleaming and intelligent eye which
seemed almost to *listen* as well as watch when Jervis was
doing a job reserved for the white hand and the European
mind. There was Asmani, for instance, small and neat and
brown, whose face glowed with intelligence and goodwill.
After Asmani had pleaded with him, he had once let him
use a tape measure to mark out part of the site for a sheep-
shearing shed, and Asmani had done it perfectly. He had
hurried the other men about, impatient for speed, like a
white man in a hurry, and had shown his knowledge of
inches and feet. He had learned this, he explained, by
listening to, and watching, the Bwana on many occasions.

"It's very clever of you, Asmani," Jervis had told him,
surprised. He had said nothing about it to Major Fawn-
Cochley. The old man would have warned him, explained
that Asmani's smartness was all mimicry, clap-trap, and

that allowing him such liberties would swell his head, spoil him. Such work was an Indian *fundi's* job and not for the *watu*, yet, anyway.

"If I ever have land in this country," Jervis would say to himself, "I'll train my own Africans. They just want a chance, that's all." He understood the Major's careful pressure on the Africans. He wished to keep his Africa of the wild beasts and the simple tribal Africans untouched as far as possible by European change, and, Jervis wondered, who was to say in the end that he was not right? But you had to start somewhere and be generous, take a risk with them. It was 1935 and this part of Africa had not greatly changed since the white men had come about fifty years before.

That night, as he lay awake, thinking about Mrs. Brinden, Jervis heard a lion roar for the first time. He sat up, trembling, his hair prickling at the roots, holding his breath and not knowing it. He had *imagined* the lion's roar to be fearsome, but not like this, this terrifying shattering of the silence, and in its utter uncaring savagery, all the hunger and anger and hate, it seemed, of Africa's forests. The roaring diminished as the beast moved in the darkness, and when it had ceased Jervis could feel his heart pounding in his throat and ears. It was the biggest experience he had ever had, he thought. Excitement, and considerable fear as well as curiosity, had all but exhausted him and he lay down and thought of what he would do if one day he must face the charge of this beast that could tear the night into a vibrating thunder with its voice. He heard the old man calling him from the veranda and he went to his window.

"D'you hear it? D'you hear it?" the old man called to him.

"Yes," Jervis cried. His voice was high and excited. His heart still thumped. "God, I'm as nervous as a bloody girl."

"Your first, isn't it? Shake you up a bit, eh?" The Major cackled in the darkness. "Well, let's hope he doesn't get in among the bulls, that's all. Good night."

Chapter VII

THE BANTU peoples stretched from the area of the Cameroons in Western Africa to Cape Town and from there to Mombasa. The northern line of their extension ran through the Congo territories until it reached somewhere in the Cameroons below the negroid lands of Nigeria and the enormous sand wastes of Sahara.

"But even here in East Africa you can't be sure who's Bantu," Helena Brinden went on, kneeling among heaps of books in what she called "the library". Humphrey Browning lay back in an arm-chair, his hands clasped behind his neck and the long cigar clenched between his teeth pointing upwards. Through its smoke he watched Helena's animation as she sought to inform Jervis of Africa's, to her, no doubt, fascinating mosaic of peoples and languages. She was not quite sound on her subject, it was said, but her personality, her flow, her zest, made the subject interesting.

She never spoke of the Kikuyu, but of the Wa'Gekoyo— "for that's what they call themselves and that's how they pronounce it," and "You see, the Masai are not Bantu, they're half Hamitic and so are the Nandi, the Suk, the Lwmbwa and the Turkana. You'll find they all love milk, worship it practically like a holy thing. They're generally tall and slender." Sometimes she spoke of them like a woman in love.

"It's the country," Jervis was thinking. "I'll be like this

soon. I wonder what *I'll* be cracked about." She had called him "Jervey," and he was trying to get used to it. It pleased him that she should call him Jervey; how thrilling it was to watch her kneeling there while he sought to keep his eyes from the soft golden swell of flesh where her shirt cut him off from her body. It was a nuisance, for what she said was interesting, but could a beautiful woman concentrate a man's interest on her mind? Well, he must try and concentrate.

"You mean that the description 'Bantu' is based on language and that it's not really the name of a people?" he asked her, settling back in his chair.

"Something like that," she replied quickly, the speed and animation of her words smothering the vagueness. "They call a man intu, mutu, muntu, and the prefix agrees with the noun. It's very exciting when you make little discoveries on your own among the languages of the tribes. There are great similarities and great difficulties." Humphrey Browning was yawning and he said: "Look here, Helena, old thing, what about the Ganners, are they in on this zebra thing or not?" He was a tall, very fair man with thin sunken features and small green eyes. His yellow hair was cropped close to his head and round his wrist a twining cobra was tattooed. It was rather a pity, that, he would sometimes explain. "Tight one night with some of the other subalterns in Peshawar, and before you knew what had happened there we all were having cobras tattooed on our arms and then chicken tandur at Wali Mohameds." He wore a violently red-and-green-striped shirt and bright green corduroy trousers. When he saw Jervis looking overlong at this ensemble, he said: "It's the country. It brings out all your self-expression. I used to wear a Mexican sombrero, too, but I could never manage the confounded chinstrap at a gallop." He was about forty-two. He had a lot of money and he was a good farmer, specialising in grade sheep.

Browning's wife, Anna, was lying on a couch in the corner, reading *The Lady*. She could never be bothered listening to Helena on Africa and the Africans. She did not like the country and she bore with it, never quite deciding that she hated it, for she was very attached to her husband. She was able to create an illusion of England on the farm. Her house was like something you find advertised in *The Field*, and you could always find the latest magazines and books from England in her house. The Brownings had a Goanese cook, and the food was renowned from Guyu to the Machango plateau.

"I can't *bear* shooting things," she would tell visitors. "Humphrey kills enough for both of us." She was a small pretty brunette, not as dark as Helena, but shrewd where Helena was emotionally certain of things, cool where Helena was violent. She despised Helena but could hide her annoyance when she saw her husband responding gladly to Helena's excitements and enthusiasms.

"I'll shoot every damn zebra you put in front of me, Helena," Browning said, laughing. "So the old Prawn-Cocktail is squeamish about shooting the foals. Well, I think your Dorobo is quite right, old thing, let's do 'em all in. I want some grass left on my farm. Now about the Ganners. If they've agreed, I say let's make the date now and send them a note telling where we all meet for the drive."

It was Helena's plan that every available African on the four farms should be spread in long lines behind the horsed Europeans. They would have drums, spears, tins and clubs, and should concentrate on preventing the zebra from breaking past the riders. The riders would drive the zebra, dismount and shoot wherever possible, and then drive again.

"But what about getting them through the forest?" Browning asked for the second time.

"Oh, you're just like the Prawn-Cocktail about that forest, Humphrey," she told him with mock patience. "We'll get them through that all right, you'll see. It's a matter of determination, that's all."

"It's all very well, Helena, relying on your feminine intuition about men and things, but zebra are different. They're more determined than even you are. I've chased them before and I know that an old zebra stallion is a good leader when he's in a stubborn mood. I can't see us getting them through the gap in that cedar forest. There are lions about now." Then addressing himself to Jervis, he said: "That lion you told us you heard last night. Ten to one it's lying up with some of its chums in that cedar forest. When we get the zebra to the forest they'll smell the lion and they won't go through. Would *you* go through if you were a zebra and you smelled lion?"

"I don't think I would," said Jervis laughing. He felt an inexperienced boy among these "old-timers." "I don't know much about game yet."

"You'll learn," Browning said, mouthing his dying cigar. "You'll learn all right."

"If you want to learn how to kill anything, Humphrey's the best teacher." Anna Browning spoke languidly from behind her magazine. "It's time you went in for a camera, darling. All the best game killers do it when they've had enough killing."

"But I *like* killing, Anna," her husband said to the magazine. "I'd be lost without it. I like nothing better. It's my nature. Why should I deny it?"

"Good, honest Humphrey," murmured his wife in the baby talk she used with him when they were alone.

"All right. I'll write to the Ganners now and send the chit with Jorogi," Helena told the two men. "Anna, *won't* you come with us, just for the ride?"

"Not for anything. Guts and blood and vultures. I saw it a couple of times with my spouse and I don't want any more. I'll stay at home and mix the drinks for when you come back."

"Let's have jugs of Pimm's, darling," Browning said. He crushed his cigar in the rhinoceros hoof which served as an ash-tray. "We've got oceans of mint in the garden too."

"I'm telling the Ganners that we all meet on your forest boundary, Humphrey, and we spread out from there and start the zebra off. It's going to be a long, long drive."

"Plenty of spare horses," Browning assured her. "But we won't get them through that forest."

"We will," said Helena.

"All right, old thing," Browning waved his hand. "We will."

"Never argue with a woman," Helena mocked softly.

"Exactly."

"To-day's Monday. I'm making the date for the drive Wednesday. Will that suit everyone here?" The men agreed. As soon as she liked.

"The Ganners will hate leaving their little love nest. The ideal couple, you know." Browning watched his wife as he said it and smiled when the magazine was lowered. He knew she had a curious respect for the Ganners and their deep attachment for each other.

"Yes, they are the ideal couple. They really love each other, and what's wrong with that?" She was vehement. Obviously the Brownings had often discussed the Ganners.

"Oh, Anna," Helena put in lightly. "You're quite starry-eyed."

"Nonsense." Anna was not quite annoyed. "But I get tired of this smart local chat about 'Have you heard Mrs. So-and-So has gone off for the week-end with Mrs. So-and-So's husband?' Or 'He's living with the other fellow's wife.'

I like the Ganners. They may be dull but it's a change after the sexy stuff that makes the gossip round here."

"It's the country," Browning told them. "It's something in the air. It brings out the worst in us, and the best too, if you take the other view. Ultra-violet rays acting on the spine or something. Everyone's a bit gone in the nut. Well, come on, wifey, let's go." They murmured with Helena about not wanting tea. They left in a soft rumble of hoofs and trotted away through the plantation of gum trees which ringed the house.

"Well, Jervey, you're looking quite nice to-day in your brown shirt and your natty shorts. You've chafed your poor bare legs on the saddle leathers. Why don't you wear jodhpurs like a sensible chap?"

"I want to get toughened up," he told her, his face serious.

They laughed.

"What a pet you are," she said, looking into his eyes. She was sitting on the floor among the books, sunlight streaming through the low, wide windows and falling on her in liquid golden light, casting a faint glow like a halo about her. "I'll just finish this note for Jorogi to take to the Ganners." She wrote a few lines of the note and then looked up into Jervis's face. He saw a change in her face. It was solemn and the red, finely-shaped mouth was open, showing the edges of her white teeth. One of them had the tiny grey metal spot of a filling, something he had noted with regret, for he was twenty.

"Jervey," she said in a low voice, "are you going to fall in love with me?" He considered it, discomfited, but not showing it by more than a pinkening at the cheekbones. She was examining his eyes, suffering a little, trying to separate the thrill from the facts of her real world. It was like toothache, but in the region of the heart.

"Yes," he told her, too casually, so that she smiled thoughtfully.

"I think we'll bring each other bad luck," she answered, in a whisper so that he almost saw artifice there but was not sure what it was that seemed false to him.

"Why do you say that?" he asked, his poise gone. He almost leaned down and took her small brown hand.

"I don't know, but it worries me," she said.

"Why should it? What's wrong if I fall in love with you?"

"You sound quite experienced," she said, laughing at him. "But it's acting, I know. D'you know much about women?"

"No one knows much about women," he told her, flushed with smartness and a sort of headiness which her interest had kindled in him.

"What a clever thing to say," she replied. "Only it's not true, like most clever things. What am I going to do with you if you fall in love with me?" That made him blush and she was sorry when she saw his eyes cloud.

"*Do* with me?" he said. "How do you mean?"

"Let's not talk any more about it," she said. "Jervey, you can love me, but privately, inside yourself. There's no harm in that."

He was stung by her words. She went on with her writing. If only he had more experience. There must be some hidden meaning in all this, or why would she mention it even? "There's no harm in that." She was treating him like a boy. As though he had silently reached her with his misery and his darkened temper, she looked up again and said: "I like *you*, Jervey. I'll teach you everything I know. If you want anything, sewing or darning, I'll do it for you." She meant it. She knew she would only do it once for him, it bored her so, but it was the most generous thing she could think of at the moment, and she knew such an offer about mending shirts or socks always touched a lonely man, even the youngest, at one of his deepest parts. She was gratified by his white, happy smile.

"That's good of you," he said, and his voice was not quite itself. "Helena," she said, smiling too. "Helena," he repeated in a low voice. "God, what bloody fools we all are," she thought, while she scribbled the rest of the note. "I want him. He's in love with me, but I probably won't do a bloody thing about it." Then cautiously she added: "Unless I can't bear it, that is."

He would have liked to ask about her husband, but she had been pointedly silent about him. He must be lying drunk in some room in this house, staring up at the ceiling. Jervis sought to imagine him but he failed. Then he thought of Helena lying with this unimaginable drunken man, and he felt the first deep scalding pain of his life. He felt jealousy and despair, and he wished to hurt her, would like to have said abruptly, "Well, good-bye," and then to have stalked out, leaving her miserable. But he sat on, sucking his pain, trying to contain the fearful longing she had conjured within him. He watched her almost sullenly, upset, his interest in the new world of forests and beasts which had so quickly captured him, now dulled, something almost hateful and without point. With her head bent and apparently intent on sealing the envelope, she felt all this like a dark flow from his silence. She knew he was watching her, and with what hunger she knew too. She sighed and said: "Now, I'll get Jorogi and then I'll give you some tea, Jervey." She smiled at him, almost sadly, no, not sadly, but like pity, like compassion, like a nurse passing a patient, and he smiled back, desolate, a little older as it were.

3

Chapter VIII

A LION in its prime, playful, hungry, glad of testing his speed, may kill about forty or fifty zebra in a year. One huge clawed pad on the zebra's nose, another in the centre of the back, one deep, crushing bite through the neck, and the zebra is dead. For an unknown number of centuries this war in nature had gone on. The leopard killed more baboons than usual when the maize of the villages was ripe. The lion killed the zebra, the eland, the oryx and all the others of the wandering antelope herds. The cheetah too, exultant in his arrow-speed during that last, grey-flashing rush on to the impala, or the Thomson's gazelle with the ever agitated stump of tail, had also helped in this fluctuating struggle of mouths seeking grass and herbs and flesh over the yellow, dusty plains of Africa. Everything which sought flesh for its meal, even the hyenas and the jackals yowling over the leavings of the lion or the leopard, found it in abundance and feasted at will. The old lion, slowing up, could turn to the herds of humped zebu cattle which grazed ahead of the sun-dazed herdsmen. The leopard, even when old, had little trouble with the baboons, though he could turn, furious, to a village dog should the baboons outwit him. The serval and the civet cats, too, had their smaller prey, and the wild round-eared hunting dogs, sadistic and painstaking, could chase herds of fat game for as far as they wished. There was always sport to salt the hunger of the beasts with the rank feline smell or the sly doggy lope. The rhinoceros, usually solitary, like a bad-tempered, dropsical, old man, rootled about for his favourite herb, piled high his mountain of dung and trampled about it as if loath to leave it, or leaned against a tree in an enormous bloated daze of grey flesh and tiny uncertain eye. The elephants in the high, dripping forests tore down the tall, slender Mukeo trees so as to eat the special, tender greenery which crowned them, and snuffled away in mud-smeared, mountainous rumblings, leaving the tangled heaps of broken trees for the rains to rot them. Every beast, from the small, screaming tree-hyrax, that little, velvet-gloved, beady-eyed creature who saw everything, to the rolling, leather trousered elephants, two tons or so in their benevolent enormity, knew his place. The black, ochre-smeared hunter, his arrowhead smeared with *sumu* or *wabayo*, might hunt them, and with his puny blade and traditional cunning, find meat for his belly, but he never threw that great assembly out of balance. The bravest could drive the poisoned spear, with its detachable head, into the belly of the elephant whose bowels rumbled above him, and then follow the wounded giant until the poison felled him in a slow, mighty collapse in some distant grove.

The Hamitics, demoniacal with their thin noses and twitching, aristocratic nostrils and their painted bodies, could, for bravery's sake and the warrior's title, corner the lion, seize his tail and pin him with the long shining blades of their spears.

In the rains, when the black cotton soil became deep and gluey, even the banana eaters of the timid river villages could run down the fat, sweating antelopes until they stood exhausted, mired to their hocks and ready for the bone-handled knives of the men who were tired of bananas.

All this made little difference. Disease would come and wipe out herd after herd of game, turning the plains into a shambles of dying animals among whom yapped the jackals and the snapping hyena made brave by windfall. The vultures cleaned the bones, the sun dried them, and the wind, the hoof and the blowing dust of the droughts pressed them down into the implacable African earth. Always, the tooth, the spear, and the germ had weighted the scales, this way and that, but the balance had seemed to remain.

The rifle of the white man altered this. When he first came, with his big, leaden bullets propelled by black powder in a swirl of muzzle-smoke, he could hardly believe his eyes. Here was a paradise. At one, two, three, four hundred paces, the amazed tribesmen saw the lion and the rhinoceros collapse after the sharp clap of rifle-thunder, collapse as though God had plucked out their hearts. The white man was amused by the rolling eye, the tribal exclamation of wonder, the ease of it all. There was something touching, too, about the way the tribe, if it was of that persuasion, and there were few that were not in a time of famine, fell on the corpses of rhinoceros and elephant and devoured them, the small, quick tribesmen kneeling, lost inside the cavernous, gaping chests as they sought for this or that tit-bit of liver or lights.

The lion began to fall in hundreds as the years passed. As white men came and built huts or houses in the far bush and tamed it, throwing herds of cattle and flocks of sheep far and wide on the sparse grass, they fought the lion, not for sport, but to protect their flocks. They fought on foot with the rifle, or with gun-traps, and in a pinch, but regretfully, with strychnine. The white man at this end of the country could tame the land for some miles about him, as could the other white man at that end, so far away; but in between, in the lands barely peopled, wild, thick with bush or forest, the lion could always find his hiding, alone, or the female with cubs, or the roaming pride of four, five, or even fourteen. The slaying of the lions went on year after year. As the years passed and the times changed, and the settler's house became more comfortable, the Overseas *Times* by sea, mail by air, the radio, the newer, faster, smokeless ammunition, and even the ice-box, Africa did not change much. The lions were far from extermination, but the herds of antelope and zebra had grown in numbers, particularly the zebra. A skilled forager, always fat, clannish and innocent, he became a destroyer, almost forgetting that he was the prey of the lion. He became the enemy of the white men, who were replacing the tribal burning of forests for grazing by agriculture and wages for the tribesmen who for so long had wandered, hungry, the prey of spears and disease, but free. They were no less free now, but until they learned the meaning of the new world which had come to them, and until they embraced it, they would fret in the pains of change. The African, still close to his forest and his lore, knew that the white man had broken the spring of nature's balance and he would talk of it to his white master, who knew that the plague of baboons in a piece of country, now devoid of leopards, proved there was something in the African's words. But the zebra were the strongest proof, perhaps, of the work the lion had done before he was killed or driven temporarily away from the haunts where men used rifles. The zebra began to teem on to the land, and when the low-lying plains dried up in the hot season they swarmed into the higher, greener country where the white man had his favourite grazing.

Browning estimated his zebra at about five thousand. The Ganners were luckier. They had something like two thousand. The Brinden farm carried far more, probably seven or eight thousand, while Fawn-Cochley estimated his at getting on for ten thousand. All these were spread over enormous acreages of wild country, where the rhinoceros still roamed and large numbers of antelope grazed from pasture to pasture. About the antelope the farmer had something of a heartache. He did not want them, for they carried ticks, yet he could not bear to part with them. They were beautiful, among the most beautiful beasts of

creation, and if they were not too numerous he turned a
blind eye, unless he shot one here or there for meat, or an
eland for his hide, which made good rawhide ropes. What
would Africa be without its game? He did not want his land
denuded of game. He would manage somehow despite the
ticks, or he could comfort himself by saying: "Anyway, if
I *did* kill them all off, the birds carry ticks, too, so what's
the point. Just have to go on dipping, that's all." But he
could seldom abide the zebra. They served no purpose.
They grazed voraciously, seemingly closer than sheep. They
galloped the dry soil into powder. They shed ticks by the
thousand, and worst of all, when they were shot they were
useless. The meat was uneatable. Those, and they were few,
who had eaten it in an emergency, knew its flesh was rank
and tasted like kipper. Its yellow fat stank and was useless,
and its hide, when dried, was like a sheet of metal. You
could make a stinking box out of a skin by wrapping it wet
round a wooden box and trimming it off with a sharp
knife. A novelty and useless.

Then some Central European government, preparing
part of the hordes so soon to be used in the second round
of the twentieth century's elimination contest, decided they
would give their troops boots of treated zebra skin. Great
was the elation in the Guyu club when this news filtered in.
"Characters" turned up, the professionals who would shoot
or capture anything if the money was good. Theirs was the
perfect life of freedom. A couple of pythons from the Chum-
bo swamp, a cheetah or two (a hundred pounds for a fully-
grown specimen, the money straight from the hands of the
Maharajah's Rajput minion who scoured Africa for the
cheetah) or, now, zebra skins, made a "character" enough
money to stand at any bar in Nairobi, Kampala or Brazza-
ville and tell about it all. They, and the settlers too, slew as
fast as they could on the plains south of Guyu, but the

Central European government was vague and the killing came to an end.

Then a night-club in America upholstered its furniture and draped its walls with zebra skin. A man in the Guyu club, stabbing with his thumb the picture of the club's interior, ornate in an American magazine, said: "There *is* money in these bloody zebra, I tell you, if only someone will use his brains." But that came to nothing too. The zebra increased. The thunder of their hoofs at night as they poured past some lonely farmhouse woke many a muttering white man. Some, like Fawn-Cochley, the Brownings and Ganners and Helena Brinden, combined to make the first big drive in the Guyu district. On the Tuesday before the drive two poor Dutchmen came and offered Helena Brinden their services. The South African Dutch, the greatest shots, and often the most indiscriminate killers in Africa, were still nearer Africa than the British in many ways. Some, like these two, had come north from their original homes, following the game and the wild vastness they loved and could not do without. They killed what they loved, but they could not help that. Better a store full of biltong, their dried antelope meat, and maize meal, than an empty belly and slavery to a job with some British *rooinek*. These were the free, roaming Dutch with the eagle eye and the hard heart for killing, and Helena was sure they would all be glad to have them.

On Tuesday night the Ganners went to stay with the Brownings. Helena Brinden, Jervis and Fawn-Cochley would ride over to the Brownings' farm by their separate ways on the Wednesday morning. All of them, even Fawn-Cochley, were a little elated when they thought of it.

Chapter IX

THE grass was wet with dew when the first cold, steely light crept from the rim of the world and lit trees and scrub with brief, unworldly greyness. Not light enough yet to cheer the two riders, the world, and there was such vastness before them that it could only be called the world, was still enveloped in its immense twilight dream of silence. The stars were there still in the slowly lightening sky, but fading quickly as the first beams of dawn turned the world below them into a softly glowing ocean of reddish gold. It seemed to tremble then, to liquefy before their eyes as the true light flowed on to it, flooding trees, hills, valleys with quivering shafts of a blinding crystal brilliance. Jervis saw giant cobwebs in the bushes, lustrous with dew, palpitating in an almost pearly iridescence as the sun's first beams played on them. So fast was the sun dissolving night that Jervis felt he was seeing the birth of the planet, for below them rolled hundreds of miles of wild country swimming out of blue mists and turning green, grey, yellow, becoming Africa again before his eyes. He could hardly contain his exultance, as his eyes sought to drink in these moments of wonder. It was like touching eternity with his hand, and he was solemn with the feeling of mystery and the almost overpowering majesty of the universe which had quivered for a moment in his being. It went from him as fast as it had come. Now eyes took in this thing and that thing, measuring again, breaking the world before him down into man's ciphers of his environment.

They were riding along the slopes of a green mountain. A few hundred yards or so above them on their left were the dark, towering rain-forests, thick, silent, sunk in the riotous luxuriance of centuries. Suddenly some colobus monkeys,

their thick, black, white-banded coats shining in the sun,
began screaming as they swung through the trees at the
forest's edge. Below the riders, far down on the gentler slopes
which fell away to the plains, the zebra herds were grazing,
grey, gold-illumined hosts, and thick among them the
browns and yellows of eland, kongoni, oryx and gazelle of
many kinds.

Fawn-Cochley and Jervis had ridden for three hours in
darkness, Jervis apprehensive and nervous following the old
man's warning: "Keep your rifle ready and your eyes open.
You never know what we'll meet on the way." They had
ridden hunched in their saddles, cold and silent, and now as
the sun's strengthening light fell on them they slowly sat
up, emerging from that daze which the steady walk of the
horses had created in them. They each carried a ·303 service rifle slung across their backs, their high-velocity sporting rifles cradled across their saddles. In the saddle-bags
they had three hundred rounds of ammunition apiece. Jervis had practised with his rifle for a whole afternoon. He
was not feeling very confident, though his shooting had
improved. "You have to know your rifle," the old man had
told him consolingly. "A rifle is like a man. It has a character of its own and you have to learn it." A slow bond had
begun to form between the old man and the young. Now
that the early, careful behaviour of the pupil had widened
into the real character of the person, Fawn-Cochley could
see his virtues and his failings. He memorised them and
increased the tasks he gave Jervis, nodding when satisfied,
irascible when displeased. He thought he might make something of Jervis if he could overcome what appeared to be a
romantic and immature view of the world.

They reached the edge of a long narrow donga, crossed
it and then the old man said in a low, urgent voice: "Stop.
And keep still. Do you see anything?" Frantically anxious

to show the eagle eye, Jervis searched the broken scrub and vegetation which was sprinkled across the open country before him. Being frantic he saw nothing moving, and forgetting his desire not to irritate the old man, he said: "Where? Where? What?" keeping his voice as low as he could. But the old man was patient, even amused.

"Use your eyes, son," he said. "Look!" He pointed and Jervis saw, his heart leaping, a huge dark shape moving slowly against some bush about two hundred yards ahead of them. He tried to absorb the sight immediately into his eyes, but he could not recognise the meaning of the bulk.

"It's a bull," whispered Fawn-Cochley. Jervis's agitation, though he had not moved, had communicated itself to his horse, which began to tremble and to shake its head.

"Keep still, for Christ's sake, son," the Major told him without turning his head. Then Jervis saw the bull emerge into the open country, saw the long curved horn of the rhinoceros on the long, low, heavy head which moved from side to side in rhythm with its strange slow-motion trot. The sun turned it into a swollen, monstrous bug of gold, its smooth hide like a mirror. There was something menacing and evil in its shape and size, in the almost malevolent swing of its great horned head. Unconscious of everything about him, gripping hard the stock of his rifle, Jervis stared at this brief visitation from the primeval world until it had passed out of sight in the bush. His sigh as he released his breath made the old man laugh. "You're seeing a lot, you know. Some people are years in Africa before they see one as easily as that, but still this place swarms with things, as you'll find soon enough."

"What a frightful brute it is," said Jervis as they rode on.

"It is not the best thing to meet in thick bush, or on a plain either for that matter. They've got a nose for a scent that takes some beating, and if you wound one you'll soon know you've hit something nasty. I've had one of them with its horn under my arse on two occasions, and believe me I didn't know I was an athlete until then."

Morbid after what he had seen, Jervis pressed him for the details and the old man gave them. It was a tale of a last-minute escape and Jervis, when the Major had finished, said, "God, how does one *shoot* that straight in a tight corner? I think I'd shake like a leaf."

"No, no," the old man said. "You shake *after*. You'd be surprised how bloody careful you are when a thing like that is coming for you and you're looking along the sights. Of course, you can always miss."

"I wonder if I *am* cut out for a life like this?" Jervis asked himself. "I wonder if I would be any good if I had to be." It was very worrying for him, for he faced a world, inexperienced as he was, which might erupt into a wild beast's charge at any time while he rode on his work about this still untamed country which Fawn-Cochley had picked for his farmlands.

Jervis liked the Ganners at once. The man was about thirty-five. He spoke with a faint Australian accent, and he was lean and rock-jawed with skin burned to a rough brick-redness. He looked just as Jervis had always imagined Australians to look. He had very light-blue eyes in deep sockets, and strong bony hands as red as his face. He was taller than Jervis, and looking at him, Jervis thought: "That's what freedom in a wide country can do for the British." He had read about the Australians at the Darda-nelles and had seen pictures of them. They looked bigger and more confident than Englishmen, and it seemed they were more direct, for Ganner said to Jervis, as soon as they had shaken hands:

"Better lower those stirrups. You're in for a long day and a sore arse."

"Tom," said his wife, her voice full of a stock disgust, the private family joke that never works for others. "Yes, dear. Yes, dear," her husband said and laughed. "These coarse words before all these ladies and gentlemen." Helena Brinden, wearing khaki jodhpurs and a jacket of soft yellow leather, laughed, and Fawn-Cochley, though not amused, nodded sardonically to Mrs. Ganner. Browning was smoking a cigar. He was wearing tight black trousers buttoned from the ankle to the knee and a yellow shirt of thick, heavy silk. The buttons were of silver.

"Like something out of a film, aren't I?" he said pleasantly, though ironically, to Jervis. "These pants are part of my Mexican get-up. Some day I'll wear the whole thing for you and you'll see what I mean by the full release of the ego which this country brings to us all. Won't he, Helena?"

"Let's all have a drink out of that big flask of yours, Humphrey," she said. "That's the most exotic thing about you as far as I'm concerned."

"Bitch," he said softly and handed her the flask. It was pure whisky, and when Jervis drank from the flask he felt the spirit strike his vitals like a flame, exhilarating him. "We look like a group of bandits, I must say. Look at the armoury." Browning was about to develop the new thought when the Africans began arriving. It was the first time Jervis had seen so many tribesmen with their spears. They were nearly all tall men, some reddish-brown, some almost black, some with negroid features, some hawk-faced and as handsome as he believed the Greeks had been, all of them naked save for short, belted-in cloths which ran from the right shoulder to the knee. Many of them carried short swords in flat red sheaths which they wore almost under their right armpits. Seeing them in that array, Jervis fell in love with Africa, he was sure, for ever. No matter what became of it, he would never, he knew, forget seeing its people like this, dressed for the hunt, trusting, yet full of confidence and an innocence which made him sentimental. He joined that band of white men which would never again be sure whether it wanted an Africa of literate and progressive people geared to the wheels of the West, or like this one before him in its tribal prime, laughing, in touch with and understanding the Africa of the forest, and the beast, and still safe in the background of their tribal world of discipline and strange freedoms. Thus began in him a dilemma he would share with many and which he would never quite solve, for to see men as all men once were, especially if they came of the great cattle-worshipping tribes, was an experience which stirred him deep. He had never believed in "the noble savage," but he saw him now before him, not more savage than he, but, he felt secretly, much more noble. He now understood the sentimental ravings of the Englishman on the ship, and what the Major meant by a Masai-worshipper. These were not Masai, though there were two somewhere among them. They were of many tribes, and as they spread out behind the riders in a long line and he saw their steady, swinging lope with spears held at the trail, he knew he was seeing the Africa which he had imagined in his boyhood and which one day would be gone.

"Nice, aren't they?" said Browning, interrupting Jervis's reverie. "But they get syph and T.B. and bad teeth. I saw you gazing at them and knew you were seeing it for the first time. It's a bloody shame, isn't it? Why can't we keep them like that? Some day they'd thank us if we did." He chewed his cigar, melancholy.

"I don't know what to think about it," Jervis answered truthfully. They had taken his mind even off Helena Brinden when the whisky had given him an elation and a hope about her. Now he wanted to ride beside her, but Browning said:

"Don't worry. Soon you'll be as full of theories as the rest of us. You'll think you know more than the district commissioners and the game wardens. You'll have downright views. You'll want to tell the Colonial Office a million things and you'll wonder sometimes, on the quiet, of course, if you're right after all. In short, you'll be a settler like the rest of us." Jervis was amused and Browning took the cigar from his mouth and smiled, rolling his eyes at Jervis like an actor. "You'll see," he said.

"But is that what you think being a settler is, really?" Jervis asked him as they rode through a deep gully towards the lower slopes. The others were riding in pairs, all talking or laughing. It was good to talk, for they seldom met each other.

"Listen," Browning said, serious, his pose gone. "Being a settler in this country is a bloody hard thing. This country is a museum, a museum containing every damned animal disease that's ever been known to man. They kill your beasts like flies when they come. Wait and see. Then, if you grow corn or maize or some other thing, there are the locusts. Never seen 'em yet, eh? Well, wait. You'll see 'em all right. You need a bloody bank account like Henry Ford to keep going. It's dip, dose, weed, all the time if you *really* want to farm. There are only a few good farmers round here and one or two very good ones, and they work like bloody slaves to keep the thing going. Turn your back and about twenty sheep are lying down dying. Fluke, wireworm, quarter-evil, footrot. The cattle get everything from rinderpest to necrosis of the tongue. Ticks everywhere. It's like being a combination of vet and hired slave. Old man Prawn-Cocktail keeps you on the go, doesn't he?"

"Yes. We work pretty hard. Harder than I thought it would be."

"That's right. Well, soon you'll be full of it all and with a lot of bloody strange views into the bargain. I'm one of the chief settler politicians round here, you know. I talk like a bloody gramophone about Whitehall and the Fabians, but like us they're half right. But besides talking I work my guts out, too, and that's why I'm still here and still got a couple of quid in the bank. You'll meet a lot of what we call bush-stiffs in the country, a couple of horses, a case of whisky and some bills with the local Indian store, but they get weeded out slowly or they have to farm. You can have a good time in this country if you like work or you can go home D.B.S."

"What's D.B.S.?" Jervis wondered if it was some strange state of mental derangement.

"Distressed British Subject," Browning told him. "That's when you're on the bones of your arse, broke, finished. They pay your passage home. They don't allow poor whites at this end of Africa, yet. After a good locust season, you can meet a few D.B.S. types in Dar-es-Salaam or Mombasa, waiting for the ship. Good chaps, some of them, but this is a hard country."

They had ridden out on to the slopes which were almost bare of bush. A mile away were the first zebra, grazing in peace.

"There they are," said Browning. "We'll gallop the bastards off the map. I feel in a particularly nasty mood to-day. The zebra have smashed up about a mile of my new fencing which I slaved to put up. I tell you it's no use fencing until we get rid of these cursed zebra."

"Rein in here," Major Fawn-Cochley was shouting. Jervis saw the two Dutchmen standing beside their horses a couple of hundred yards away. Ganner shouted to them and they mounted and came at a canter across the side of the slope.

"You'll see some real shooting when these *Kaburu* get to work, and you'll see a couple of real trained gun horses too," Browning said.

"What's a *Kaburu*?"

Browning coughed affectedly and said: "It is what the *watu* call the Dutch South Africans."

"But what does it mean?" Jervis pressed him, his curiosity aroused.

"I just don't know but I don't think it's very nice. But you'll find the *watu* have already given you a nickname too. Probably Bwana Dungface or Bwana Stinker or something like that. They call me Bwana Bigmouth. Apt, isn't it?" They laughed, Jervis heartily and Browning like a woman, falsetto, back in his pose again.

The two Dutchmen were young, one of medium height, rawboned, with eyes as pale and cold as spring water, and the other short and squat and dark. They both carried rifles of ·256 calibre and their slouch hats were old and faded. The one with the pale eyes wore the tuft of a lion's tail in his hatband. They looked like men who fear nothing on earth.

"Tough, aren't they?" said Browning in an undertone to Jervis. "They look like pictures I've seen of them in books," he replied in a low voice.

The Dutchmen looked at the people who had stolen their country, who had burned farms, built the first modern concentration camps, the red-necks who had taken their South Africa away. It didn't matter a damn, man, about Slim Janny Smuts, and his chat about friendship. The red-necks had pinched Suid Afrika, a land where a Boer could once ride as far as his horse would stagger and still find land and game and niggers to work. Christ, man, but there they were, the red-necks, owners of Africa and the world. But they'd killed forty thousand red-necks before they went down.

Sure, man, it was wrong to remember the bloody past, but it happened, man, it happened.

Fawn-Cochley looked at the Dutchmen and was sorry once again that white men were so far down the nick in front of the *watu*. They had no standard of life, they lived only a little above the standard of the *watu*. True, they had not had the right school, the right background, the right outlook trained into them, but after all they were pretty far gone, too far gone in a country like this. They should not allow poor whites and that's what these were. They worked hard but they had been too long in Africa, too close to it, had too much of it. The Major knew they thought of him as a red-neck, but because he was Major Fawn-Cochley the Dutch-men would never open their hearts to him and show him their real goodness, and that sharper thing, their bitterness. For if there was one thing an Englishman could not believe, it was that his race had ever been brutal, caught up in desperation, revenge, anger, and the Dutchmen knew this and were tight-mouthed, respectful and careful, locked in-side that long arid memory of veld and kopje and defeat by a huge army.

It came about that the Major, the oldest settler among them, made the suggestions as to how the drive would be done. His plan was clear, simple and easy to understand. He did not shy from the direct order but said: "And you, Ganner, you can work with your wife and follow the line direct from here to Sabuga at the bottom of my place. We'll all have to do a lot of to and fro riding, but we'll stick to our lines as close as possible. Shoot when we can." He could not resist one cry back to the army: "Targets of opportunity you can call it. The main thing is to get the zebra to that gap in the forest below Sabuga and to the right of the Brinden boundary. Any questions?" Everyone was silent. "Right. We'll spread out now and start. Keep an eye on the *watu*. They can kill when they get the chance, but their main job is to keep a line behind us and drive back any zebra that break through us. You can convey that to them, Helena. You're the language and custom expert around here."

Helena blushed with pleasure, because it was true, and Browning said: "That's right, old thing. Get it across to the *watu*."

"*N'atererei*," she said in the rhetoric of the Wa'Kikuyu, and those who were of that tribe smiled and listened. "*Moigwa*. You will do this and this and not this."

"*N'aterei*" to the Wa'Meru. And to the Masai, that tongue less sibilant than the others, less cadence and smoothness in its flow. There were some Samburu who laughed good-humouredly as they listened to her halting Masai, but the two Masai were grave, for this was their holy language of the owners of all the cattle in the world, for that was how it had once been until they lost them all, it was said. The Rendille, tall, black, with a face like a hungry bird, his great fuzz of hair like a cap, defeated her, and he was glad when she went over the instructions again in Ki'Swahili. Too shy to use the correct Ki'Swahili she had learned from the book, and which no one west of the coast ever used, save for the learned district commissioner, she used what was called Ki'Settler, but even that had music in it.

"*Watu wote na fanya laini nyuma yetu. Nueza uua punda milia lakini kaa kama sisi na kaa, tembia upesi kama sisi na tembia. Lakini kazi yaku kuona punda milia haweza taroka nyuma.*"

"What terrible Swahili, Helena," said Browning. "After all that learned other stuff."

"What's the use of learning proper Ki'Swahili when no one uses it?" she flashed back, cross with him, for she was vain about her African lore.

"Take it out on the zebra, old thing," he said soothingly.

"By Christ, man," said one Dutchman to another quietly. "There's a woman who knows these black bastards like one of us."

"Christ, man, you're right there," said the other. They nodded to each other, grim and thoughtful, the dispossessed, but anxious to begin the chase.

Jervis lengthened the stirrup leathers until the balls of his feet took the weight in the stirrups. He half-filled the pockets of his khaki bush-shirt with ·256 calibre ammunition. He gave his ·303 rifle to an African to carry and then sat in his saddle beside Browning, ready to move. The other horsemen spread right and left until they became small in the oceans of grass and scrub.

"Anchor your hat down, sonny boy," Browning told him. "Want a cigar?"

"No, thanks." Jervis pulled the chin-strap of his cork helmet down and tightened it under his chin. "That's right," Browning said. "Now you look like a subaltern ready to ride with the Colonel. Don't forget we work together. We'll ride these bastards to death, we'll ride the bloody stripes right off them. We'll try this baby-shooting scheme of Helena's. You're going to be a tired man tonight, but we'll have a good feed of booze when we get back, I promise you that. Come on, we're off. At a walk for now."

Chapter X

THEY rode down the slow incline towards the zebra, and when they were about five hundred yards from them, the striped comical horses looked up from their feeding and became shifty, trotting about, standing, drifting.

The herd, a couple of hundred of them, began to move friskily, circling, and then trotted away for a while. They were puzzled, unhappy, anxious to graze again.

"Plenty of time," Browning cautioned Jervis when he saw him rise in his stirrups. "Lull them, see? Let them get used to us. We'll do the galloping soon enough."

While the main body of the zebra slowly moved ahead of them, a few, wedded to their bellies, bent to their grazing again. They stood until the two men were less than two hundred paces from them. There was a small foal circling slowly about its mother, who was too busy with her grazing to look up. Like all zebra foals, it had an appearance of bewilderment and trusting idiocy.

"Well," said Browning, "who's going to have first crack?"

"You." Jervis was keyed up, but to kill that small toy horse with its faint immature rusty stripes was still beyond his growing lust to kill. Browning swung gently from the saddle and gave Jervis his reins to hold. He aimed standing, fired and the toy horse buckled on to its neck and then fell over, still. The sound of the explosion rolled across the plain. The others, and the herd beyond them, reared, swerved and were off, their hoofs kicking up a low veil of dust. The mother of the dead foal ran round the corpse, uncertain, until she, too, fell to Browning's next bullet, thrashing on her side.

"She'll take a bit longer but she's finished," Browning announced as he mounted again. "Come on." They went off at a trot towards the subsiding dust. They could hear a stallion hee-hawing beyond them and the rumble of hundreds of hoofs.

Jervis began to feel an increasing desire to close with the zebra and to get over his nervousness with the rifle. Now was the time to practise, to learn about his rifle. The faint distaste which had become almost horror when he had seen the baby zebra fall, was fading fast. Excitement mastered squeamishness and he drove his heel into the horse's belly, and Browning, amused, did likewise. The zebra kept up a steady pace; occasionally they swerved slowly and gracefully in grey and black dazzlings as the sun fell on their flanks. They were without panic, or real fear as yet. In their collective and instinctive way they were enjoying the move. It was not until they heard the cracking of rifle shots away on their right that they put on speed. Many reared and plunged, causing a desperate commotion in the herd, and all swung this way and that while the two riders closed on them. Forgetting Browning, Jervis dismounted and Browning took the reins from him. He sat down to aim, but his arms trembled even when he rested his elbows on his knees. The rifle barrel was warm from the sun, and in his eyes its glint was like a white fire as he depressed it slowly until the sights met. He followed a trotting zebra mare, fired, reloaded in a second as he saw her plunge and fired again. She ran on and his next shot brought her down. He knew he had aimed the last shot anywhere between her shoulders and haunches and had been lucky. He must control himself.

"Try one in the rear," Browning shouted. They were running straight ahead, their fat haunches dipping as they gathered speed. Jervis picked a fat stallion and this time at three hundred yards sent the zebra skidding in an arc on to its right side, and as it slid at speed in the grass a wake of yellow dust shot from under it. It kicked feebly, broken by the shattering power of the bullet.

"That's better," Browning said, with little conviction. "You don't know that rifle yet, do you?"

"Getting to know it," Jervis replied as calmly as he could manage. That last shot had changed him. He could shoot at last and now the bloodlust was strong in him. "Come on, let's get on." Browning was already off at a canter while Jervis mounted. When they crossed a low roll of country they saw an amazing sight. Below them on the rolling grey and green country were thousands of zebra in five separate herds, separated by a mile or so from each other. They were racing aimlessly for hundreds of yards and then turning, at last sensing the frightening plan of all the horsemen. In the glaring light of the sun they scintillated like metal. They had begun to panic and in the warm air there was a smell of sweat and salt.

"Stop and you'll see some shooting. Look!" yelled Browning to Jervis. He pointed to a small rise on their right. The two Dutchmen, about four hundred yards from them, had flung their reins over their horses' heads and were aiming. They opened fire like trained soldiers. "Look," said Browning. Zebra began to fall even as they galloped at three hundred yards from the marksmen. "That's shooting," Browning said, but Jervis only nodded. He had never seen anything like it. The Dutchmen's horses stood perfectly still while their masters, comfortable in the saddle, killed zebra one after the other, dropping them right and left, a line of them from which the herd fled in a rush of hoofs and dust.

"Those horses are trained specially," Browning said. "You just throw the reins over the head and they stand doggo. These Dutchmen could shoot a fly wing off if they wanted to. Come on. We're getting the zebra nicely collected now."

"In a way, it's rather terrible, isn't it?" Jervis seemed to Browning to have turned a little pale and he smiled sympathetically. "Wait till the *watu* get into them," he said. "Then you'll see how terrible it can be. But it's got to be done." They cantered again, past the dead zebra. They

were so like horses. Perhaps that was what made Jervis feel
sickened. They broke into a gallop and his emotions
changed again. He would, he must, try and shoot like those
Dutchmen. Only if he learned to shoot well could he feel
he really belonged to this Africa across which they were
galloping, the wind tugging at his helmet.

Eland, about thirty of them, fat, sleek and soft with a
glow of sun on their smooth coats, flashed past them,
almost close enough to touch. Browning saw a bull with
long white-tipped horns. "Steaks, fat chops, a lovely head,"
he thought, and then it was gone. A stream of kongoni,
their hunched forequarters and ugly heads straining,
crossed their front at great speed. About them all was movement, swerve, skid, dust, drumming of hoofs, and to right
and left, far away, the snap of rifle fire. They went through
a wall of dust, the hoofs of their horses urgent in one continuous rolling beneath their tight, gripping legs, and a
quarter of a mile ahead the long racing lines of zebra ran
from end to end of the yellow prairie. Their hee-hawing
now was loud and anxious. They seemed to know in one
great, collective despair that they were being driven down
into the scorching heat of the plains, that these men on
horseback would massacre them, would drive them from
the cool luscious grazing to which they had been drawn by
the urge of centuries of seasons. Bunched together now in
one pouring mass across the rolling country, they had to
slow down to an awkward trot. The riders were herding
them towards the boundary of the Brinden and Fawn-
Cochley ranches, and already the unsuspecting herds of
zebra on those lands could hear the low thunder of the
waves of their own kind slowly bearing down to join them.

Behind the riders, the vultures, who since morning when
they had seen men and the glint of rifle barrels, generally
the equation of noise and death and food, were pouring

down from the sky on to the corpses which lay spread across ten miles of country.

Major Fawn-Cochley cantered up to Browning and Jervis and, after wiping his face with a handkerchief, said: "We're going to wait now, all of us, while the *watu* move forward and drive for a bit. No use panicking the zebra too much yet. And anyone who needs a change of horse can get one from the *watu* bringing them up." He explained that once the herds in front of them joined up with the thousands on Brinden's and his own place, the real drive could begin, for below Fawn-Cochley's ridge was the break in the forest and then the plains.

"Right." Browning dismounted and the old man rode on in search of the Ganners. The zebra moved on until they were lost in dust and haze.

"D'you like this life?" Browning wanted to know when they were seated in the grass, which already, a thousand feet below the starting point of the drive, was drier, with more grey in the green.

"I love it," said Jervis. "I only wonder if I'll ever be able to shoot like you and the rest of them. It's necessary, isn't it?"

Browning nodded, looking up at Jervis from where he had curled up on his side, his eyes playful.

"Yes, it's necessary," he agreed, "but nothing to worry about. You'll shoot better all the time. You'll learn to be cruel. You have to be. It's not like home with the quiet lanes and the village pub, and where the only exciting thing that happens is when someone puts one of the maids in the family way. No, it's different here. But you'll never feel quite permanent here. You'll never feel you quite belong."

"Why not?" Jervis was curious. He could sense the other Browning now, the one under the bright shirts and the easy flow of nonsense.

"Because the place isn't empty. Not like Australia with a few Stone Age blacks cutting designs into themselves and waiting for the end. No, this place is not like that. It's full of Africans who are going to change and somehow, even when I'm working my guts out, I wonder what I'm doing here. There's something almost artificial about it at times, and at others it feels worth it. There, that's something for you to chew on."

"You mean we don't really belong here?"

"In a way, that's what I mean. It can't last like this. It's only about forty years since this place was swarming with Masai ravaging the country and one or two Europeans hunting for ivory. We've brought a bit of order but it hasn't altered Africa much, yet. But it can't last. I love it too and I hate to think of it going."

"I was thinking about that only a couple of hours ago," Jervis said, remembering the emotion he had felt when watching the tribesmen with their spears and their bodies so at home in this scenery.

"Africa gets a grip on you. You love it. You hate to think of it not being this Africa. And that's wrong, but that's what I feel sometimes. We're seeing the best of it. Look out there." Browning pointed to the plains below them, which were like an endless reddish-yellow floor sprinkled with grey jungle until they dissolved into a bluish quivering haze of heat. The sky where it reached the horizon was like grey-blue aching metal. A dust devil, miles away on the dead, seemingly deserted floor of Africa, whirled slowly away into the haze.

"That way to Congo and the Sudan. That way to Abyssinia and the Gallas. It's huge. It swarms with game and the tribes are still in the blue. You see it every day, from where you are at the Prawn-Cocktail's place. You'll want to go down there. It draws you. When this place is covered with buildings there'll always be that to go to. There's not much water there. It'll always be the same. I like to think of that when I read the bloody newspapers from home and think of this place full of civilisation. So you see you're not the only one who dreams round here." He laughed, feeling he had given too much away, but Jervis was the kind of kid you could talk like that with. With one of the others, it would have sounded just a little queer, as though he had drunk too much.

"I always wanted to come to Africa," said Jervis, warming to Browning's mood. "I always knew I would come too. Strange, it's just as I imagined it. I didn't really feel that until I saw the Africans this morning with their spears and the whole thing."

"You'll always come back too," Browning replied. "It's true that the bloody claws of the lion will pull you back just as the *watu* say."

They heard shouting, and behind them they saw the tribesmen in a long chanting line, their spears resting on their right shoulders, moving at a lope downhill. As they passed the two white men, some shook their spears, slapping them in their quiverings against the palms of their hands. "*Na'uua*," they shouted, laughing with fierce teeth gleaming. "*Na'uua*. We are going to kill." They loped on towards the far dust-clouds of the zebra, intent; they would release themselves through their blades from the as yet slight constriction that even in this wilderness a few white men had begun to build about them and their ancient dream of blood.

"They *are* savage," mused Browning as they got to their feet. "Because they're quiet with us and do their jobs we forget what goes on inside them. But sometimes you get a surprise and you sort of see for an instant what a big difference there is between you."

"I know that," Jervis told him with curious conviction so that Browning looked at him as he drew in his reins. "How do you know it?" he asked.

"I don't know. But I *knew* these people as soon as I came amongst them. They didn't feel strange to me at all. I knew I would soon understand them." Browning knew that Jervis was beginning to trust him and he was touched. Jervis looked so young and yet he knew what Jervis had experienced.

"I think you will get on with them. The main thing is never to lose your temper. That's the curse of most of us out here. We get into a temper in a couple of seconds and the *watu* don't understand that. Ready?"

They went forward towards the zebra at a trot. The sun was high now, blazing like a candle in the sky. The saddle was hot between Jervis's legs and his rifle barrel felt as though it had come straight from a fire. He screwed up his eyes in the increasing glare as the sun poured back at them from the yellowing grass which was already more sparse, drier than the lushness they were leaving behind.

They rode for nearly half an hour, the Africans keeping pace with them. A mile ahead the zebra were beginning to tire, imperceptibly to Jervis, but to Browning obvious in the air of listlessness which marked the movements of the herd.

"A couple more hours and they're going to be tired," Browning called out. "They're fat. They're a bit puffed now, but in a couple of hours they're going to be really ready."

It was among the foals that the first exhaustion became apparent to Jervis. They ran about aimlessly and then stood panting, sad, while the mothers distractedly sought to escape with the herd but were pulled back to their young. The thousands of zebra milled on until they joined the herds on Fawn-Cochley's land which already the two Dutchmen with Helena Brinden were driving into their first panic.

The spearmen, screaming, beating drums and tins, ran forward to despatch the foals and those mothers that stood by them. It was then that Jervis understood what Browning had meant. He saw one tall thin tribesman, lips twisted back from his teeth, devilish, frighteningly magnificent, stab a mare with his long spear, while his companion finished her off with a club, striking her head as though she were a tree. "Oh, God," said Jervis, but all about him the Africans were falling on the zebra, slashing, beating, worrying them like dogs. One mare, her terrible teeth snapping, sat on her haunches, moving her snarling head from side to side, hamstrung, while an African drew back some ten paces, raised his spear, hopped on his right leg, then, howling, thrust the spear through her body. Then he beat his hands together and jumped about, ecstatic with this death he had given her. The bone plugs in his ears shone as he danced, and then Jervis found himself shooting at the wandering foals ahead of the Africans, hearing the strike of the bullets, his mind gathered up in the daze of killing which had overcome them all. Then he was galloping ahead of the yelling Africans, dismounting, shooting, galloping on, Browning working to his left.

"We've got them," Jervis was shouting. "We've got them." To those Africans who passed him as he sat, firing between each gallop, he cried: "Kill. Go on. Kill." He felt desperate, anxious to end it, to see the zebra through that forest gap and end this slaughter. But the slaughter had hardly begun.

Helena Brinden found that she could not do what she had hoped she could do. She could not shoot the foals and she sat in her saddle, pale and shaken, while the two Dutchmen shot them down before her eyes. It was her plan and here it was in a welter of blood, in writhings and jumpings and quiverings. She shot several mares and a stallion, but the thrill of hunting was not there for her. She watched the two Dutchmen, grim in their business, shoot everything that came within their range. They were keen and careful. They were happy.

The Brownings' land, the Ganners' and the Brindens' were now clear of zebra. All of them were concentrated on Fawn-Cochley's farm where it began to run down past the Sabuyu hills to the forest. For miles about sixteen thousand zebra were swirling slowly towards the escarpment, and the riders, eight of them, were closing in and behind the riders came the Africans, their blades wet with blood, not caring about the saving of the white man's grazing, unconscious of a plan, not squeamish, but full of desire to hunt down and annihilate. They had not known how bored they were. Now, they were lit up with an almost sadistic energy, for this was all that was left for the spears to do in the world of wages and white men. In this part of the land the raiding was finished and the old chiefs sucked their gums in the sun, bald with comfort. Now a man could use his right arm again and see blood spray in the sun. One day there would not even be zebra to hunt and kill.

Major Fawn-Cochley was tired. He noticed it after the first long gallop of the morning. "Don't know why that should be," he mused. It came as a slight faintness first, then an overpowering desire to lie down, but he fought it, reining in near a tree and leaning against it. The sharp scent of his horse's first sweat seemed to nauseate him and he rested against the tree, his eyes closed. No one could see him thus. In five minutes he would be well again. Was it all this reading late at night? And what good was it doing him? He had read over a hundred books about the soul after death, about the spirit world, all of them absorbing, but there was no proof, and without proof he could not believe. A cool breeze caressed his face and for a second he thought he would fall from the saddle, so powerful a faintness came over him. He was sixty-seven and perhaps those years had caught up with him. He had a fear of illness and death, not an ordinary fear, but a fear that was sometimes like being a prisoner at the bottom of a dark, silent pit when he woke in the morning. He shook it off and entered life on such mornings with an almost brutal resolve, to live, to do, to escape. Those sixty-seven years, twenty of them in India and twenty-six in Africa. India was a far memory, a weirdness of heat and swarming people and flowers trampled before a million silent, unanswerable gods, an endless cycle of dilemma for its children and all its conquerors. Africa was like seeing the first dawn, a land which had called from its every corner to him to strike out, march on, camp, stay for a while, and then wander past mountains, through forests and along deep-flowing brown rivers. He had hunted elephant across dried, baked mudflats which shook with heat at midday, in the great Sud where the tall, gangling ash-covered negroes still lived in a mystery of signs and symbols, nailed by the sun to their blazing plains. He had walked through the red lava dust and the scattered seas of black basalt which by midday were almost as hot as when first flung from the heart of the great explosion which had torn the country's breast open for hundreds of miles. Galbanti, where the Somalis and the Masai had wiped out stockades, houses and that first glimmer of foreign light only forty years before. Lokwadang, Yombo, El Marodi, Chambambo, all the names which brought up visions of squat black men, some almost ape-like, of thin red men like pharaohs lost in wildernesses of sand and scrub, of black, brown and red men of all kinds who had lived for thousands of years on the very edge of the world's centre. Rome and

Greece had died and Europe's dark age had passed before these men had seen the white men and the terrible choices they offered. Raided for generations by the Arab slavers, the banana eaters had hidden in the forests. It was only forty years since this land had seen its first few dozen white men staring amazed at the Mountains of the Moon, at the new world which had lain silently behind their backs, touching them, for two thousand years. Fawn-Cochley had often thought how strange it was that this land he farmed had not seen a white man until four hundred years after Columbus had discovered America. Several times he had wished to leave it, once had even left it, but he could not go, why he could not say. There was something, no one could say what it was, in the Africans that captured him. They might make his temper bad, they might make him despair, but always they were forgiven for that curious quality, it might be trust, won in the end.

"There are no ghosts," he had brusquely told Jeru one day when that now creaking figure had told him of a strange visitation in the night. "No, there are no ghosts. You're always talking about ghosts but you've never seen one. How can there be a ghost if you can't see it? Tell me that."

"Bwana," the old cook had said after sucking his black cheeks for a time, "Bwana, have you seen the wind? Yet, it is there."

What answer could you give to that? They were born for religion, there was no doubt of it. One had to watch that the best one, the unspoiled, the splendid, did not go away to the mission at Gombo. He had a deep distrust of the missions. They were out to destroy his Africa of which he was jealously fond. When he saw an African in torn shorts it was pain. When he met one who said his name was Josiah he lost his temper in slow barkings and cruel questionings.

"What's your real name? What was the name the tribe gave you? That's good, isn't it? It's better than Josiah, isn't it? Go on, clear out. I don't want you around here. Go and get a job in town." He knew it was mean and yet he could not help it. He knew they wanted to come in, to get into the warm after the crash of so many legends of cut bodies and filed teeth and bunches of smeared entrails at midnight in the giant nettles. He recognised that leaning forward, that small supplication of hands and the black face with its soft eyes saying: "But I'm a good man, Bwana, I have been to the mission school." He had to walk away then, angry, and ashamed of himself, but how could he deny that other enormous Africa of sun and beasts and wilderness in which he had wandered with tall spearmen or small black, cruel hunters with their poisoned darts?

The faintness left him and he opened his eyes and looked down again at the zebra a mile or two away, shimmering with a heat he could all but feel. The air above them quaked and some thorn trees seemed to swirl like green smoke in the heat. He had lost interest in the game. He had to go on with it, but there was no joy for him as he had seen in the young Jervis, who was seeing his Africa with fresh eyes and responding to it with the heart and muscles of twenty years. The old man watched the riders moving in on the herds of thousands, and behind them the Africans shining like small red copper figures as they advanced. Best to get on. The sooner it was over the better. He longed to lie down and he did not look forward to the furnace heat of the plains below where the chase would end. He struggled against the alarm he felt in his years. The alarm that he was old at last and had lost that steel and leather strength which had carried him through country where even the beasts had panted.

Chapter XI

THE zebra were tired at last. Their bodies were dark and shining with sweat. At last they were terrified, too, and they stampeded like explosions of ants from the earth when the rifle fire opened on them. Trails of corpses, now struggling mounds of vultures, marked the chase from the mountain forest to the escarpment where it began to fall away rapidly to the plains. The Ganners had driven them slowly down towards the forest while the others, by shooting, had pressed them into one rolling, hee-hawing multitude of terror. Stallions burst out ahead of the herd and drummed at speed towards the forest gap, but wheeled again in long parabolas of stripes and hoofs, their nostrils dilated, back to the herd. Now it was massacre as the black and white walked slowly on to them and slew them with blade and bullet. The Africans went mad, leaping and dancing with their spears and clubs, as they ran from victim to victim. At times the beasts would surge like grey waves towards the men, seeking to break out until several stumbled to the bullets and they fled back again to the milling herd. There was a deep, continuous thundering of hoofs, and the men were close enough to hear the concerted panting which underlay the neighing and hee-hawing of the thousands of tired zebra.

Slowly they were driven towards the gap in the cedar forest. It was rocky, washed out by many seasons of flooding rains. As they moved to the gully, skittish, shying, Browning called off the Africans, but they took no notice. They went on with their killing, grunting, like machines. One held aloft an embryo in its gelatinous casing which the sun turned to silver, shouting: "*Na zaa! Na zaa!*" "It is born! It is born!" Jervis leaned from his saddle and vomited, and

4

in his ears he could hear the good-humoured laughter of the
Africans who stood beside him clapping their bloody hands.

They followed the zebra down into the aching heat of
boulders and sand and dead bitter grass, Jervis alone now,
listening to the wind whistling in the white ant-eaten bulbs
of the mimosa thorns. He saw a scorpion scuttle under a
rock and a blue lizard staring at him from the sand. The
smell of the zebra was strong in the airless gully. Their
thousands of hoofs created a veil of dust through which
the sun appeared as a disc of dull white fire.

One zebra, worn, its head hanging, dropped from the
herd and stood in the shade of a giant euphorbia. It heard
Jervis coming and turned. He dismounted, holding the reins
in the crook of his left arm. As he raised the rifle, the zebra,
as if seeking the death which he now knew the men always
carried, began to trot towards him. He waited until it was
fifty yards from him and then shot it, watching it fall on to
its knees with bent head, and as though digesting the bullet
it swallowed, working its neck and head. Then it rolled over
slowly, sighing, and Jervis rode on. The sweat poured from
his body as he descended towards the plains. On each side
of him the dead cedar, bearded with green lichenous foam,
gave back the low muttering echo of the moving hoofs. He
found a foal lying on its side under a boulder, lying quietly
as though resting near its mother. He saw its glazed eyes,
which did not move when he walked to its side. Against
his will he leaned down and stroked the sodden coat and
rubbed one coarse wagging ear. He shirked the next move
after aiming at it, and he pressed over the safety catch,
mounted and rode on, leaving the small beast in its shade,
alive. He could hear shots at intervals. He saw troops of
zebra breaking up the sides of the gully and racing over the
ridge. More began to follow them. They were breaking back
with renewed energy and a determination. He opened fire,

missing three times, then dropping one as it heaved itself on to the edge of the gully. It rolled down in a long thickening plume of dust and an avalanche of sand and stones, but the others did not stop. The whole herd began to turn and he saw silhouetted against the blue of the sky, Browning and Helena Brinden firing into them, but unable to stop them. Jervis rode half-way up the side of the gully, from where he could cover both flanks of the zebra, but as he did so they began to race back along the gully and he could hear Browning shouting: "Get down again, Jervis, and stop them." He did stop them, but not until over a hundred had escaped. "There's something going on in front," Browning was roaring at him. "They're stampeding. They won't go through." Even as he spoke Jervis saw the zebra coming towards him in one charging solid mass. Like mad cavalry they came, and from where he sat on his plunging rearing horse he looked down on them as they tore past him, acrid, soaked in sweat and utterly desperate. They brushed against his legs and knocked his horse from side to side. There was a break for a few seconds and he galloped up the side of the hill, and as he got down from his horse the second wave came charging up the gully. He shot one after another, but the tearing, clattering hoofs went on over the dead. The drive was over. He watched hundreds after hundreds escape. "Get on down the donga," Browning was calling. "There are still some down there. Quick. Drive them before they break back."

It was two o'clock. They had been riding and killing since an hour after dawn. It had seemed only a short time, the whole amazing day, until he began to move, and then he could feel his tiredness. The heat of the sun-glare weighed on him, and the disappointment of the drive's failure made the next effort pointless, dreary. He rode slowly down the donga. Far down on the plains he could see zebra streaming away in lines from the escarpment. There were some hundreds of them and this was a solace. He watched Browning and Helena Brinden a long way ahead, riding down the donga. He looked forward to meeting her again but wished Browning was not there. Browning was a good way ahead of Helena, and he thought of riding over to her and delaying her while Browning went on, and while he idled over this plan he saw Browning dismount and start waving to Helena, waving her back and shouting. He could never remember perfectly what happened after that. He saw Browning leave his horse and walk forward. He heard Browning's shout of "Look out, Jervis," and some other words which he did not hear in his shock, and then terror as he saw a long, heavy, brownish-yellow shape bound out from the rocks, rear, and then come slashing down on to Browning like a flash, disappearing with him behind some ragged bush. He galloped forward, his heart in his throat, seeing the woman raise her rifle, aim, then bring it down again, raise it again, drop it. He heard her scream and he could hear his own brutish panting as he kicked his horse, leaning forward almost on her neck in an effort to get up the ridge.

"It's too late," the woman was screaming. "It's too late." He saw her firing and then she burst into tears as he reached her. She had her face in her hands and her rifle was at her feet. In seconds he saw what had happened. Down in the gully was Browning's hat, part of his shirt, and, most shocking of all, nearby, Browning's body, but strangely mangled and with one leg missing. He ran down with the woman following him, and though suffering from great shock so that he trembled as he ran, his eyes ranged the thick grey bush which ran up to the forest. "It went in there, into the bush," he heard Helena weeping. When he reached Browning his eyes took in a dead zebra which lay farther on, slashed and half disembowelled. Browning was quite dead, the first dead man Jervis had ever seen, lying in the sand which had soaked up his blood thirstily. Helena burst into tears when she saw Browning's mutilated body, so lately experienced and confident. It was as though Africa had put out a swift, sweeping paw and removed him from his small and puny attempt to pacify her. What those fearful claws had done to him shook Jervis down to the fibre of his body, and after one look the woman had turned away, swaying.

Africa had always been so easy up to now. She could not believe it had sprung like this from its darkness and shown her its fierceness, its lightning-fast ferocity. She had never seen the beast win before, and it was incredible that the huge, muscled, yellow shadow had sprung and mauled Browning, biting him to death with one growling crunch of its fangs.

"It was standing on that zebra," she whispered. "We saw it when all the other zebra broke away. It had killed right in the middle of the herd and there it was. It growled when—when Humphrey went forward to get a shot and before he could move it had him down. Oh, God, it was dreadful. He cried and he tried to get hold of its jaws, and I tried to shoot but I couldn't because I would have shot poor Humphrey. It went away with his leg and I fired twice and missed it." She broke down again into bitter tears, and Jervis said: "Where did it go? I'll have to go after it." She pointed into the grey scrub, and while Jervis was reloading the magazine of his scorching rifle, Major Fawn-Cochley and the Ganners arrived.

"Christ Almighty," said Ganner when he saw the body of Browning from some distance away. They all came galloping, and the old man said: "My God, this is a nasty business. A nasty business. My God. What happened?" He knelt beside Browning and listened while Helena described again those few paralysing moments of horror. There was a silence when she had finished, that awful silence when the men wonder if enough was done, if the survivor could not have done something despite all the difficulties described. Not being a man, the woman did not feel the import of this brief silence, for about death and destruction and all its facets men have a clannishness and a code which women never quite grasp.

"It must have been a terrible thing for you to see, Helena," the Major consoled her. "I know. I've seen it twice, and it's so quick you can't believe it. And there's nothing more terrible than trying to shoot when the brute's on top of the victim."

"That's true," said Ganner. His wife, a small, pretty blonde girl, was staring in a dazed kind of way at the ground, her face ashen. Helena had recovered from the hysteria into which the killing had thrown her. She was calmer now and she listened while the old man said: "We'll have to get this lion, and soon too." To Jervis he said as though he were a servant: "Go and get the Dutchmen. And all the *watu*, quickly."

Chapter XII

ONCE it had been agreed that Jervis and Mrs. Brinden should go back on fresh horses to the Brinden house for a car, and two heavy rifles, they left the others to scour the bush. The Major had ordered some of the tribesmen to pile thorns on top of Browning's remains. They laughed and joked as they did this, solemn when the white men were there, but themselves when they were absent. They did not laugh because they were callous. They laughed because they were moved, as some Europeans are to the point of laughter at funerals, for there is a point where grief and laughter meet and are one. They laughed because of the flutter in the diaphragm whence their laughter, and their grief, came, as they had come in exclamations of wonder or pain when the men had been moved and uttered sounds to convey the tremulous feeling in their centres. Politeness, as such, when a death or a great joy was concerned, was not a part of the few hypocrisies, or refinements, that their primitive life-patterns had formed in them.

One of them, a thin youth with ear lobes hung with coiled copper wire and stretched to the breaking point, had hoped to get a job one day as one of Browning's herdsmen. "This one," he was thinking, "gave with a big hand—and I would have shared in that giving. Now, he is taken up into his God's hand and it is finished. Now, I will have to go on under the tongue of Muntu Mareti, the old one whom the white woman trusts." He was one of Helena Brinden's assistant herdsman and now he would have to stay with her. But five minutes after covering Browning with thorns he forgot him, for death was the end of a man and he was gone.

Jervis was quiet as he rode beside the woman. He had wanted to comfort her, to put his arms about her small shoulders, but he could see she had had a great shock, greater than he had himself. He had been in this country only a few weeks and had half-expected violence daily, ever since hearing the roaring of the lion for the first time. Even though he had always begun the fantasy of meeting his first lion by a long slow prelude, the killing of a cow, the riding to the place of the kill, the tracking and the hunt and *then* the lion, he had thought of it so much, that the sight of one bearing Browning down in a second had not upset him as it had the woman. He was shaken, but had got over it quickly. Helena, after twelve years of growing complacency about the wild country in which she lived, had thought of herself as an expert, and of the country and its beasts as sport. Lions had killed cattle, had escaped or had stayed and been trapped, or shot. She had never shot one herself. But they had been hunted and killed and were sport. But she had never before known one to win and had never expected it. That lashing tail, those yellow eyes staring up from the head which had its teeth buried in the zebra's belly, the stiffening tail as Browning had gone forward a few paces to get a better shot, and then that incredible speed of the charge and the kill, she would never forget. It was so quickly over that it might have been a dream but for the greater horror of it eating the fallen man.

Jervis did not know what to say to her, but at length, noticing that she was riding as if in a dream, he said: "We'd better hurry, Helena." It was the first time he had used her name, and she smiled weakly and said: "Yes, you're right, Jervey. I'll be all right soon. It was a shock. I've known Humphrey so long, and there's poor Anna to hear it yet. What shall we do?"

"Do nothing yet," he said, only half conscious that she had turned to him for advice and that he would make the decisions from now on until they joined the hunt again. "Let's get the lion first." But it was not the same thing, he thought, as hunting a man who had killed a woman's husband, hunting him for revenge. It was not the same thing at all. He knew that the only reason they had for hunting and killing the lion as fast as possible was because it had killed a man and had found it easy. Much easier than killing a beast, for a man is nothing, having no speed, no claws, no teeth or hoofs, only his rifle, which is not within the lion's conception of opposition. This lion would kill more men now, for it was easy.

They went at a canter the rest of the way, and Jervis knew that he would meet her husband now and he was in a mood of expectancy and knew a kind of guilty nervousness, for he thought that the man might guess his feelings about the woman.

Louis Brinden was lying back on a divan on the front veranda when they arrived. He did not get up as they approached, but Jervis could see his eyes following them. He was a short man, with big shoulders, strong and well knit. He had a red face and a dark-blue chin and mouth where he shaved. There was a deep white scar across his forehead. It was a kindly, thoughtful face, and when Helena introduced Jervis, he got up and shook hands, saying pleasantly: "So you're the new slave at Fawn-Cochley's? How d'you like it?"

"Louie," she said, holding up her hand, "we've got some bad news. Humphrey Browning's been killed by a lion."

"Killed by a lion," he said, his eyes opening under raised brows. "Good lord, when?"

"Just an hour ago. I was there. It was over in a flash." She was afraid he could see her distress and would walk over and comfort her, lay his hand on her, but he did not move. He offered Jervis a cigarette and lit one himself, thoughtful and quiet. When the smoke was pouring from his mouth in a blue haze he said: "You'd better have a drink. Did you see it?"

"Your wife did. I saw the lion get him down from some way away, but your wife saw the whole thing," Jervis told him, adding: "I think a brandy or something *would* be a good idea."

"Right," said Brinden. "Poor Browning. I wouldn't have thought a lion would get him, but you can't tell in this bloody world." He shouted for a servant, and a young man in a clean white *Kanzu* and red fez came, reminding Jervis of the hotel on the coast, novel after the slap-dashing Kyonga and Nyangi. The house was well furnished, almost sumptuous, and the living-room into which they went had windows all along one wall so that the room sparkled with light, unlike the gloom of Fawn-Cochley's house.

"I'll get the rifles," Helena told them. Brinden was about to say something but she had gone before he could begin. When they were alone, Brinden said: "Sit down." He smoked for a time and then said in a good-natured way, but with a hook in the words:

"I suppose you expected to find me lying drunk on a bed." He sucked at his cigarette, regarding the young man observantly through the smoke. He could see that Jervis did not know what to say, and he smiled thinly and said: "Surely? She tells everyone I'm drunk most of the time. I must be rather a surprise for you." Jervis was irritated by this playfulness and he said brusquely:

"What does it matter? Does it matter to you?"

The other man sat up, and for want of something to do, squashed his cigarette out, rather carefully Jervis thought, in an ash-tray. Then he said: "It does as a matter of fact. You don't have to tell me that everyone round here has the idea that I'm drunk day and night. I was merely suggesting that it must be a surprise for you to find it's untrue. Ah, here's the brandy."

Helena came back carrying two heavy, double-barrelled rifles, and some packets of ammunition, and while he poured the brandy, Brinden said lightly to her:

"What are you going to do with those?"

"We're going back after the lion with them. The others are waiting for us," she told him. She could sense his antagonism. She knew that lightness of voice, that narrowed eye.

"You don't have to go," he told her and handed

her a small, heavy glass of brandy. "Here, drink it," he added.

"No," she said and sipped the spirit, "but I'm going."

"You're not," he countered at once, quietly. "Much better stay here. You can't make any difference. Jervis can go back with the car and the rifles."

"No, I'm going," she said. "I want to see it through."

"See it through?" His voice had changed. In it there was an edge of hostility, and Jervis wondered if he should go out of the room for a while. She saw his movement and said:

"It's all right, Jervey. We often talk like this. Don't go."

That seemed to break Brinden's calm and he was almost shouting when he said: "Well, you're not going. That's all. What damned good can you do? From what you've told me you've had one chance to shoot the bloody thing and didn't. Now leave it to the others." As though to soften his words he added: "It's dangerous and I don't see any reason why you should take risks."

But the row had begun. They were experienced people. They knew each other's armoury, they knew where the skin was raw, where a word was like salt and where to go slowly, probing into another deeper wound. She took the end he had thrown her, that bit about having had the chance to shoot it already, and she shouted:

"That's a dirty thing to say. I had no chance of shooting it. You're blaming me for his death. It's not fair."

"Well, you did, didn't you? You had a chance. You had a rifle and you did nothing. So why beat about the bloody bush?" She began to cry. As though it were the most natural thing to do, Brinden took her glass and filled it again, saying: "Here. This is that five star I got from Abdul Hafiz." She took it, her face misshapen with tears.

"Must hurry," said Jervis in a low voice.

"Well, hurry," Brinden said jovially. "Here's the key of

the car." Jervis took it and rose, saying: "Well, it's nice meeting you. I hope we'll meet again."

"You hope no such thing," Brinden said, his false smile failing to hide the bite in his words.

"I'm coming too," said his wife. She walked to the door. If they had been alone, Jervis knew, Brinden would not have taken his dogged and now ludicrous stand. He tried to make it less ludicrous by shouting: "You go, and you'll regret it. I've told you you're not to go. You do what you like around here, at any time you like to, but this time I draw the line. You go, and you can bloody well stay."

"What *nonsense*, Louie," she snapped at him. "What's the matter with you? Are you mad?" Jervis made a mistake by saying half-heartedly: "You can't really stop her, you know."

"She's attractive, I'll give you that," Brinden said, smiling sardonically. "She's had more than you put in a good word before now. But you go and sit in the car. *We'll* attend to this." Jervis left them and he heard their voices rise immediately.

"You bitch," he cried.

"You ill-mannered bastard," she shouted back. "Why don't you mind your own business? What are you trying to do? Are you trying to show the guest that you own me? Because you don't, damn you." Her voice became sibilant then. "Own you?" he asked. "In what way? Why? Does anyone else own you in any particular way?"

"Don't be a fool," she shouted. "Instead of trying to stop me going, why don't you come yourself?"

"Did you ever see me hunt anything?" he said. "Do you think I'm going to start now?"

"It'd be a bloody more use to you than sitting reading your T. S. Eliot and your James Joyce, wouldn't it?" she wanted to know.

"You read them too, don't you, you silly bitch," he shouted back, and like routine she replied with: "But I work as well."

"You like it, that's why." He showed his teeth.

"I have to."

"Liar."

"I have to, I tell you. Or nothing would be done." Her voice was filled with rage now. They were closer to each other now.

"When you stay here and look after this damned house, then *I'll* do the farming," he roared at her, following her on to the veranda. "If I sacked Jomo, the place would be a pigsty again, wouldn't it?"

"Oh, do shut up," she screamed at him. "Do shut up."

They were both very relieved, even pleased in their fuming silence as they looked at each other. Then she began to cry again. Brinden motioned with his thumb to Jervis to go. His nerves were on edge and he felt almost a hatred for Brinden, but something of the bright, lyrical warmth he had felt for Helena was tarnished, and he was angry. He started up the engine and he saw Brinden grip his wife's wrist as she tried to go towards the car. He heard her call him. "Jervey, Jervey!" But he revved the engine, drowning her voice, and let in the clutch. He knew that Brinden was determined she would not go, because he had said she would not in front of a stranger. Helena knew this too and was beside herself with fury. Jervis drove away, gloomy, chewing his lower lip, a pain in his heart when he thought of her, the lust he had vaguely felt dimmed by the sight of the aboriginal selves they had shown him. He looked back and saw her sitting on the veranda with her head in her hands, sobbing he could see. Brinden was smoking a cigarette and brushing back his thick black hair with the other hand. While she wept he hummed a little song to himself, and then he stroked her neck and said: "Now you can get out the old Ford and go and see Anna Browning. That's a better thing for a woman to do than sodding about after lions. Go on. Tell her the news before she sees the body. Was he much chewed up?" She nodded, thinking perhaps he was right about seeing Anna. She could do that job well, and it would be interesting to see just how Anna took it. Plenty of people in the club at Guyu had said often enough that Anna Browning was bored with her husband. It would be interesting to see how poor Anna took it. She cheered up a little and then shook her husband's hand from her neck.

"It's the last time you'll insult me like that before a guest," she said, staring at nothing.

"It was a pity I wasn't tight, wasn't it?" he said jocularly. "But I did my best to live up to my reputation. You've got to admit that, dear. Why don't you go off and have a good cry with Anna Browning? Remind her what a good fellow Humphrey was and that'll cheer her no end."

"You're a pig," she hissed at him, forcing anger.

"I know," he said. "But I can't stand all this bloody public lying we all do. There's no need for us to talk like characters in a morality play, is there? We're sick of each other and we can be honest. Anna Browning didn't give a damn for Humphrey, nor he for her. They were two machines living together, that's all, and we all knew it. They were just like us only he had more money than me and Anna has more taste than you." He had a lot more to say, but she was sneering and he was watching her, wondering why it was that despite her great physical attraction he felt nothing for her but boredom. She had never given him anything but that body, and he was bored with it and with the cold private mind that inhabited it. Strange how he had hungered for it once and how soon it had gone dead on the palate of his longing.

"You don't look very good with a sneer like that," he told her as though commenting quietly on a dress or a brooch. She was silent and after giving him a look of contempt, at which he smiled, as though affectionately, she left him. Once, she had waited to see how long he could do without her, but he knew, and he kept away from her, and they had fought a long silent and polite struggle over a period of months until he had got over her and she knew that their marriage had come to an end, and she was glad. Neither knew why they went on with it, and often, after a quarrel, he or she would decide to go, but they never went. "Someone," she often thought, "will have to take me anyway, or I'll stay here for ever living like a man." But she liked the life and the power she wielded, the pleasure of making decisions, sacking men and paying others, seeing the farm improve under her care. There were times when she felt there was something missing, but some sharp words with a labourer or a herdsman soon dispelled that longing for what was dead between her and this quiet, waiting man who lived with her. She did not know what he was waiting for and neither did he. It was a fairly normal marriage but with a little more control than in most, he thought. He heard her driving away in the Ford and aloud he said: "Thank the lord for that." It was deep pleasure to be alone again. To himself he repeated his most recent favourite line, feeling its strange, green, fathomless mystery: "A crab scuttling across the floor of silent seas." In such words he could live, feeling as though he shared in the secret spring of the poet's mystery.

Chapter XIII

WHEN Jervis told the Major that Helena had been unable to come back with him the old man raised his
eyebrows for an instant and then said: "Good job too.
She's all right, but I'm a bit old-fashioned and don't wel-
come women on a lion hunt. She was shaken up anyway.
Let's have a look at those guns you've got." One was a
·450, firing a heavy, dull slug of metal. The other fired an
even bigger bullet, a ·500, and Fawn-Cochley said: "Right.
Two can back up with these things and the others can use
the light rifles. We haven't got much time. Did you bring
trap guns?" When Jervis shook his head, the old man
showed anger with him. "God damn it, why didn't you
bring them? Why? What's the matter with you? We're not
hunting rabbits, you know." His severity upset the youth
and he said: "I'm terribly sorry, Major, but I'm afraid this
is a bit new to me."

"Nonsense," he was told with some coldness, "sheer
bloody carelessness. Now you can get on up to my house.
Here are the keys of the store. Bring four of the old rifles
you'll find in the wooden chests near the wall. Any will do.
The ammunition's tied in a bag on each rifle. I'll get the
watu to start on the traps now. And hurry." As Jervis
turned to go, the old man said: "Don't fret too much. You
were careless, that's all, but this isn't a game, not to-day
anyway. We've got to get this lion, and as fast as possible
too. Now get a move on."

Miserable, Jervis got into the Brindens' car and drove
away. Would it not have been better to have gone into the
Army after all? Everyone else here seemed to know what he
was doing. It had been a long day, a day of violence and
horror. He had seen a man torn up like a doll, and the

nausea and fear returned when he thought of the awful savage strength of the lion which had been until now represented in his mind as a magnificently kindly beast padding about in a zoo. Week by week he had gone deeper and deeper into this fierce nature which was so different from the quiet, ordered hedgerows of home which had contained the only nature he had known, small and gentle. "Not hunting for rabbits now, you know." No, this was larger, bloodier, relentless. What would he do if he came face to face with that lion and it charged? He trod hard on the accelerator and bounced the car over rocks and bush. "Poor Helena," he thought. "If only I could talk to her!" He missed Browning. They had taken to each other and Jervis felt loss as well as pity for his brutal death. He felt that in six weeks he had grown much older but not much wiser; he had felt like a stupid boy when the Major had shouted at him just now. At twenty, and in a country where there was so much to learn, it was hard to know just how to behave when one was shouted at. To shout back or to stand quietly and learn, but he knew the old man was right. He had been told about trap-guns, had even questioned the old man about their preparation. No, there was no excuse. He must learn, more and more he must learn.

The Dutchmen and Ganner, with four Africans, had sought for the lion in the thick scrub while Fawn-Cochley had sat with Mrs. Ganner. The sun was sinking, but they found signs, marks of a drag in the sand and some blood smears which ended in bush so thick that it was dark within and even the Dutchmen cried off, saying that it would be better to wait until morning. Then the tall, thin Dutchman voiced what all the men had thought about but had not thought fit to speak of. He suggested that they sit up over the corpse of Browning. It was a horrible and cold-bloodedly practical thing to suggest, and the Major, who had once sat up for a tiger over the torn body of an Indian peasant, tried to assure himself that there was no difference between these two bodies, between the brown one of a poor unknown Indian thirty years ago and this white one of a rich man. "Would Browning have sat up over mine, I wonder," the Major speculated and decided that he would have done. "I don't know whether Mrs. Browning would agree to a thing like that," he said firmly to the two Dutchmen, who were squatting on their heels smoking cigarettes. "What do you think, Ganner?"

Ganner scratched his lean jaw and said: "Well, you know, Major, it depends on how you look at it. Browning won't mind and we *might* get the lion that killed him. But anyway, there's the zebra the lion killed. Why not sit up over that?" The Major said yes, that was true. A zebra was as good as a man for a lion who had killed both, but the Dutchmen, in some dogged, almost superstitious way, said that a human victim was better.

"No," the old man said at length. "The zebra'll do the job. We'll get Browning's body back to his wife." The Dutchmen looked at their cigarettes and were silent.

The Africans sat in groups under the bushes, talking in low voices. One said to some others: "The other white woman did not come back. Why is that? Is it that she could have killed the lion and was afraid, being a woman, for though these white women wear trousers like their men, are they not after all women? All men are men, white or black, and all women are women. Is this not so?" The others said it was so. It was not a right thing that a woman should face and kill a lion. Those that could were men-women and had hard breasts covering stone hearts. Did they not think that that was so? Yes, it was so, they said. Then they began to tell stories of the differences between

men and women, even men and women among the beasts
who were man's brothers.

Now, in this low country, though the sun was low on the
horizon, it was hot and almost airless. They could hear
jackals yelping in the distance and once the booming of an
ostrich, and Mrs. Ganner thought it was a lion. She had
been in Africa only a year and had seen little of its carni-
vora. She was nervous and liked to stay in the house, but
her attachment to her husband still forced her to do things
which were against her temperament. She was sure he was
worth it. There was no man like him, she was certain. She
wanted *him* to find the lion and shoot it. She was afraid for
him, fearing he would be killed, but something deeper than
the fear for him wished him to be the hero. He knew this
and hoped to kill the lion. He had never shot one, or even
at one, but he was eager now to show his wife that she was
fortunate in her husband. All this beneath a calm, even
phlegmatic bearing. The old man was glad he was there.
He had recovered from his faintness but not from the
tiredness he had felt since midday. It was age all right. He
would have to try and accept it but it was hard, harder than
anything he had ever experienced. He went off in one
direction with some Africans to build the frameworks of two
traps. Ganner went with a Dutchman and two Africans in
another direction. Mrs. Ganner and the other Dutchman
sat in silence, waiting for Jervis.

When Jervis told Jeru and Kyonga of Browning's death,
Jeru exaggerated his concern and grief in the manner of old
African servants who feel they understand the white man.
Though upset to hear the news, he threw up his hands in
great and false concern and said in a hoarse voice: "A fine
strong, kindly Bwana. And he is gone. He has left us." He
rolled his eyes, and Jervis could see that such magnification
of emotions had become a habit with the old man.

"While I'm getting the rifles out," he said sternly to Jeru, "make many sandwiches and two flasks of tea, and very quickly." He was pleased to see the way they both scurried off. It was the first time he had ever been stern and he found it impossible not to be highly gratified with the results. He could not take his mind off the scene which the Brindens had created together. With a sense of loss was connected the figure of Brinden, who had shown a surprising ownership of his wife, and going over it again, Jervis was conscious of a sense of humiliation in his youth and in his apparently pointless attraction to the woman. He had been given a glimpse, during their quarrel, of that deep relationship between a man and woman, deep even if it was founded on the ashes of dead passion. For Jervis it was as if they had rejoiced before him in their bitterness and failure, as in something exclusively their own, something of hers from which he would be for ever shut out. She might give him what she considered everything, but he could not share in that ruined intimacy she had known, and this was a strange stab of pain for him. Their adult ways with each other during that flare of personalities had shut him out from her and he felt like a boy crushed by a new despair. Self-pity caused him to look back on his carefree enjoyment of the new world he had entered only a few weeks before. How dead it tasted now when there was time for reflection.

He put the rifles in the car and sat waiting for Jeru, moping, yet making efforts to dismiss her from his mind. He thought, too, about Brinden's ironic remarks about his drinking. Could it be that Helena had maliciously created the legend of his drunkenness for some reason of her own? He could recall hearing so often when among older men their humorous remarks about "women," about their scheming and planning, about their depth and their many wiles. They wanted to warn him of his doom, they said, for he was only a boy. He felt on the edge of manhood but not of it yet. There was still mystery ahead. A woman was still part of fantasy, part of the untasted promise of adolescent folk-lore.

Jeru brought the sandwiches and the flasks and said: "It is not right that Bwana Major tries to live like a young man. He should be in his house, eating like an old man. To chase zebra and hunt lions is the work of the young." He went on mumbling and fretting until Jervis put the car in gear, and, still in a deep study of that awful scene between the Brindens, he drove off towards the Sabuga hills.

Mrs. Ganner had cheered up by the time Jervis arrived. She took the food and drink from him and laid out the cloth in which Jeru had wrapped them. Jervis watched her neat, pretty movements, her quiet absorption in her task, and thought how lucky Ganner was to have this person as his wife. Why was it more moving to see a woman laying out a place to eat, with such somehow touching charm, than in trousers, with a rifle, seeking a lion? He did not know, but he was sure it was unfair to even think of it, for women had to be freed from slavery and drudgery, he knew.

He went towards the sound of digging, carrying the trap-guns. He found the old man sitting on a rock, smoking a cigarette and watching the grunting Africans digging with their machets. "You weren't long, anyway," the Major told him. "Come on and I'll show you what a trap looks like. We've got one up already and only waiting for the rifle." In thick bush, not far from where Browning lay under his mound of thorns, the trap stood like an African hut, but made of tightly packed thornbush. The trap was circular, with a high narrow gateway with two crosspieces. Looking in through the gateway, Jervis saw the interior and the roof of branches and thorns, but with gaps to let in some light. In the centre of the floor was a heap of bloody zebra meat, its strong smell already beginning to hint of decay. "They like their meat a bit high, you know," the Major told him. "Now give me a rifle." Wrapped round the rifle stock was a coil of thin baling wire. The old man unwrapped this and stretched it out, measuring it with his eye. Then he took a long, sharpened peg which an African had fashioned from a piece of thick branch and drove it with a stone into the trap-floor on the near side of the heaped meat, leaving about an inch protruding. Then he tied the rifle with lengths of thin pliable creeper to the crosspieces of the gateway so that the rifle muzzle was fixed about three feet from the earth and pointing downwards. He did all this with great care, for the wire, which had to reach a plug of wood he had inserted in the trigger-guard, would be pressed by the lion's sniffing head, and the positioning of the wire and the rifle muzzle had to be of such a nature that the pressure of the beast's head on the wire would fire the rifle so that he received the bullet into his skull. Many times the old man moved the wire, whistling to himself, and when eventually he tied it and it ran from the plug in the trigger-guard to the peg in the trap-floor, he cocked the rifle action and then with a long stick gently pressed the wire until the rifle action clicked. "Just right," he said. Jervis was very taken with the simple ingenuity of the trap, thinking that against man, when he had time to plan, the lion had no chance. But he was to find that some lions are cleverer than others.

When all the traps were ready it was nearly dusk, and when the sandwiches had been eaten and the tea drunk, the question came up as to who should take Browning's body to his house. Ganner's wife at length said that she and her husband would take it, and the others were relieved. The Dutchmen promised they would be at the trap shortly after dawn. The idea of sitting up over part of the zebra kill had been abandoned. Ganner would come in the morning too, and with Fawn-Cochley and Jervis and the two Dutchmen would hunt the lion if the traps had failed. There was gloom over them all when they placed Browning's remains in the box body of the car. Only then, for Jervis, did the tragedy of the man's end truly oppress him. Browning had ridden here with him, laughing and talking all day, and after violence, that casual, expert violence of the good shot, had died violently, and now returned to his house in the form of quiet mangled remains. Fawn-Cochley, on the other hand, showed no emotion at all. He had seen a lot of dead men in his time, had lunched among their corpses, keyed up for his own death, too, on many occasions. It was the luck of the game, he would have said, if asked. The young man, though, morbid, sentimental, felt a sorrow which raked him, even when he and the Major sat on their veranda and watched the car disappearing on its way to the Brownings' house.

"It's been quite a day for you," he said to Jervis, sensing the young man's depression. "Don't take it too badly, you know. It's very sad and Browning was a nice chap. But you see now how careful you've got to be. The lion is fast and you don't often get second chances." He had decided earlier in the afternoon not to ask questions about Helena Brinden's actions after the lion had felled Browning. He had never believed in women hunting lions and he did not expect much of them in a crisis. In this he was unfair, he had been told so and given proof on several occasions, but he would always maintain that hunting was a man's job. "But *they're* unusual women," he would say when this or that woman was mentioned in denial of his strictures. If it had been a man who had seen Browning killed by the lion, he would have questioned Jervis doggedly, but he said nothing about it. It was Jervis who brought it up by saying:

"Poor Helena. She was terribly upset. I think she felt she ought to have killed it, but it was so quickly over. By the time I got there, only about a minute all told, Browning was dead and the lion had gone." Now the shock of it all seemed to well up in him and he shuddered when he envisioned that leaping, yellow shape again. He even imagined he had seen its bared fangs and its distended claws as it knocked Browning to the earth.

"A whisky, I think," said the old man. "It's been quite a day. You've only been a few weeks in the country but you've already had more experience than some people I know who've been here for years." Then, unusual for him, he said: "Cheer up, son. You might get the lion in the morning. How would you like that?" It was on Jervis's tongue to say: "I don't want to go near it or see it. I don't want any more to do with lions, ever again." But he nodded and said: "It'd be a great thing to shoot it. But I wonder if I can shoot that straight when it comes to the push."

"You'll shoot all right," the Major replied. "You shot well to-day from what I've heard." He let this sink in and he was right, for Jervis was pleased to hear that his shooting had earned favourable comment. His vanity awakened, he already imagined the lion falling to the bullet he would put in the right place, and the old man smiled to himself when he heard his pupil say, in a livelier voice: "Where is the best place, other than the head, to hit a lion?"

"Through the shoulders, with a solid, not a soft-nose unless it is a heavy-calibre rifle," the Major explained. "Try and break bones and arteries. Straight through the shoulders, not behind them."

"D'you think we'll find the lion if it doesn't get shot in one of the traps?"

"We've got to," the old man told him. "It's a man-eater now. It may have killed men before, we don't know. But it's somewhere in that bush or forest and we've got to get it, that's all."

The whisky, after the day's emotional storms, made Jervis feel drunk and he excused himself from dinner and went to bed. Major Fawn-Cochley sat on, chewing his moustache and thinking about a variety of things, the most important of them being nostalgic, wishing he was twenty again. He stared at his cigarette and then suddenly flung it into the dark garden below the veranda. It was no use thinking like that. It was all over with that. The thing now was to solve this damned problem of what happened after death. "Nothing," the shreds of his youth called. "There's nothing." But the sprouting seeds of the end seemed to shake their heads. There must be *something*.

Chapter XIV

THERE was no moon that night. Down beyond Sabuga on the plains the zebra stampeded and raced in long rumblings of hoofs, their bellies hungry for the green grass from which they had been driven. They could hear the howling of the hyenas from beyond the escarpment as they foraged among the dead, and packs of jackals went yapping through the darkness. The gazelles stood with one leg raised, listening, for the upheaval of the day's drive had permeated with fear the forest and the plains for many miles. The convulsion of many thousands of beasts in terror had disturbed the baboons, the antelopes, even some buffalo who had retreated deeper into the forest from the heavy smell of fear and blood which hung in the warm, dark air. The zebra could not rest. They cropped the dry grass fitfully, anxious for water but afraid to approach the water-hole they had always used when grazing the plains. At the slightest sound they plunged desperately, and galloped after their barking, hee-hawing leader, joining him in frantic chorus until he stood, panting, and the herd panted with him, all loaded with the disaster of the day they had survived. They could smell the lion too at times, his acrid, ammoniac scent thinned on a puff of wind, and then they would lose their senses and thunder across the plains through the darkness until they lost that odour of their unseen, merciless enemy.

The lion was about four years old, young, and with all his fearful powers gathered at their peak. He had very little mane, what there was being of coarse, wiry, brassy hair. He stood about forty inches at the shoulder, and from his nose to the dark tip of his twitching tail he measured about nine feet six inches. His pads, each about the size of a small plate, were firm, and the claws retracted in them were still thick with the blood of the zebra and of the man. He came out of the bush noiselessly in long, gliding paddings, sniffing quietly and looking about him. Small beasts in the vicinity became still, cocked, as though springs within them had been wound up. The lion walked through the thin grass, without fear, as if he owned the world, for there was nothing he feared here. There were men in this world and he had come to know something of them. They fell easily, he had discovered. He had killed two, one a woman walking near her village, but other men had driven him off. The other, he had eaten a part of and he walked on now in search of the man's body.

He found the smell of blood where Browning had lain, and the heavy smell of many living men who had walked here. Once this smell had sickened and frightened him, but now it had a sweetness, like meat, which caused him pangs of desire to kill again. He searched the ground, but the man was gone. He could smell zebra meat and he glided softly towards it, into the thick bush. When he came to the gateway of the trap he stopped and, like a cat, he sniffed delicately, then growled low in his throat. There was something of man here, and though hungry, he was not hungry enough to lose his caution. He peered into the trap from where he stood and began to sniff with deep brutish snufflings, walking round the trap. When he returned to the gateway he stared in again, and after clawing the ground in a rage, coughing and spitting, he chewed furiously at a rock nearby, breaking off flakes of it and pawing them about. He moved off again, as smoothly as flowing water, grunting until he reached another trap. Here again there was something of man. He visited each trap, and familiarity by now with that certain gateway, that dull gleam of the rifle barrel's metal, caused him to stand some way off and growl before the opening of the last of the traps he visited. He moved closer, breathing in the rank smell of the meat, and in a playful sensual fury he drew one heavy clawing pad down one of the upright poles of the gateway, tearing it like cloth. Then he flailed it with both sets of his foreclaws. He turned round, lashing his tail, struck the wire with its tip, and immediately there was a livid flash and an explosion and the bullet from the trap-gun thudded into the shale behind him. He uttered a low, coughing roar and sprang into the air through the darkness, landing into a bush, which he ripped to pieces in a paroxysm which paralysed every creature within hearing.

He went off at a swinging, effortless lope up the gully until he reached the escarpment, carrying on until he had covered the seven miles to the cattle *boma* at the edge of the Brindens' boundary. He caught the thick, hot breath of the huddled cattle, and, full of murder, he padded round it, past the smoky hut of the herdsman, who sat dozing, his spear impaled in the ground between his legs. The herdsman heard the jumbled rush of the cattle from one side of the *boma* to the other, and even before he came out of his doze, knew that a lion had come. He had heard some time ago the far thump of the trap-gun and had assumed it had killed its victim. He stood up, took his spear and undid the thong securing the narrow covering of greased leather which ran around the edge of the blade, protecting its sharpness. His wages were forty shillings a month and sixty pounds of maize flour. He had worked six years for the Brindens and he was thirty-four years old and was strong and sensible. He tore off the thick grey blanket which he wore knotted at the shoulder and wrapped it round his left arm. Then, naked, save for a bracelet of copper and the small, flat, brass box hanging under his armpit and containing his *kipande*, the paper of contract with his employer, he went carefully out of the hut. He held the long spear resting on his right shoulder, but drawn well back and ready to stab with all the strength of his arm. At that moment the lion, his great weight propelled by the thrust of terrific muscular force, sailed over the six-foot-high fencing of the *boma* and landed on the back of the cow it had chosen, killing it with one snap of its jaws over the beast's sweating neck. The lion, ecstatic, almost musing in the feel of the quivering neck locked in his jaws, crouched in the position in which he had killed, his tail moving slowly from side to side while the demented cattle crushed and struggled in a mass at one side of the *boma*, moaning and bellowing. The herdsman stood on the top rail of the *boma* overlooking the lion and, in the brief seconds in which the lion luxuriated on his victim, flung his spear. It pierced the lion's neck where the muscle was bunched, and stayed there, when, with a short coughing roar, the lion leaped into the air, spun, and then sprang over the milling cattle, over the fence and into the darkness, leaving the herdsman lamenting over his beloved spear. He had missed his aim and had lost his spear, and he sat for some time on the rail of the fence, numbed by these disasters, and looking at the dead cow whose white belly was firm and solid in the starlight.

Then he began to yell in that certain pitch of voice used by herdsmen from Ras Kyamboni to the Cape, his cries cutting like thin swords of sound through the silence. "*Simba*," he called, "*Simba*," announcing the lion. Herdsmen in huts beside other cattle and sheep *bomas* who heard it, ran out and took up the cry in the same high, yelling pitch until, in the darkness from the edges of Browning's land to the broken, dry country beyond Sabuga on Fawn-Cochley's farm, the herdsmen were awake, listening and watching. They lit fires and stared into the darkness, their spears near their right hands, waiting for the panic of their cattle or sheep, or the snuffle of the lion. Then they heard it roaring from the forest below the escarpment as the damp mist of the high country rolled greyly about not long before dawn. It roared as if challenging the world, and it was some time before that strange stillness, a stillness which seems unearthly after a lion has roared, settled again over the plains and hills.

The herdsman, still muttering over the loss of his spear, said to the cattle who still stood in a jammed and shaken mass: "I have speared him, *n'gombe*, and his neck will burn like a fire." He whistled to them, coaxing, consoling. He addressed the dead one, too, in his dialect, saying he would disembowel her later. "*Ngeja nandi-nandi ku'tufura ngombe*," he advised the others, sad for them. He hoped he might find in her belly the *Kiolengo*, the hairball from long lickings of her coat, which would bring him luck after her bloody end.

The lion went through the forest in a series of crashings and snarls, until he cast the spear from his neck, and then plunged on to the plains just as the sky was lightening. Before his bleeding neck stiffened, he fell on an eland cow before she ran very far, and slew for the fourth time in twenty-four hours, and this time dragged his kill, after gutting it, and feasted on the brisket.

"D'you hear it, Major," Jervis called when the distant roar of the lion had awakened him. "D'you hear it?" But there was no answer and he walked under the old man's window and called again. He heard a grunt and the creak of bed-springs as the Major turned over in his bed in deep sleep. "He's done. He's fagged out at last," the young man thought, feeling warmth for him, but he nodded in self-satisfaction too, cruel in his youth, like all the young who live in action and recognise age's signs in their companions. "Been doing too much," he reflected as he got back into bed. "Knocked himself up this time, though. Poor old bugger." Then he lay down and passed into dreamless sleep.

Chapter XV

THE hunt went on all next day from dawn until dusk, but they did not flush the lion. When they stood round the fired trap-gun and examined the torn wood of the gate-way, the splintered, broken bush and the gnawed rock, the short, squat Dutchman said in English to his companion: "Christ, man, but this lion's got a brain." The other replied: "You're right there, man."

Major Fawn-Cochley stayed in bed, calling out to Jervis before he left for Sabuga: "I'm not coming, son. I'm as stiff as a poker. Take the ·450 with you and be careful, and if you *do* come on the lion, remember the ·450's got two barrels and doesn't fire five rounds like your ·256." Then he had groaned and said: "Good God, but my confounded back feels like a board." When Jervis began to murmur sympathy the old man became testy and shouted: "I'm not dying, you know, and I'm not twenty either. Go on. Get that lion if you can."

His nerves pitched high for hours, Jervis stalked quietly through bush and forest with two spearmen and one of the Dutchmen. He learned things about flattened grass, how to walk round and round until a pug-mark, at first hardly visible, showed faintly when seen in the right light, and about the difference between a hyena's dung and a lion's. The Dutchman was patient with him, anxious to get on, but sorry for the young *rooinek* who carried his rifle as though his next moment would be his last.

"He's gone a long way," the Dutchman said in the afternoon. "A hell of a long way." Then, after a pause: "Or he's looking at us right now," and that made Jervis say: "God! Do you think so," so surprisedly that the Dutchman gave him a long look and then smiled. "We're not the only ones who can hunt, you know," he said, and Jervis almost shivered. They were in thick bush and they were sweating. There was no breeze and the sun poured down in yellow waves. In the stillness he could smell the fragrant, pungent sap of the vegetation they had bruised in their passage.

"Aye, you've got to remember, man, that this lion's not one of the ordinary ones. He's a bloody man-killer and he's sharp too. But we won't find him to-day. He's lying up somewhere."

"Then let's go back," Jervis suggested, and, relieved that the young *rooinek* gentleman had made the suggestion at last, the Dutchman agreed, but not too eagerly as to seem over-anxious. He was not afraid. He was bored. He was sure that, alone, he would have found the lion, but he was quiet and held his tongue. He was very surprised when Jervis said during their walk back: "You might have found him if I hadn't been with you, eh?" The Dutchman appeared to think this over for a time, and then said, "Aye, man. I might," and Jervis was unreasonably annoyed, though silent. The Dutchman continued, though, saying: "You've got a good eye, but you need practice, see?" He hinted that because the lion was a man-killer, if not a man-eater, and he *had*, after all, taken Browning's leg with him, it might be better if Jervis thought he could hunt alone. Jervis had not enough confidence to hunt alone, though he longed to do so, and they said little to each other until they reached their horses. They would try again the next day. They bade each other good-night and separated, and all the way back to the house, with the Africans trailing behind his horse, Jervis sulked to himself, wishing he had been years in the country and had shot lions before. It was a depressing thing to be young in a country where everyone else knew so much and was stamped with so much experience.

The old man was in a very eccentric mood when Jervis returned. He was massaging his head with paraffin oil, apparently absorbed in the task. Jervis sat down in an arm-chair and watched this with some interest. To the accompaniment of fevered rubbings and snortings, the old man said: "The sun, you know. Nothing like paraffin if you've been sun-touched. Cools the brain and eases the scalp."

"I've never heard of that before," Jervis replied, choosing a gentle and non-committal tone.

"It's my own remedy, you know. I've *drunk* paraffin when I've had a touch of Guyu-gut or colic or indigestion. There's nothing like it, son, believe me." He went on rubbing.

"Does everyone use it round here?"

"Everyone? No, only me. But everyone's got a favourite remedy of some kind, you know. I know a chap the other side of Guyu who eats candle grease if he's got dysentery. He claims it works like a charm."

"It's the country, you know," Jervis could hear Browning's ironic voice, and missed him, remembering he was dead, had become a name and a quick flash of a few memories.

"No luck with the lion," he said.

"I know. You'd have come rushing in here like a man who's just killed his first lion, if you'd had any luck. Want to try some of this stuff on your head?" He offered Jervis the cigarette tin of oil, but his pupil thanked him and said he did not think he would.

"Nothing wrong with it, you know," said the Major with a slight frown. "It's kept me going for years."

"It's very good of you, Major," he countered, "but I always use olive oil myself."

"H'm. A lot of damned good that'll do you," he was told. "Still, it's your own remedy and everyone is right about his own ideas in the end." Kyonga brought a bowl of water, and as he washed his hands the old man said: "Look here, Jervis, I think I'm getting too old for a lot of the work I used to do." He turned his face then to Jervis, his dripping hands suspended over the bowl, and continued: "That's private information I'm giving you, though. I don't think you're a gabber, but still, I don't want you to tell anyone I've said that to you, understand?" Jervis nodded. "Yes, I'm feeling as old as the hills to-day," the Major went on, drying his hands. Jervis could see Kyonga's dark eyes flicking from white man to white man, sensitively, sensing that words of importance were going to and fro between them. "I think you're going to be all right, Jervis, and I'm thinking of employing you. I know the contract

5

with your uncle is as a pupil for a year, but if you'd like to work full time for me I'll pay you, not much, for you don't know much yet, but I think you want to and that's more than some of the pupils I've had wanted to do. How are you off for money?"

"I haven't got much," Jervis told him. "I've got five pounds a month from my uncle going into the bank, but that's only for this year. Then I've got to get a job."

"Do you want to be a farmer out here? Do you think you're going to like it?" To Kyonga, who was hovering, the old man snapped: "*Kwenda*. Go on. Clear off." As Kyonga went he mumbled: "Wonder how much English that chap can understand. The day'll come when they can read, too, read everything in the desk. Won't be a single thing they won't know."

Jervis drew him back slowly from his reflection on the future. "I like it," he said. "I don't know if I'll make a very good farmer, but I'm going to try anyway."

"You come from farming stock, don't you?"

"I don't know if that means much," Jervis put in. "My grandfather was a Scotch crofter——"

"Scottish, not Scotch," the Major interrupted him.

"Scottish," said Jervis, but not wearily enough to change the old man's mood. "My father went into insurance and then he rented a small farm in England, but I didn't learn much about farming. I wanted to go into the Army."

"How?"

"As a private. We hadn't the money. My father died broke."

"As a private? H'm. Much better to do what you're doing. If you want a life of action, then here it is. You ought to do a bit of studying. I've got some books here on cattle and sheep diseases that'll keep you busy for a long time."

"Did you want to be a farmer, Major?"

The old man was silent, thinking of his answer to this question. He had never been one to discuss his private motives, his failures, his doubts and hopes. He could feel a temptation to voice some of them now. He had hoped to retire from the Army as a Brigadier, but his temper had once got the better of him during an action against some savage tribesmen. He had told his Brigadier, a big bumbling man who knew more about fishing than about soldiering, that he was a fool. The Brigadier was a good-tempered man and he had eyed his irascible major curiously, but with such a dull glint in his eyes that Fawn-Cochley might have made his plans for retirement right then. But he had mistaken the Brigadier's silence for acquiescence, and had gone on to explain how the campaign should have been fought from the start, warming to the theme when he got on to supplies. The Brigadier had thanked him with what, years later, Fawn-Cochley realised was a particularly gentle humility. Not long after that the Major found himself in charge of some ration dumps in a temperature of one hundred and fifteen, and some months of this had the anticipated effect: after long correspondence he resigned his commission. He went to Africa hoping to become a white hunter, but his temper lost him clients. Europeans and Americans, many of them fat businessmen used to buying docility from those whom they paid to serve them, were outraged when they were told sharply by their white hunter what was and what was not sporting. There was something revolting for Fawn-Cochley, too, in the way most of them worked their way through the list of game allowed for slaughter by their licence, like going through a menu from top to bottom, the full value. He had given it up when a large sum of money came to him from his mother's will. He had bought this farm and had found freedom. He did not think very highly of the human race and he had to be careful of those odd members of it who began to infiltrate through the breastworks of his suspicion. Like this young-ster, for instance.

"It gave me freedom anyway," he told Jervis. "That's something in this world as you'll soon find. It was a better world when it was only half discovered. D'you realise that this land we're sitting on was full of savages only forty years ago and that all the tribes for miles lived in terror of them? But it was a good world to be young in. Not like this one, full of bloody committees and women voting for better houses for the Eskimos." He sighed, looking as though into a mirror. "The war finished that world. It's no use moaning about it, but it was a good world to be young in."

Jervis did not know what he was talking about. He could not imagine any other world than this. He had been born just as the first blows were raining on to the framework of a world which had gone along at the ox's pace for two thousand years. Crises, leagues, committees, votes and the dim roaring of disgruntled voices some way off, were normal to Jervis, as were the small wars for various slogans which went on in different parts of the world. He missed the newspapers here, the papers which drew the cartoon of the world's anguish twice a day. He wondered how it was getting on. He had no views yet. He still thought of it as a world to walk in. He had reached no cross-road yet other than about what would suit him in what his elders had called "life, making his way in the world."

The old man told him something of that lost world, of the low cost of things, of the freedom, the sense of a world still unconquered by the map-makers and the technicians. It must have been a good world. "But," he asked the old man, "this country is still what you call in its natural state, isn't it?"

"Not for long," was the Major's sombre reply, and Jervis

did not understand his despondency. "We can't stop change, though, can we?" he suggested. "It's got to come. We should be ready for it."

"We can't stop it. No," said the old man. "But we can regret it. We are still able to do that. When you are as old as I am you'll wish you were back with things as they are now." He laughed. "There'll be no lions here then. The only ones left will be in the Zoo." It was attractive to mourn in this way; Jervis could feel its comfort, but he distrusted it. He was sure that Asmani would be a friend if the walls of ignorance and custom were broken, but there was a dark future of conflict, he knew intuitively, before that time could come. He kept his thoughts to himself, just as he kept back from the old man the story of how Asmani had measured out the site of the sheep-shearing shed.

"Well, what do you say?" the Major asked him. "Would you like to work here?"

"I still don't know enough," Jervis replied. He did not wish to commit himself. If he thought Helena Brinden—but it was stupid. She thought him a boy, only a boy. There seemed nothing here any longer to attract him, all pleasure being dead. He enjoyed once again his lost youth, happy in his sorrow.

"Well, we'll talk it over again some time," Fawn-Cochley said. He was thinking: "He's not as bright and all that as he was a couple of weeks ago. I wonder if there's anything going on. The way Helena had that other pupil of mine going on started like this. Or I wonder if this Browning business has shaken him up too much."

"You know this lion killed a cow down on the Brindens' boundary last night?" He would like to know how anxious Jervis was about this lion. A queer boy in a way, deep.

"Yes," said Jervis. "Their herdsman told us this morning.

He said he put his spear into it, into its neck, and it went away with it."

"Probably not true," the old man was sceptical. "And if it is true we've got a *wounded* man-killer to deal with now."

"But it was rather brave, wasn't it, to tackle a lion with a spear in the dark?"

Fawn-Cochley thought this over and then grudgingly said: "Well, yes, I suppose so. But it's his job. He's paid to do it." This youngster was inclined to sentimentalise about the *watu* and he must knock it on the head, but gently, but nevertheless knock it on the head.

"I'm going to have a look for the lion on my own to-morrow," and when he heard this the old man raised his thick white eyebrows and said: "Oh? On your own?"

"With two spearmen, that is. I'd like to take the ·450. Can't you come too, Major?"

"No. I don't feel up to it. You go after it, but you'll have to be very careful. It's wounded if that herdsman's telling the truth, and a wounded lion is very dangerous."

"Then it's not the lion," he thought. "I knew it. It's this damned woman. He's feeling his oats. What a damned confounded nuisance women are, just when he was getting his feet."

During dinner Jervis kept up a long description of the day's hunt. Then he asked the old man how many lions he had shot, and when he was told "Forty-three," it made his day's effort a waste of time.

"Forty-three," he said. "Good lord!" It was with respect that he looked at the old man now.

"Some chaps have shot over a hundred," the Major went on. "But that's making it into a habit, of course." He began to complain about the food again, cursing Jeru. "I'll sack him, by God, that's what I'll do. I'll sack him."

"You'll never sack Jeru," his pupil told him, and the old

man was very surprised by this and almost reprimanded
Jervis. It was the tone. Had he detected a note of irritation
there? He could not be sure.

"Oh?" he said, waiting, but Jervis laughed and told
him: "You couldn't do without Jeru now, you've had him
so long. You couldn't sack him. Could you?"

So it was well meant. "I'm getting to be a touchy old
bugger," Fawn-Cochley said to himself. "No, I couldn't
sack him. When you're on your own here your servant be-
comes a part of you and you don't notice it at first. But Jeru
is too clever. He thinks he can read my mind."

"And can he?"

The old man became indignant. "Of course he can't," he
said. "How can an old man whom I took out of the trees
—out of the trees, I say—how can *he* read *my* mind? Damn
silly. He thinks he can and it makes me livid at times.
You've got to watch them, you know. You mustn't have a
soft heart about them. They're as cute as monkeys if they
see you're soft." Jervis was sleepy and the old man said:
"Better get to bed." He looked forward to the chapter he
was reading in the new book, *Is there another World?* As they
rose from the plain table of polished cedar boards, Fawn-
Cochley said: "I'm going to do something about that lion
if you have no luck to-morrow. Not very nice, but we're
going to have real trouble with the brute if we don't get him
soon. I'm going to lay poison out for him." Jervis did not
seem to think that there was anything unusual about that,
and the old man said: "It's not considered very sporting,
you know, to poison a lion. You should really take it on in
the open and give it a chance, you see."

"Well, it wasn't very sporting what the lion did to
Browning, was it?" He had said the wrong thing, he knew
it at once. Fawn-Cochley reacted as though Jervis thought
him over-sporting about a man-killer, a man-eater if it came

to that. There was iron in the old man's voice when he
said: "Well, damn it, isn't that why I'm thinking of
poisoning it?" He glared at Jervis as though awaiting an
answer. Jervis said: "That's true. Pardon me." He moved
to the door. "You know, son, you're a bit difficult to understand at times." Fawn-Cochley threw the words after him.
"Am I a very difficult person to live with?" Jervis turned
round, his eyes twinkling. He had to make them twinkle.
"You're not easy, Major. You're set in your ways, that's
all. But I'm getting to understand you."

"Oh, good," said the Major with mock gratitude. "I
just wondered, that's all."

Jervis said: "Good night, Major." The old man gave a
peal of almost insane laughter and went to his room,
saying: "Good night, son. Good night."

Passing his window Jervis heard the Major walking about
his room and saying, "Bloody young fellows to-day. I don't
know. Not easy, eh? Not easy, eh?"

Chapter XVI

SO you had to come? And you mean the old man actually
lent you the car and let you come to Guyu? He must be
becoming fond of you." Helena drained the whisky in her
glass and then looked at Jervis and smiled, affectionately,
he could swear to it, affectionately. He put his hand on hers
where it rested on the table between them. "Oh, Helena,"
he said, "why am I so fond of you? I was thinking about it
the other night and I saw how everything else seems dull
since I got to know you." She frowned, an intimate frown,
he saw, and said: "Not here, Jervy. Not among all these
people. They'll make wonderful things of it if they see you

do that." She moved her hand and he took his away, despair in his eyes.

It was rather nice to have a boy in love with you, she mused, watching the clouds and lights moving in his eyes. But a nuisance unless you could do something about it. If she were able she would let it run its course, but how steady was this boy? Would he do something silly? She was twelve, no, ten—ten—years older than him. Useless even to think about it, as a possibility, that was. No, he was attractive and he was genuinely drawn to her, fascinated was the word.

"Have you ever loved another woman, Jervy?" she asked him. He shook his head. "No, this is my first calf love," he said. Was he joking, being sarcastic, or did he mean it? No, he was piqued. She laughed. "Jervy, you are a dear," she told him and saw his eyes light up again, but he liked his other mood and they darkened again when he said: "Just a boy, that's all. But I am in love with you. I think you are with me too." She looked at him with thoughtful eyes and said:

"Yes, I am in love with you but it's stupid, that's what it is, stupid." She thought he would have exhibited joy, but he nodded slowly, she was not sure it was not smugly, and said: "I knew you were from the beginning." How could she hurt him, break that self-satisfaction? She was at once cross and touched, but she would have to be careful with this boy. He had a confidence that warned her of torture if he ever had too much of her.

"From the beginning?" she asked him, her will floating between desire and hilarity, remembering that pang when she had first seen him. He ignored her question. It was over, that part of the journey with her.

"How long are you going to go on living with that brute?" he said. The boy brought more whisky and she saw Jervis wave him away when he had put it on the table. His eyes were intent on her. He wanted nothing to interrupt his pursuit of her.

"He's not a brute, Jervy. He liked you. How could he be a brute if he liked you?" He was uncertain of what to reply, his cheeks flushed a little and she laughed, throwing back her head to show him her throat. He ignored it. When she looked at him again he was staring at her breasts, and she shuddered in her dress under an instantaneous vision, a riot of titillations. "Jervy," she said, and her voice was thick. "You mustn't."

"Mustn't what?" His mouth and eyes were sullen with longing.

"Look at me like that."

"You love it. You love me to look at you like that." He could not contain his misery. "It's terrible knowing you," he said. "I wish I'd never met you." He snarled the words and she divined his misery.

"Poor darling," she said, meaning it. He was like a sick man. Most men were like sick men when they were in love.

A week had gone by since Browning's death. Three times Jervis and the Dutchmen had gone after the lion and found nothing. For the rest of the week Jervis had been cutting and branding calves, hard work in the sun and dust, the semi-wild cattle bellowing in the crushes when they smelt the burning hair and the blood of their calves. The lion had not killed again.

"I wish you were my wife," he told her.

"You're morose, Jervy," she said. "Cheer up."

"You don't like that brute you're married to. Why do you go on with it?"

"He's not a brute. He's a very intelligent and generous man. We're just sick of each other, that's all. I like the farm and it's his farm, so there we are."

"But why go on with it? Don't you ever want love?" His nostrils were quivering. He almost said: "You're deeper than you let on. You're cool and calculating." He felt her coldness, not a fleshly coldness, oh no, but in her mind. It was like glass. Why was she not unhappy with Brinden? Why would she not admit she was bored?

"Love?" she said, raising her dark eyebrows. "What's love? You don't know what love is. What you're feeling now is simply the need of a woman, that's all. I'm handy and I'm attractive. So it's me." Her smile was warm and real. It was true, he knew. He was hurt, though, but he would hurt her too. No, he wouldn't. If he said that he would lose her. Better to hang on, hang on, oh, curse it. But he said it. "That's true," he admitted. "It's what you feel, too, isn't it?"

"Yes," she told him. She had gone pale, sad. He was full of hope and his heart sang, whirled up like a bird to his throat, until she cut him again, saying: "That's why nothing's going to happen. You'll get over this, Jervy."

"Damn it," he said. His lips were pressed tight together and he appeared as though he would strike her. Lust is anger, she thought, thrilled.

"Jervy," she said, "what's the matter?"

He shook his head and looked at his glass, turned it in his hand like a man inspecting a rare object. "I'll never mention it again." His voice was hard and she knew by the flutter in her heart that he had got inside her after all and she was afraid and resentful at the same time.

"Don't be angry, Jervy," she pleaded.

"You're putting it on," he almost snapped at her.

"I'm not, I'm not, Jervy." He watched her, satisfied, smug again. He saw the trouble she would bring to him, the gossip, the quarrels, the antagonism of Brinden, and it was not worth it, but he would go on with it now. Her lips

had swollen slightly and he stared at them. There was
longing in her eyes. "What a queer woman you are,
Helena," he told her. "You're cold and I don't know how.
But I told you I won't mention it again."

"You're quite the masterful man, Jervy, aren't you?" she
said. "So *I'll* have to mention it, will I?"

"Yes, *you'll* have to mention it. When you're ready, tell
me."

They had entered a conspiracy and they felt it around
them, close to them, like darkness. He knew foreboding as
he looked at her, telling himself he was the stronger, he was
the one who would begin and end it, but he could not con-
vert his mood to confidence. He saw trouble. He felt this
darkness about him, like her perfume, and he saw Brinden's
face in this darkness, a man older, experienced, rivalled by
a boy, and he began to worry for the first time. His desire
had cooled and he saw the room again, the smart women in
their green and yellow corduroys, tweed skirts, the men in
khaki, some fat and red-faced, the faces of retired officers
who had not got very far, and others lean and brown, or
pale, he saw them all quickly. The men wore khaki shorts
and stockings, and usually brightly-coloured shirts. There
was a roar of noise from the bar. It was Saturday night at
the Guyu Club. The dinner jacket had not penetrated to
here yet. Jervis was drawn back into this atmosphere which
he must learn.

"I don't know a soul here," he said.

"What does it matter, Jervy? Aren't you happy with
me?" Her eyes sparkled and he said: "Let's have lots more
whisky."

"All right," she agreed.

"I've only got a pound on me," he said, and she saw a
boy there again; his face was young as he clapped his
pocket, remembering.

"That'll do," she told him. "The whisky's cheap here. A shilling a tot."

He got drunk. "I wonder if the old Major will expect me back," he said. She had a little revenge. He was not smug now. "You'd better go and be ill," she advised him.

"Go and be ill?" he said, trying to take in her words. He could not focus his eyes on her. "Do you see two Helenas?" she said. "Yes. Two of you. But I thought that was just a story. But I do see two of you." He peered. "I haven't had a lot, though," he said.

"You're tight, Jervy. Go and be ill." She was gentle. "You don't want me to take you, do you?"

"Oh no. God, no. You mean go and be ill out there?" He jerked his head at the window.

"That's it, sweet," she said. She longed to have him in her arms. It was like swooning, she thought, like starting to faint. It was not what she had felt for Louie once, that almost habitual rite, a certainty which was there. No, this was another thing altogether, like a fever, and it hurt. She knew he had forgotten his desire for her, bewildered with whisky. It was the first time he had been drunk, he told her.

"So many first times for everything out here. I hadn't lived till I came. Could you tell I was drunk by looking at me, Helena?"

"Go and be ill, Jervy." He walked well, went through the door into the moonlit bush which stood dark like a wall near the club. He saw the moon enormous. He could hear the planets humming.

"Who's that nice young boy you've been filling up with Scotch, Helena?" It was Doreen Withers-Hamden, a big swollen woman. "Good for one more man and then finish," Helena thought, saying:

"Why, Doreen, it's you. He *is* rather sweet, isn't he? He's the Prawn-Cocktail's new pupil."

"And what will you teach him, dear?"

"*Doreen!*" They always talked like this.

"I hear you were there when Humphrey Browning got killed." Mrs. Withers-Hamden's eyes were fishy with tenderness. "Poor Helena. Is it true you nearly got the lion?" How pale Helena had gone. She watched her swallow and patted her shoulder. "How awful for you, my sweet. Did you get a shot at it or were you just *shattered*?"

"No," said Helena. She suddenly imagined all the talk that must have gone on. Even Louie had hinted at it. Panic almost caught hold of her.

"Everyone was amazed, for we know how much of a thruster you are. I would have backed you any old time to get that lion. Was it all very sudden?"

"Yes." She looked ill. All that smart starch had gone out of her.

"There, Helena, sweet. Don't think about it." She patted Helena again with her fat white hand. Helena looked down into the great, pale, powdered cavern that separated the woman's breasts, in a dream, hearing what everybody must have said.

"Hallo," said Jervis. He had sobered but was a little green near the eyes. He looked about him at the people, almost arrogantly.

"This is Mrs. Withers-Hamden. Mr. Jervis." He heard her voice, small, sniffed worry between them, and looked into the bright, pouched eyes of the strange woman's face.

"I was just saying, Mr. Jervis, how we were all shocked to hear of Humphrey Browning's ghastly end. It must have been awful for poor Helena. Don't you think she's a sweety?" She smiled coyly, her head on one side, wondering if he had had her yet. Everyone knew about Louie Brinden. A nice chance for this boy. He did not reply, so she had to go on. "We all thought it amazing that Helena didn't get the lion. She's one of the best women shots in this district. So it must have shaken her." She turned to Helena. "Did it upset you very much, sweet? I mean did you have a chance or were you just paralysed there, *rooted* to the spot? I don't know what *I'd* have done." Helena began to cry, and Jervis turned white with rage. "Oh, Helena. I shouldn't have," she said, putting her hands on Helena's shoulders.

"Clear out," said Jervis. The woman faced him.

"*What* did you say?" Mrs. Withers-Hamden appeared not to have heard him aright. "Please, Jervy," Helena said.

"I said clear out." He seemed quiet enough, yet it was amazing.

"Are you out of your mind?" the big woman asked him, indignant.

He hated her big, swollen body. He must be drunk.

"Well, I'd better go, I suppose. You'll have to watch this young man, Helena, dear." She stroked Helena's hair. "Do go, Doreen. I'm sorry I got upset." There was embarrassment, silence, and then the woman sailed away to the crowd at the bar.

"You've done it now, Jervy," she said without looking at him. Her face was drawn. "Get me another whisky, there's a pet." He called a boy and ordered more drinks. He sat down and they shared a dim misery in silence until he said:

"They think you bungled it. That's what they think." His voice was flat and she shivered, hearing it.

"I didn't, though. You know that."

He put all the conviction he could summon into his voice when he said: "No. There was nothing you could do." But she was not satisfied. "But how do *you* know, anyway? You didn't see it. It was over when you got there."

"I know, though. I saw him go down. I was there in a moment."

"But you don't know I couldn't have shot it. You don't

know if I was too frightened to move. How can you be so sure?" Now he looked at her, her eyes were glassy and cold.

"What are you trying to do?" he said in a low, hissing voice. "Are you trying to tell me you could have shot it and didn't? That you could have saved him?" All noise about them disappeared; the tension between them cut them off from the world and there was a growing ringing of strange echoes in his ears. He stared at her and saw her eyes cowed, crushed by his waiting face and his intensity.

"Yes," she spoke in a whisper. "I could have shot it but I was terrified to move. Oh Jervy, Jervy." Her face had gone hollow.

"You're making it up," he coaxed her.

"No." She shook her head again and again. "I'm not, Jervy. I could have shot it. They all know."

"Let's go away from here," he said and they left, people watching them. Here, their faces seemed to say, Humphrey Browning was at his best, one of the boys. He would have been there to-night.

"That's why nobody came to say hallo to me," she told Jervis. He had his arm around her. He was trying to decide what he felt. Should she be blamed?

"You're making it up," he kept saying, but she said: "No. I'm not, Jervy. I lost my nerve. Oh, if you could have seen it and heard the noise its teeth made." She hid her face and he had to guide her to the car. "Anna just sat there and listened to me and never said a word. I had to go on talking, talking, talking, and she just looked at me. It was horrible. She *knew*. Oh, Jervy. I could have saved him. I only had a few seconds but it felt like years. I fired twice at it and missed. I didn't aim properly. I didn't know what I was doing. Even when it ran away I fired again and missed. It's finished me in a way. I wanted to tell you but I couldn't. But they all know."

They sat in the car, liquid with moonlight, their eyes and hands silver. The moonlight almost had heat in it, so powerful was it in its flowing, translucent force. He could smell her black hair under his nostrils, pity melting into desire, forgetting the lion and her sorrow, her useless sobs, then back again into her voice telling of those seconds.

"I seemed to know when I fired that I couldn't kill it. I was too afraid to aim straight and it killed Humphrey. He screamed and that finished me. He was trying to push its head away. He beat its face but it went on and killed him." Jervis trembled as he saw the lion in the picture she had given him.

"Did you tell this to *him*?" he murmured.

"Who?" she whispered.

"*Him*," he said loudly. "S'sh!" she whispered. Him.

"No," she said. "But he knew. You heard what he said. He knows me. Oh, he knows me, everything about me."

"Everything," he said savagely, thinking of everything. She was not there with him in his animal jealousy. She went on about Him. "He always knows. He knew right away that moment as soon as I told him what happened. You were there. I wanted to go and kill the lion, but he wouldn't let me. He stopped me." She wept. He could not hold in the fire of his envy, hearing of Louie knowing her, everything. "You were glad he stopped you," he said in a hard, cruel voice. "You were glad." She knew he would not talk like that if she could have had him in bed with her. She could feel his dammed-in force through the wall of his body, desire like a moaning. She burst out crying, shaking with this blow of his cruel voice. He sat still, holding her, tormented, sick of her, but nagged by that other longing. She cried for a long time. He heard men singing in the club, drunkenly: "I belong to Glasgow. Common old workin' chap."

She became quiet and lay with her head against his chest, afraid to speak, and he, knowing this, waited, remembering.

"Jervy," she whispered at last. "I love you." He did not answer. Her heart trembled. "Jervy," she said, "I love you." She looked up at him and he saw her eyes, great and black, silvered as they searched his face.

"It's no good, though, is it?"

"Why, darling?"

"It's what you said before. That's all it can be." His voice was hoarse and he did not know why he kept thinking of Brinden. "He'll know," he told her. "He'll know, won't he?" She said he could not know *that*. That? Oh, yes, that. He kissed her, his mind sinking down through the areas of Brinden's personality, that grown, adult man, down into the softness and urgings he had not imagined.

"Drive us away from here," she said in his ear.

"I wonder if we should go on with it," he said over her head, fretfully. He could not visualise the mystery she was offering him. It made him quiver.

"Drive us away from here and we'll see," she whispered. His throat dried. His mouth moved but nothing came from it. He started the engine. They said nothing as the car moved away, down the drive, along the dirt-track, out into the bush. They were immense with guilt and the ache to confirm it. Lamely, he said: "I don't know much about it. About love, I mean." "*Darling*," she whispered, watching his long silver face as he drove. "*Darling*."

Chapter XVII

IT was nearly dawn when he drove up to the house. The veranda light was on. Sitting on the top step was the old man, smoking a cigarette. Jervis braked the car at the foot of the steps, still new with the night's failure, thinking the old man was up because he knew something, guessed something, for the first guilt was heavy on Jervis.

"Did I wake you, Major?" he shouted.

"No," the old man called back. "It's been again, an hour ago."

"The lion?"

"Yes. It killed one of our best bulls and mauled Charanga. I think he'll peg out."

"Charanga? Hell, I'm sorry to hear that." Charanga was one of his favourites. Jervis ran up the steps and sat down below Major Fawn-Cochley. "He's been badly chewed up and the bull's dead," said the Major. Was it worth it, trying to farm out here?

"Which bull?"

"The young Aberdeen Angus, Sweetmeat."

"Oh, I'm sorry it's Sweetmeat. He was rather a pet of mine. I got him to eat kale the other day for the first time." He knew what a blow it must be to Fawn-Cochley. A new, young bull only four months out from England. Thousands of miles by rail, ship and road, and killed near the Equator just after he had eaten his first kale. But try as he might, he could not focus his interest on the lion, the bull, and Charanga. He needed to be alone, to go over the failure of the night. In one way he was glad it had failed, but he was still cut off from the real world of men, and women.

"You'll have to go in with Charanga to Loltugi. There's a doctor there and it's nearer than Guyu."

"Now?" It would be a relief. "Yes, I'll take him."

"Doc Punter's an Army doctor but he's always on tap for anyone who turns up." The old man's eyes became grave when he spoke of Charanga. "I didn't know I was so fond of Charanga until I saw the poor chap lying there. He never uttered a sound. Just looked at me."

"Is that because they don't feel pain like us? That's what I've been told."

"No," the Major shook his head. "We kick up a fuss when we're hurt because we know we'll get sympathy. We expect it and we usually give it to each other. But the *watu* don't feel that. They just keep quiet. But it doesn't mean they don't feel pain like us."

The moon was gone, and the darkness which began where the flood of lamplight ended was deep and warm. There were no stars, no hint of the universe, only black silence. It was twenty-six miles to Loltugi.

"I should do it in an hour or so," said Jervis.

"You have to go through a thick forest this side of the Malanga river. But the road's good. Dry. A bit bumpy. Bottom gear on Godlummey hill."

He had heard of Godlummey hill, christened by a British sergeant attached to the Loltugi platoon of the King's African Rifles.

They spoke as men do in the early hours, short sentences, silences, each pondering for a time, as though one of them might suddenly say: "Well, I feel like bed."

Charanga was lying on some sheepskins, and as Jervis held the hurricane lamp over him he saw the deep holes of teeth and claws, in the shoulders, the arms, like holes made by sharp spikes.

"*Jambo*, Bwana," Charanga said in a low voice. There was nothing very *jambo* about it, Jervis felt, but he replied in the same way as though all was well.

"I'm taking you to Loltugi to the doctor." Charanga was covered with a skin of dried blood. The Major had packed salt into the holes in his body and Charanga lay still, his torment like the heat of fever, like the deep glowing ache before the *titamaka*, the shiverings of malaria.

"It's no use, Bwana," said Charanga. He had a long nilotic face, a thin, almost Greek nose, and his purple lips were firm and finely shaped. His face was greyish now, its brown shining skin faded under pain and despair. For it is only when a man is fit and strong that his heart is free. When he is cut down by fever, by the knife or the beast, or by *uchawi*, the witchcraft, then he is half-way to his end, and death is the finish of all things. No man could cope with death. It came and ate him up, swallowed him, wiped him out of the world. Jervis saw this and knew the first struggle with tribal Africa's acceptance of catastrophe. He laughed as all white men do when they deny a fact.

"Nonsense," he said. "The doctor'll have you all right in a week." Charanga shook his head, his eyes fixed on his doom, far away, beyond the straw roof of the store shed in which he lay.

They laid Charanga on a thick pile of skins in the back of the car. Mirangi, one of Jervis's friends now, sat holding the young Bwana's rifle, and Jervis climbed in beside him and took the wheel.

"Give Doc Punter my salaams," the old man said to Jervis. "He'll give you a whisky when you get there. You'll find him in a little white house this side of the Army post near the river. Keep your eyes open in the forest. There's plenty of big stuff living there. Get back as soon as you can. I'm laying out poison everywhere to-day and I'll need your help."

As he drove, Jervis drank the clean wind, glad now that she had refused him. Was it true, after all, that women were strange, unaccountable? In the midst of sighing passion, when hands, lips, eyes were becoming the body's anguish, were seeking relief for it from the mindless storm, she had panted: "No. No, Jervy. No. I can't do it. I want to but I can't." He had hissed something in her ear, anything, words, moans, sounds, but on the edge of mystery's door she shook her head, skilled, familiar with the man's ox eye, with its light between tenderness and violence, the yearn of lust, familiar with the way to change all this to normality again. He had sat up in the sea of moonlight, loving her with a surge of baffled hatred, not seeing where they began as one, puzzled by her refusal.

"It's no good," she had said. And it was no good. He did not ask her why. She told him, though.

"I love *him*," she explained. "I could love him better if we could only separate from each other. Together it is hell. You can't understand, I know." He shook his head, fierce and contemptuous, sick with desire gone cold. At last, he was sure, he knew that women were cruel in their love for man, more calculating than men, having to be, for man was a savage. "You can't even remember the names of your first women after a few years," a thin, cynical man had once told him. "But it's not like that for a woman. They are in love all their lives." He tried to connect this now with Helena, but it would not connect. Perhaps she was frightened.

"You want me, though, don't you?" he had asked her.

"Yes," she told him. "But I'm not having you. Something horrible will start if we do." She did not want any more love with any more men. When she had come to the point she knew she had not shaken off that hopeless knowledge of the turmoil of possession. No, enough. It was a thing he could not understand. He was too young. She would not try to explain it.

"You're angry with me, aren't you?" she had said. She was sitting up then arranging her hair, her slender body in the tweeds undulant with the poise of some statue he had seen somewhere.

"Not angry, Helena," he said. "Not now. I feel better now. I think perhaps you're right." His heart was still thudding, his throat tight, but the storm was gone. It was enough to know that she had longed for him. It made him a man. He did not tell her this. He was amused by it and thoughtful as to why it should be, this secret masculine pride. Being young, that's what it was. He began to laugh and she, quizzical at first, had laughed with him, saying: "Jervy, you *are* a sweetheart. One day you're going to be a very clever and understanding man and some woman will have you for herself alone—for a time." She would not explain, would not fondle his awakened vanity, but smiled to herself in the way women were supposed to smile when they were thinking a secret thought. Then he was bored, not knowing why. He had hurried her to the car, driven her back to the club, where she was staying for the week-end, and had then stood silent with her at the door of her little hut in the garden.

Then: "I love you in a funny way, Jervy. It would be horrible to love you in *that* way, like incest." It was a lie and he had nodded understandingly, hurt but bored with her now. She knew it would take some time to overcome this crisis of flesh between them, for she could feel his vanity like clothes on him. Could she be torturing him? He thought not. He was relieved that she had restrained them both from intimacy. He felt free again. She saw him anxious to go but could not accept his relief, his unhidden air of freedom. It gave her pain. What *do* I want? she thought. She kissed him, her mouth cool on his cheek, and though he did not move she could feel him strain for her again. "You need a woman like Ganner's wife," she whispered. "A good woman. Simple and sweet, Jervy. I'm bad. Bad." She meant it, he saw, and tenderness bathed his heart again. He did not say: "I know, I know. I love you for it," but thought it angrily. What a mystery it all was, this thing between men and women, this torment so that the world could be ever populated. He would have liked to have asked her about this, for she knew. She saw he had lost his boredom with her, was staying, so she said:

"Good night, Jervy, sweet. Come over to the house and see me. Soon."

"Yes," he said. "I will. Good night."

"Say darling."

"No," he said. "What a tease you are." He put on his pith helmet, miserable again. "Good night."

"Good night, sweet." She was sorry for him as he walked back to the car. "What *do* I want?" she asked herself again. "I think it's this country. I need a trip home. *Are* we all mad out here?"

Mirangi said: "Here's the forest, Bwana." They drove into the high cathedral of dark trees, the headlights lighting the red soil of the road on which the blue flowers of the jacarandas had fallen like precious stones. He smelled the forest, the heavy warmth of sap and dead vegetation. Green eyes glowed in the darkness ahead, moving off into the forest again. "Antelope, Bwana. But there are many leopards here too, and sometimes elephants stand on the road and cannot be moved. Stubborn, they are, Bwana, like old women."

Charanga was silent in the bumping car. He lay thinking of his death, not afraid, for there was nothing to fear; there was only an end. No more eating, no more lying with women, no more stories over fires. An end to all this. A hyena carrying a human thigh bone in its steel trap of

a mouth ran in front of the car for a time, blinded in the
headlights. His low hindquarters were those of a sneak.
"Jangau," said Mirangi. "The carriers of our fathers and
grandfathers."

"Do you still throw your dead to the hyenas?" Jervis
wanted to know. "Yes," Mirangi told him. "And we cannot
touch or kill hyenas because of that. He may have eaten my
father." Thrown away like a worn shoe, thought Jervis.
The end. It is used. Throw it away. But was it not honest?
No, it was heartless. He could not decide.

"That hyena will soon eat Charanga," Mirangi said to
him in a low voice. He was laughing. He had to when he
thought of the trouble the white men were taking for
Charanga, who knew he was going to die.

"Why do you laugh?" Jervis was severe, and Mirangi,
remembering that this was a white man, made his face
solemn again. "We laugh at death, Bwana," he said. "We
laugh because it is the end." He could not tell this white
man that things which moved the heart like a spirit made
men laugh. "You swine," thought Jervis, not understanding, the child of an old religious civilisation. He shuddered
when he thought of the dark, savage world all about him,
the Africans in their villages acquiescent to death, singing
their sad, almost devilish, and monotonous little songs. He
did not know yet what they sang of, but when he heard them
it was like hearing the beginning of the world with men lost
in it, afraid. Mirangi was thinking: "I would like to be like
the white man. Why do I want to be like this white man?" He
did not know. He did not think much beyond the parables
of the folk stories. He did not question yet. There was the
earth, the beasts, the women, the food, the beer, the death
and the hyenas. It was the world. Only those who came
from the mission schools, loaded with strange clues, saw the
lie of the world and the savagery of which to be ashamed.

Jervis was glad when they left the forest. Here was God-lummey hill. He put the car into low gear and it groaned and steamed its way up through the cold air, past the twined, rubbery castor-oil bushes growing in the red soil. He smelled the villages, smoke and cattle in the darkness. It was nearly dawn and cold greyness was shivering over the world.

Captain Punter was lying asleep in an arm-chair. On its right arm was an ash-tray on a tiny saddle from which the stirrup leathers hung on either side. "To Doc Punter from 'A' Company, Rawalpindi, 1926" was inscribed round the edges of the silver ash-tray. It was the only prized possession he had never lost.

Doc Punter had white hair and his red face was puckered in sleep. He had a big grey moustache which he twitched as he dreamed. On his lap was a book about the local tribe by a German anthropologist. A bottle of whisky and a glass stood on a small table by the side of his chair. The room was simply furnished, a table, two chairs, two arm-chairs, an untidy bookcase. Since his wife had died he had gone to the dogs. Everybody knew that. Not that he drank much. He simply did not care about anything but his work and his books. The officers of this infantry battalion, which had one company at Loltugi, all loved him. They called him "Daddy" and he liked it.

He woke up at once when he heard Jervis on the veranda. "Hallo," he said, "you're early. Come far?"

"I'm looking for Dr. Punter."

"That's me. Have a whisky?"

"No, thanks, Doctor."

"Come on. It's early but it's cold. It'll warm you up." He poured out a large whisky and gave it to Jervis. "No water handy," he said. "Not till my boy comes. I've used it all up. I had some of the officers in last night. Go on, drink it. Sit down."

Jervis told him about Charanga, "He says he's going to die." The doctor nodded. "That's it, then. He'll die."

"But you haven't seen him yet. How do you know?"

"Once one of these chaps decides his number's up, it's up. I can half convince a mission boy sometimes that he's not going to die, but not one of the primitives. We haven't got any properly educated ones yet so I can't speak about them. But the primitives can die whenever they want to. I envy them that. But it'll go with civilisation and then they'll hang on to the bitter end, terrified of heaven." He laughed and got up. "Where is he, poor chap? A lion makes a really bloody mess usually."

They carried Charanga to the veranda, where the light fell on him and the doctor examined him. For the first time Jervis saw Charanga's torn back and chewed arms. The grey, noble face was calm and the eyes watched the doctor interestedly, who questioned him in his own dialect.

"Says he'll die in two hours. Look, it's just quarter to six now. He'll pass on at about eight. I'll give him an injection. You'd think he had no pain, wouldn't you? They're wonderful chaps, I tell you. Been out long?" He worked as he talked, kneeling beside the quiet tribesman.

"Never seen one of these chaps make his mind up he's finished, you say? Well, there it is. I was once driving through the bush, across country, in a car, and I startled an African, who fell against the car. It knocked him down. Didn't hurt him though. He lay quite still with his eyes closed and began to pass out. He went grey, like this chap. Have you noticed, by the way, how they go grey when they're ill? Same colour as a rhino's skin, exactly. Well, anyway, there was this chap pegging out, thinking he'd been badly hurt: the fright was enough, you see. Hadn't expected to see a car that far into the bush. He may have thought it was a rhino. I was pretty puzzled for a minute. Then I had an idea. I got down and I fairly roared down that chap's ear.

"'*Simama*,' I told him, 'get up.' And he got up, shook his head, said: '*Jambo*, Bwana,' and started getting better. I gave him a couple of bob and drove on. Now what do you think about that?"

"It's a queer country," was all Jervis could think of to say. He was sad to think that Charanga, of whom he was fond, was determined to die. He went across to him and said: "Charanga, don't die. If you will live I'll give you the money to buy a cow. Don't die, Charanga." The doctor watched this scene, smiling faintly, touched by this young man's pleading with the dispossessed warrior of another world.

"I must die now, Bwana. It is the law. The *amri ya mungu*." *Mungu*, God. Which God was this of whom he spoke? "Do they believe in God, Doc?" he asked.

"In a way, yes. The sky is God, so is the sun, so is the river. So is any power or force in nature. A bull is God too. They don't worry about it much. But we're putting that right. Very soon they'll be like us. You know, while you've got the chance you should study these people. They won't be here very long and they'll never come again." The doctor could not quite convey his sympathy for this Africa which was soon to be sick before its death and then its rebirth among the tractors and the buses and the rational life. He knew that the tribes were now poised between the long savage dream of their past and the beginning of the political mythology which so soon would envelop them. The search for Utopia among the buildings and the clinics and the miles of books. To understand it, eventually, they would have to wear glasses. To live in it they would need rubber goods. To sin in it they would need help, instruction. He said nothing of this to Jervis. It fascinated him privately. He would stay here to watch it, leave his bones here in the dry grass of Africa. He loved it. Why, he did not know.

A little after eight, Charanga died, Jervis and the doctor holding his hands. Mirangi looked on, watching the white men who were not fierce with words now with the black men. They held this one's hands and the young one was pale, he noticed. The young white man was staring like a witch at Charanga, willing him to live, fighting against the queer, dark, African death which was flowing like blackness into Charanga's eyes.

"He is finished, Bwana," said Mirangi. Yes, he was finished.

"Don't worry, son," the doctor said, patting Jervis's shoulder as they went into the room. He saw tears in Jervis's eyes. He would soon get over this, these tears when an African died. The other Europeans would not like to see a thing like that. He understood Jervis's sorrow. It was the heart of the young before it hardened into that of the practical white man who was determined to make Africa into a new kind of country. He had seen it before. You kept your own counsel about these things in the end, silently agreeing that all would be for the best in the best possible of Africas, but not to sentimentalise, not to feel doubt about the task ahead, but to press on with civilisation. The long muddled journey through hinged doors, down rubber roads, along the skies of petrol vapour into the never answered question. It was wonderful. It was a fact of the world and the doctor regarded it always, patient with it, curious and acceptant of his doubt. He did what he could for the sick, but he could do nothing with the destruction of worlds, with the steady breaking down of the last fences of innocence and savagery.

He gave Jervis breakfast of eggs and tinned bacon. One day there would be a piggery here and cured ham. The doctor longed for ham and he knew, too, that it was the kind of wish which would hasten the new Africa, and in a way that was very funny. He sighed at the death of the tribes and he wanted ham. There was nothing that could stop it. He began to explain this to Jervis, who was eating slowly, his mind full of Charanga's death, the eyes, the defeat, the hopeless shrug of the spirit.

"It's only forty years since the Masai ruled here, and everywhere else they could reach with their raiding parties," the doctor was saying. "They even reached Bagamoyo on the coast, and a fellow told me that Masai spies used to enter Mombasa at night. They spared nothing. The whole country was frightened of them. The road you came on to-night was once a Masai warpath. They used it only forty years ago. Queer, isn't it, and here we are with cars and microscopes and the beginnings of political agitation." He spoke of the *Watu Wa Mungu*, the mad sect, the men of God, who lived in the forest near Nairobi, coming out at times to kill. They had lost their tribal pattern, had been shut out from the White God, and now lived in a fantasy of bloodlust and the Old Testament. It was only a beginning, a hint of despair. It was the beginning of the struggle against civilisation, the yell from the swamp before the experts came with the blue-prints for the pursuit of happiness. He told Jervis in his bright dry way of the Africa he was living in. He explained the dilemma of sentimentality and the wish for progress. "Nothing can stop changes now we've come," he said. "In the near future the Africans will fight us for political power, but whether they like it or not, they can't do without us. Africa's just a big melting-pot at present, full of black curios from the past. They learn quickly when they want to, but they've never in a thousand years invented anything beyond the firestick. They were lucky. But we've come now and in the future they're going to have to depend on us, and we on them. You'll live to see it too. Me? Well, I'll be out there somewhere, turned into a tree or something. I wish I could see it." He smiled and called for more fried eggs.

"Do you think we should have come here, Doc?" Jervis asked.

"Should have? What's the good of thinking about that? We're here. That's all about it. The question is what to do. Do we simply take a look round, examine the tribal system, pronounce it useless in the modern world, and so smash it up? Or do we keep it, nurse it, change the worst bits and see the African of the future grateful we saved it for him? What do we do? Do we wreck it all now and try to make an imitation white man, or do we go slowly? That's the problem. Remember, the African has no past that consists of anything more than a few clay pots, some spears, some good rules of tribal living, and tom-toms. But he could build on that. But how? D'you see?"

"I say sweep the tribal system away," said Jervis. He had forgotten Charanga and he was hungry. He was given more eggs by the boy. "You won't be so sure when you've been here a bit longer," the doctor said, his eyes twinkling. "It's a queer country. The tribal system is sometimes a marvellous thing. It's all there is, anyway. You can live in this country and just enjoy yourself, but one day you'll feel the volcanoes under you. It's going to be the biggest problem on earth."

There was more talk like that right through breakfast, and Jervis knew, after listening to the doctor's talk, that he was living in a museum of man's beginnings.

"It's not nice to feel superior to the African," the doctor told him. "I've never quite made my mind up about that.

I like him, not because he's the happy savage, but because he has a good heart and trusts us. He trusts me anyway because I trust him. You can be progressive-minded without being sentimental too. One of the first things we've got to make the African realise is that we can teach him how to make life easier. But I'm not sure we'll get the time."

"Somebody told me that the British spend most of their time teaching people how to chuck us out of their countries. He said we were fools." Jervis spoke his heart to this old doctor, knowing that he would not meet such another European for a long time. "Do you think we should just sit tight and build a civilisation here on our own? Do you believe in teaching Africans the truth, in letting them see us as we are, and letting them work with us?"

"Yes," said the doctor. "It's the only way. At present this country is a park in which we ride around. Nothing much is happening yet. It's like a period of waiting. Enjoy it while you can, but don't become the average white man with the average distrust of the wog, or one day he'll stamp on you. He's pretty sharp and he knows who he likes and who he doesn't. There's a big problem coming here, and, whatever it works out, whites and blacks will need each other. If we show some imagination we can make a fine, happy Africa." Jervis could see the doctor's enthusiasm shining in his eyes, but then the doctor added: "But I don't see it working out that way. It's going to be hell."

"Hell?"

"Yes, hell." Jervis could not coax any more from the doctor. They had finished their breakfast. "You can bury your herdsman now, Mr. Jervis," Dr. Punter said quietly. "You were fond of him, I think."

"Yes. He was a good fellow. He taught me a lot of things in his own way."

"Hard luck. But one day you may have African friends

who don't give up the ghost so easily. Let's hope so, any-way."

Charanga was buried in a plot of red soil near the forest which ran down to the edge of the company lines. Some African soldiers, tall, slender men in dark-blue jerseys and khaki shorts, watched the burial. There was no religion here yet, no ceremony, no solemnisation of the mysterious act of returning a man into the earth's crust, nothing. Still, it was better than thinking of the gulping hyenas dragging Charanga in the dark, thought Jervis.

"Come in any time, son, and have a chat. I'll give you a camp-bed any time. Would you like to read a couple of good books about the tribes you're living amongst?" He gave Jervis two books. "They'll explain a few things that puzzle you now and again," he said. "One day these chaps will be reading books about us, so you'd better get in first." He asked about Major Fawn-Cochley. "He *is* mad, you know," he said, "but he hides it pretty well. Give him my salaams, won't you."

Driving back, Jervis saw the Africa about him with new eyes. It was an Africa at a standstill, but here and there he knew there were stirrings, openings of eyes, questions. How long would this calm last, this atmosphere of a slow, enor-mous primitive world? He felt excitement and a sort of gladness that he had come in time to see this Africa of the ochre-painted men and women who were as yet uncon-scious of what the explorers had brought so short a time ago. Why, that old man there was a boy when they came. How extraordinary that was, he thought, as he fumbled the gears of the Box Body Ford, Model T.

Chapter XVIII

THE lion took some of the poisoned meat. But when it felt the first light seeking fingers of the strychnine in its belly it turned the patch of bush into a pandemonium.

Jervis and Fawn-Cochley saw where it had struggled. The flattened and torn-up grass, the broken bushes, the vomit, the purgings. It must have thrown itself into a paroxysm in its struggle to expel the deadly meal.

"I've never known that before," said the Major, shaking his head. "It's the strangest damn lion I've ever met. Knows what a trap is, and then pukes up strychnine. I wonder if I gave it too much, or too little." He had put into each piece of meat the usual dose. Enough to cover the point of his jack-knife, about as much as would cover an English shilling. "Curse it," he said. "That's the last chance we'll get. He'll never touch bait again." It was a very serious matter now. A man-killer which would not touch a trap and which had actually succeeded in vomiting a lethal dose of strychnine.

"There's only one thing left now, apart from hunting the bloody pest," said the Major. "That's the spring-trap. We'll put a couple of those about."

They laid the big traps at the edge of the forest, the great toothed jaws open, the traps chained to the long steel stakes which Jervis had driven into the earth.

Two mornings later a herdsman came to say something was in one of the traps, and Jervis and the old man went down with heavy-calibre rifles. Jervis was keyed up as they approached the forest's edge. The herdsman pointed. "The grass moving there." Jervis saw nothing, and then the old man yelled "Look out!" as a dark, coughing shape sprang out of the grass until held by the trap and its chain. It was a big leopard. It lay crouched in the grass, its mouthful of glistening fangs open, its two eyes blazing with the fiercest hatred Jervis had ever seen.

"Shoot it," said the old man. "Go on, shoot it. Quick." Jervis raised the heavy double-barrelled rifle, after slipping the safety catch. He drew two imaginary diagonal lines from each ear to each eye. In the centre of this he laid the ivory-tipped foresight and pressed the butt with its thick, red rubber pad into his shoulder. The jolt of the heavy weapon shook him. He did not hear the explosion, only the loud clap of the big bullet as it smashed home between those yellow, burning eyes.

"Nice work," said the Major. Jervis sat down, weak from excitement. "I've actually killed a leopard," he said to himself, "killed it." True it was trapped, but he had killed it and it was easy.

"Nice skin, son. Come on, what are you sitting there for?"

The leopard was beautiful, his coat smooth with the black rosettes shining in it. He was warm to the touch, and the old man seized one of the pads and squeezed out the long claws for Jervis to see. "Nice, aren't they?" he said. He pulled one of the thick whiskers out and gave it to Jervis. "That'll bring you luck."

The old man supervised the skinning, particularly the delicate task of removing the skin over the pads where the knuckle bones and tendons were. "They always mess that part up if you don't look out," he explained. "Wrap it up in plenty of salt when you get back and hand it in to old Tampley at Guyu. What he doesn't know about taxidermy isn't worth knowing." When the skinning was over, the Major said: "Well, you've got a real beauty there. Think you could face a lion now?" They looked at each other.

"You might have to sooner than you think," the old man warned him. They set the trap again and rode home.

Chapter XIX

TWO months passed. Two months full of hard work among the cattle and the sheep. There was Helena, too, and the Abyssinian war.

One day Helena came over in her car, and the old man seemed genuinely pleased to see her. "You know," she told Jervis later, "you're good for the old Prawn-Cocktail. He's actually becoming quite nice."

She asked Jervis to go into Loltugi with her. She was going to see Dr. Punter.

"Aren't you well, Helena?" Fawn-Cochley asked her. He poured out tea for her.

"It's nothing," she said. "Just something routine."

"Oh, of course," the Major said, meaning to be discreet. "Of course." There were a few uncomfortable moments which Jervis did not share.

"Will you come, Jervy?" she said. "Will you let him come, Major?" she asked the old man, her smile reaching into his lonely crag of heart.

"He's got a lot of work, you know," he said, feeling it was due from him.

"He's in need of a trip, I think. There must be something he can do for you there, surely?"

"He can see his friend, the doctor, and he can bring me a couple of melons out of his garden if he's got any. All right, son?" He eyed them both. Perhaps something *was* going on between them, but perhaps not. She was a fine-looking woman. He had never had much to do with women in his young days and he felt regret for that now, when, from the security of tired blood, he regarded Helena.

"Jervy and I have become great friends," she said confidingly to Fawn-Cochley. "We talk about everything under the sun."

"Jervy," said the old man with a comic distaste. "You'll spoil the lad calling him a damned silly name like that." He saw Jervis's thick blond hair shining in the sun which poured in at the doorway. The young fellow was quite brown now. He was certainly good-looking, something Helena might not be able to keep her hands off, particularly as she was so unhappy with Brinden. He only hoped nothing would start between them. He liked Jervis. He had grown on him slowly. He seemed fairly level-headed, but what did that count for if a woman started work on him? Aye, it would be a bloody shame if anything started between them. He examined them both as they drank their tea, but could discover nothing, none of those little signs of the fever.

When they had driven beyond the first cattle *boma*, Helena turned to Jervis and said: "I was dying to see you again. It's over a week since you came over. Do you know that Louie really likes you?"

"Oh, good," he said mechanically.

"I wish you weren't such a pet," she went on. "Are you still in love with me? Or do you hate me?" Her eyes were shining, lively. She was like a bird in her curiosity.

"I suppose so," he answered, looking into her eyes with an expression as of seeking something there.

"What," she said, "loving or hating?" She made her voice breathless. He was never sure where her acting began and her real self ended. Were all women like this with men? God, sometimes he felt weary from the long, uncertain lusting.

"Both, I think," he said. "But we've got it nicely under control now, haven't we?" He was sardonic with her. "Oh, Jervy," she said, "why must you be cross?" He looked away on to the rolling plains below the ridge, the landscape numbed and hazy in the sun, vultures wheeling like specks over some god-forsaken kill.

"You're very tiresome sometimes, Helena," he told her. "You enjoy knowing that I want you, don't you? You just manage to stop yourself from being cruel. It's part of your own frustration, isn't it?" He did not sound at all worked up, just flat and sort of malicious. Poor darling. She drove fast, thinking of his words. He went on: "I forget about you when I'm working. It's when you turn up, or when I've been to your place that I feel so damn miserable. I wish at times that I'd never met you."

"Jervy," she said, "I'm good for you. Just because I couldn't go through with it that night at Guyu doesn't mean I wish I hadn't." She got mixed up. "I mean I wish I had, but I'm glad I didn't. You'd have hated me after a bit. I only did what you'd wish your own wife to do."

"Virtuous of you," he said. "What's the difference between wanting a thing and having it?"

"A great deal," she replied.

"H'mm!"

"Don't say 'h'm' like that." She stopped the car and took his face in her hands. Then she kissed him on the mouth. He did not move, did not respond. She kissed harder until he put his arms around her. "That's better," she said. "Oh, what a horrible mess I've made of my life." He was sullen, having given in, grasped her, awakened himself again.

"If we could only go on like this always," she whispered.

"If only," he said, mocking her tone. "It'd be wonderful, wouldn't it?" He did not see her face when she spoke next, but what she said turned him cold. "I've gone back to Louie, Jervy." She said it in what he thought of as her small voice. "Back?" he asked. "Yes," she said. He took his arms away. "You mean——" He could not finish his question but she said "Yes," gazing ahead of her through the windscreen. He saw tears falling from her cheeks. "I wish I hadn't but I have," she murmured. "I couldn't hold out any longer." In those words for him was the unknown, the guessed-at forces of marriage. Couldn't hold out any longer. He repeated it to himself.

"It's not like you think," she said. "Marriage."

"Isn't it?" He was dull. It was the end of something.

"No," she said, wiping her eyes. "He won."

"Won what?"

"Holding out the longest. It went on and on. And I think loving you has done it."

"How bloody silly," he said, "holding out the longest. And you think I helped you to lose your competition. Well, I'm sorry. I'm really sorry." She began to cry again, deep sobs this time in the voice of a woman, not the girl in the tweeds, but the woman drawn into another's quiet will. Louie's quiet satiric waiting will. So it was like that, just flesh in the end after the habit began. Like a meal. Fasting and then the meal. He could not believe it. It could not be like that for ordinary people, people who had warmth in them, who worked hard for a living, who could not afford the time to have a neurosis. He saw through the murky window of the world. All "turmoil there with the leisured ones standing aside, winding their souls up like watches." "That's us," he said aloud. "Us. We're all diseased." Fling yourself into work, he thought, try and be tired, deserve to sleep. Ugh!

"Come on," he said gently, shaking her. "No use weeping about it. Drive us to Loltugi. I must say you've surprised me, but I've been a bloody fool. I've been imagining you were mine. Idiot. You've done the right thing. Now we can have some peace."

"You don't care, do you?" She wanted to be hurt, there was not enough pain for her yet, she could not think why. "You don't care." He would not reply. "Come on, Helena, drive," he said. She started the engine. They said nothing as the car rolled forward over the red dust. She stole glances at him. He looked calm. What a strange and useless affair it had been, all because she had lacked courage to seize happiness when it came. He was so lovable too, and she had only racked and hurt him.

"You'll hate women now, I suppose," she spoke in a low voice.

"I'll be more careful, that's all."

"Men are worse than women, though, Jervy." Their talk was lightening again. She could feel him responding to her tone.

"They're only worse so that they can please women," he said. He began to laugh and when she was curious he would not tell her why. He was laughing because of the pathetic mess that life appeared to be just then. Perhaps a horse was the best creature on earth after all, or an honest rabbit in a hedge. It took humans to make a mess of the world, all swarming about in their satanic tragic mess. He was a bit older than an hour ago, he thought. Boyhood must have really departed.

"I'm glad nothing took place between us," he told her. "You were right. I might have got tied up in you and then you'd have done this. There is a lot of bitch in you, Helena. We all meet the wrong people, I think. I wonder why. God, I wonder why."

Loltugi was dozing in the afternoon sun, save for two soldiers on punishment drill. They ran up and down in full equipment on the army compound while a corporal stood in the shade and barked at them. Jervis and Helena were dumb with their knowledge of each other, two people again, neighbours from adjacent farms, no longing in him now, but an unwilling feeling like loathing for her. Charity would take time to come.

He sat in the doctor's garden when Helena went in to see him. He watched the soldiers sweating, paying for the rule they had broken. How useless it seemed. A young officer wearing black puttees came in from the road and said to Jervis: "Hallo, who are you?"

"And who are you?" replied Jervis. The officer laughed. "That's right. You're quite right. I *was* rather rude. Just down from the frontier. I'm Mitten, attached to this company for a rest."

"I'm Jervis in that case," he told the officer.

"It's started at last." Mitten spoke with relish. "At last."

"What has?"

"The Italians have invaded Abyssina, and about bloody time too."

"Invaded Abyssinia?" He looked out into the distant blue mists of heat beyond which lay Abyssinia. "When?"

"You *must* be from the back of beyond all right," said Mitten. "They've been preparing for ages. And now they've started. I saw them from one of our outposts, thousands of them moving north. I'm just going in to start on the doc's radio and I'll sit there all night if necessary. No more raids from the Abyssinians now for us. No more bloody massacres and chaps being castrated. D'you know that up our way if a wog's been castrated by the Habash he doesn't have to pay poll tax."

There was something comical in this piece of tragic information and Jervis burst out laughing, Mitten joining him. "Pretty good, isn't it? Well, no more of that now. The Italians will knock the bloody manure out of them. Wish it was us doing the job." He sighed with a kind of schoolboy regret. "Yes, I loathe the Habash. Anyone who's had any-thing to do with them loathes them. They're always killing somebody or castrating somebody. Bit off, isn't it, that kind of thing?"

"It's certainly a bit off," said Jervis, and Mitten was con-vulsed with laughter. "Bloody good the way you said that. Bloody good. I must tell that to the C.O. He'll pee himself laughing." He began to tell Jervis about life on the frontier. There was one fort where everybody went a bit mad. The only amusement there was to stand in the doorway at night with a tennis racket and bash the bats as they flew in and out. There were millions of them.

"It's either that or sitting going slowly potty. It's hot too. If the Habash make a raid then we all toddle off into the bush after them. I wish I could shoot one of the sods. I just loathe them. But never mind, the Italians will fix all that now."

"Do you think they'll win?"

"No trouble at all. They've got simply millions of chaps, and our C.O. says they're using stacks of Somali troops, who just *loathe* the Habash. You see, the Habash have been raiding the Somalis for years, and now the Somalis are going into Abyssinia at last. The Italians have been bomb-ing like hell." His enthusiasm made Jervis feel old, though they were about the same age. He told the subaltern that the doctor had a lady with him at present so he would not be available for some time. The subaltern sat down and told him more stories of the frontier. It was his first outpost duty, and Jervis was the first civilian to listen to him. "It's not like this, you know. Nice soil and lots of trees. Up there, there's absolutely damn all except sand. I've promised the chaps I'll drink all the beer in Loltugi for them. Gosh, it's nice being here." He had a fresh pink face under the huge regulation helmet.

"Are you one of these settler chaps?" he wanted to know.

"More or less," said Jervis.

"Shot anything much?"

"A leopard and a few things like that," Jervis replied nonchalantly. The other was greatly impressed, so Jervis said nothing about the leopard being in a trap. After all, it *was* a leopard, there was no getting away from that. He basked in the other's respectful gaze. Then he told him about the lion.

"I say, you settler chaps certainly see a bit of life, don't you," said the subaltern. Jervis said nothing, content with the impression he had made.

"You can come in now," they heard Punter shouting.

Helena was sitting back in an arm-chair. She looked pale, Jervis thought. "Everything all right?" he asked her. She said yes, everything was all right. He shook hands with the doctor, who greeted him warmly. To Mitten the doctor said: "Well, come down for a drink, have you? When did you get in?"

"I came in this morning on an Indian ration lorry. It was some trip, I can tell you, Doc. Heard the great news?" He could not wait, though, for an answer. "The Italians have invaded Abyssinia. Good, eh? Wish it was us. I'm dying to twiddle your radio, Doc."

"You want to fight, do you? Well, you'll get all you want before you're thirty, my lad. So they've gone in among the Habash at last, have they? Well, better they than us. I wonder if we'll fight them."

"Fight the Italians? What for, Doc?" The subaltern was derisive. "The Italians are doing the right thing. Why should we fight them?"

"I'm not sure but it looks as if we might. The British Government's not very keen on the conquest of Abyssinia." The doctor smiled at Mitten. Only a kid, a schoolboy, he thought. He would never get past the rank of major. That brain was already frozen in its innocence of adolescence. There was nothing to beat a middle-aged adolescent major in this mess when some inane chat was required. Mitten was born for the part. He had all the stock requirements which would one day almost certainly create chaos in the midst of battle.

"Now run along and play with the radio, Mitten," the doctor said. "It's by my bed in the next room."

"If we go to war with the Italians we'll have a warm time in East Africa," he said to Helena and Jervis.

"We won't go to war with anybody," said Helena. "Louie says we wouldn't fight even if they invaded Britain. He says we've had enough."

"We'll fight all right," Punter mused to her. "There'll be fighting for the rest of this horrible century. Still, I can't complain. I saw some good years, some good, sane years before 1914."

They talked about Germany's demand for the return of her colonies, and of Hitler's racial mania. Jervis did not listen. It was all so far away, that European idiocy. It could never reach out to here, into this bush and jungle. He asked the doctor for some melons for Major Fawn-Cochley and a boy was sent to fetch some.

"Had any luck with that lion of yours?" the doctor inquired. Jervis and Helena shook their heads, Jervis telling him that it had not killed since the death of Charanga. He told about the lion vomiting the poisoned bait.

"H'mm, you'd better be very sharp if you meet that lion, son. Don't forget what it did to your herdsman." Jervis said he was not likely to. Since he had shot the leopard, he had noticed, his ambition to kill this lion was growing.

"I have a feeling I'm going to get that lion," he announced to Helena and the doctor. No one referred to its killing of Browning. The story had gone round and the doctor was discreet, like everyone else save Mrs. Withers-Hamden of Guyu. Queer how it was often what was not said which revealed people's minds, Jervis reflected. "If you shoot that lion, I'll give you a bottle of whisky, son," the doctor promised him.

Driving out of Loltugi, Helena said: "Jervy, I'm going to have a baby."

"I guessed as much," he lied. She showed her surprise. "How did you know—no one knows?" He refused to tell her, and came to believe he had really known. Inside, he seethed, not with jealousy, but with humiliation, that he had panted over her, implored for peace into her ear.

"I'm glad, now I know," she said. "But it's the end of my farming for a long time. Now Louie'll have to do a bit." Yes, he had got her into the house at last, woman's place, and now he could gloat over it.

"Jervy," she went on, "I'm sorry for all this mess I've made between us. Please forgive me. I think I'd gone a little crazy." He could not soften, though.

"Never mind," he replied grudgingly. "You've taught me quite a lot in one way and another."

"Don't be bitter," she said. It's like film dialogue, he was thinking. Gee, Jervy, but you're a grand person, the film actress would have added, but we're all washed up, see?

It was dark when they neared Fawn-Cochley's house. Jervis laid his hand on her arm and said: "Stop the car a minute." She obeyed. "There. Listen." It was the lion roaring from the direction of the escarpment. "He's back again," said Jervis. "My God, there are two of them. Listen." Far away they heard another one roaring.

"It's going to be very lively up here soon," she said. She dropped him at the house. "Be careful on your way home," he advised her. Was it anxiety for her she could detect in his voice? No, only the usual thing one said on such an occasion.

"Good night, Jervy."

"Good-bye," he answered.

"Good-bye? Oh, Jervy, no."

"Good-bye, Helena. And thanks for the trip. I enjoyed it." He spoke quietly. "You hate me, don't you?" she said, but he waved his hand and ran up the steps.

Chapter XX

ASMANI was born in the year of the apple. An English missionary had given some of the new wisdom to Asmani's chief and from this had come the apple tree, and when it fruited it was the year of the apple. Asmani was nearly thirty years old when Jervis came as Fawn-Cochley's pupil. He was a bright-eyed, brown-skinned man of slim build.

"Why do the men of your race all have the two bottom front teeth missing?" Jervis had asked him one day. It was strange. Perhaps that was why Asmani's tribe all pronounced ell as r, a pleasant soft guttural resulting.

"It is an old custom, Bwana," Asmani explained. "When we get the disease which stiffens us like this"—he made his body rigid and clenched his jaws—"our mouths lock and a man cannot eat. If a man gets this sickness we put a reed through the hole here where the two teeth are missing and we blow food down it so that the man cannot die of hunger." Tetanus, lockjaw, perhaps, thought Jervis. He was surprised once again. He had expected, had taken it for granted, that the Africans would know nothing, had discovered no antidote to nature's tyranny, but from Asmani he learned otherwise. Asmani told him many things which men knew about nature. Of herbal drugs and poisons, of how the women could avoid having children if they wished, of how men had discovered the properties of the castor-oil plant and how they could drug a man so that he became an entertaining idiot. There was much nonsense, too, but only enough to give colour to a fact. There was a race of men in some forest, too, according to Asmani, whose bodies were white and their faces black. If a man could only find this race he would learn everything that could be known.

Asmani's face reminded Jervis of the portrait of some Egyptian king. Who brought him that face? There were so many of these faces sprinkled among the thick-lipped and heavy-browed black men of the Bantu. They had come, it was said, from the north, killing and stealing on their way. There were men whose language was without music, brackish and hard, like a memory of the Sudanese wilderness and the burning laterite of the frontier deserts. Asmani was strong and he could not wait to learn. He drove a nail with two blows of a hammer, and could imagine a shape in his mind and draw it in the soil with a stick. More and more Jervis relied on him. He noticed that he would trust Asmani to remember what should be done at a certain time, or when such and such happened. It was not that Asmani had ambition or sought place and money for himself. He could not help being what he was, a fallen brilliant, not knowing why he thirsted to do things and to learn. He knew what Jervis wanted before this Bwana had half spoken a wish. It was almost a clairvoyance. The other Africans who worked on the farm, digging, tending the lucerne patch, driving ox-teams, or the herdsmen, all respected Asmani. He knew everything there was to know, it seemed, and he could read a man's mind.

"I wonder what would happen if Asmani went to the

mission at Loltugi," Jervis would think occasionally. "I wonder if he would be destroyed. I wonder if he would become a new kind of man." He always decided that Asmani would be destroyed, perhaps because he did not want to lose him as he was. So many curious things happened to a tribesman when the doors of abstraction were opened and he saw the world of money, whores, lies and crippled greatness before him, the key, as he thought in his head, the book, the ciphers mingling in his mind. It was like sickness, this yearning which the book brought, for he was like one lost among his savage fellows in the village, cut off from them by new habits and the dregs of the old and now spurned superstitions.

Jervis saw that this period for Africa was the "in between" one, in between two worlds, the one the mission boy aspired to being barred here and there with thorns, the thorny barriers of race and privilege, the privilege of those who had invented the tools and the ciphers. When they reached the barriers they would be puzzled and then distorted with hatred, for it was not as the missionaries had said, one God and one people in His world. There must be a God with a black face, then. No, said the missionary and then lost him in worlds of conjecture. That world barred with thorns; it is not only the taste of that world a man wants, it is the whole meal, for the taste awakens appetite.

Asmani then was happy enough, thought Jervis. He felt mean at first, making these secret decisions as to what was good for Asmani, but he grew used to such decisions as week followed week, and he was conditioned by his place in that world and by that of the tribes wandering in their unawareness.

"Let me, Bwana," said Asmani one day. "Let me dip the cattle. I will look after every one of them."

"No," he was told, and then he watched the Bwana

thinking after he had said no. He tried to read Jervis's thoughts but failed.

"It's not that I don't believe you will do it well. But the Bwana Major would not like it. And then there is this other thing of trust. You might do it well, and do it well several times, but one day you may leave it to another to do and cattle will drown or a calf will die. It is this thing that makes me hard to you with my mouth. Do you understand?" He did not like to admit it to himself, but he had to. They were not ready yet for responsibility, not knowing what it was to value another's goods as if they were their own, or worrying, thinking: "Am I doing it well? Is this good enough?" It was there, though, that goodwill and that urge to achieve, but clouded in a fog of laziness from poor feeding and struggling childhood. Who was there who could collapse under a tree in the shade and appear to die of sleep, like an African? Who was there who enjoyed this practice for death so much? It was a shame that it should end, the long sleep of centuries in the sun while Persian, Greek and Roman empires rose and fell and the engine was born in Europe. But end it would, by shouting, by economic threat, by longing for cigarettes, and the paying of rent which would be charged in the future. God, how sad it was.

"No," he told Asmani, "it is like that." Asmani laughed. He wore a pair of Jervis's English shorts which Abdul Hafiz had pronounced not quite the thing. He wore nothing else save a pair of rawhide sandals and there was a warm bloom of sun on his brown muscles. Chains of small ritual blisters ran from shoulder to shoulder, like hard grey bubbles rising from the brown flesh. Jervis always thought of Asmani affectionately, and Asmani had come a little beyond that usual African glumness and returned this affection, almost sure of Jervis's.

"I will teach you a lot of things as you teach me,

Asmani," he said. "But I cannot trust you yet in all things, for this trust is like a thing you can't see." No, he could not describe responsibility. He had not enough words in the language, but Asmani said: "I understand this thing. It is a thing done for nothing, or for money too, but it is the same thing."

"That's it," Jervis agreed, smiling. What a sharp one you are, he thought, looking into Asmani's dark, restless eyes. How much *did* they know? Could a white man ever find out? "I'll find out if it's the last thing I do," Jervis promised himself.

He would always take Asmani with him when he went shooting for the pot and they would talk as they walked. Jervis expected Asmani to ask one day for permission to use the rifle, but he never did. It was as though he knew that would be too much to ask, to request the symbol of power, for they seemed to think of it as that, the noise of M'zinga locked in its barrel.

"It is the fire from the barrel which follows the bullet and goes into the animal through the hole made by the bullet, which kills the animal," the other men argued, but Asmani could laugh at them.

"It is not true that a small bullet can kill a rhinoceros," they said. "It is the fire which goes into the hole, burning up the heart, *na choma roho yaki*."

The lion, avoiding the foot-traps, came three times more in the months that followed the opening of the Abyssinian war. He killed a cow each time. Helena grew big and Louie Brinden slowly changed, becoming active about the land. One day he came over to Fawn-Cochley's place to see Fawn-Cochley. When they were seated on the veranda, where Jervis was cutting up eland and oryx hides with Asmani to make ropes for the work-oxen, Brinden said: "I've had enough now of this lion. I'm sure it's the same one that's working all along the escarpment. I'm getting hold of a couple of Wa'Ndarobo blokes and let them track it. And I'm getting one of those Dutchmen at ten quid a month to camp on the escarpment until he gets the lion. Now, Major, will you split the costs with me?"

Yes, thought Jervis, eyeing Brinden from where he sat with the thick hides spread across his legs, he's changed all right. More confident, fitter-looking. Quite the proud father-to-be. The old man considered Brinden's suggestion, his withering brown face vacant with thought as he stared towards Abyssinia.

"Why can't Jervis here sit on the ridge instead of a Dutchman?" he wanted to know. "It's not that I begrudge the money. Though, I must say, there's plenty of work for him to do."

"Well, he can't shoot as well as the Dutchmen, can he?" Brinden was frank. Jervis looked at him and smiled. "I'm not such a great shot myself, but this isn't sport now. I say, let's get an expert on this job. The Wa'Ndarobo should soon find that lion."

"What d'you think, Jervis?" the old man asked, surprising his pupil. It was the first time the Major had sought his opinion and he was grateful, as though he had come of age.

"I'd say Brinden's right," he replied. "The Dutchman is the answer, though I would like to get that lion myself. But it's serious. It's not sport any more, as Brinden says. This lion is killing right and left."

Brinden had lost a couple of cows in the last six months. They were all agreed that it was the same lion. Brinden's herdsmen had told him that during its absence the lion was down in the plains. There were good rocky hiding-places there to lie up in, and if he wanted sport there was plenty of game.

"You know all the zebra are back, I suppose," said Brinden. "Every damned one of them." The others nodded. There was nothing to be done there save slow, steady shooting. The zebra were just another problem along with the ticks and the diseases and the hundred other pests that fought remorselessly against the settlers. "All right," Major Fawn-Cochley said at length, "I'll go halves with you on the Dutchman and the Wa'Ndarobo. But keep your eyes on those Wa'Ndarobo or they'll be lifting our cattle and sheep. I had an experience of them a couple of years ago."

Brinden told them that his wife was well, keeping to the house as much as possible. He was very nervous when he spoke of her coming confinement. He had never thought of himself as a father and he was afraid that something would go wrong.

"You can get old Punter in when it's time. He'd like the trip and you can have him as a guest for a couple of days."

Having a baby in this part of Africa was not the simple matter of the confinement in the city. Distances were long, and an emergency was something real and frightening, Brinden told them. But he would take the Major's tip.

"If the Wa'Ndarobo strike the lion, couldn't we be warned, if there's time, so that we can all have a go at it?" Jervis asked the old man. Brinden said: "Why not? I'd like a go myself. All right. I'll fix it up, if it's possible."

Asmani was working quietly with his sharp knife on the hide Jervis had given him to prepare. He was now able to separate the English talk into words as he listened. Next there was the problem of learning the meaning of the words. White men were strange about their language. They did not encourage black men to learn it, and he knew that they wished to keep their affairs and their secrets to themselves. He had once heard the Bwana Major quarrel with a mission boy who had come looking for work and had spoken in

English. Each time the mission boy had spoken in English the Bwana Major had replied in Ki'Swahili, but still the stupid mission one would speak that tongue before him. "I don't understand what you're saying," he had shouted. "What is it supposed to be? English?" This was an interesting thing, the way the white men held on to their strongest key. But he would learn it, Asmani had made up his mind. One day he would ask the young Bwana to teach him English, the Ki'zungu tongue of the Wa'zungu.

The Wa'Ndarobo had lived on the edge of the Masai wars and away from the tracks of the marauding Arab slave-traders who would come from the coast and plunder men and women for sale in the markets of the Arab seaboard. The Wa'Ndarobo lived in the forests, hunting with poisoned spears and arrows. They had lived in small groups throughout the Masai country, owning no cattle or goats, but keeping bees in the long drums they placed in the trees, and hunting anything they could eat, especially elephant. Ndarobo, the Masai called them, sneeringly or pityingly, the men who had no cattle, who had nothing. The Arab and Swahili traders had added the Ki'Swahili prefix they used for living things, calling them Wa'Ndarobo. They still lived cut off from the tribes, still hunted, awaiting the spirochete and the cheap, natty suiting which would one day be the prelude to their new world. They looked like the Masai, aping them, having a language of their own but able to speak Masai at times. Now the great fighting clans of the Masai were gone, for the white men had moved them south, and cut off from their masters, the Wa'Ndarobo lived on in their precarious freedom of the trees.

With the juices of certain euphorbia, the white milky sap which could blind a man, some roots, and, the legend said, the venom of certain insects, they brewed their poison in the quiet forests. They were the last of an ancient struggle of men in the wilderness and the forest. They kept to themselves, no bridge between their freedom of darkness and the outposts of the white men's world, except for the odd Englishman who studied them or became their friend, writing down things they said in small books.

Brinden told Jervis what he knew about these hunting people. He had once used a Wa'Ndarobo tracker to follow some thieves and had taken an interest in them ever since. "They're one people in the country about whom my wife lays no claim to knowledge," said Brinden in his deliberate way. Everything he said seemed to be tinged with irony, even when none was intended. Jervis was surprised to find how widely he had read. Everyone in the country seemed to have a favourite tribe and Brinden's was the Wa'Ndarobo. He promised Jervis that he would like them if he met them in their own surroundings. Jervis found himself liking Brinden. It was easier to do so after his failure with Helena. He was sorry for Brinden with a wife like that, but Brinden's irony did not allow of a growing intimacy, and he did not appear to need sympathy. He was the kind of man, thought Jervis, who might have guessed what had gone on between his wife and Jervis, and one day might refer to it with a note of irony.

"Well, I'm glad to see you again, Brinden," the old man told him when Brinden rose to go.

"Yes, since my wife became pregnant I get a look-in on my own farm. It's quite pleasant." Always he said these things seriously and with a straight face, and Fawn-Cochley looked puzzled, murmuring "H'm. Yes." What a queer chap Brinden was. It was the country that had done it, of course. Most people were a bit cracked, and so quietly too, never violent. There was that one in Mombasa, who, people said, thought he was a poached egg, and when he went visiting always carried a piece of toast to sit on, and people were very understanding about it. A host would always have a piece of toast made if anything went wrong. It was a good-hearted and hospitable community, the settler community. It made every allowance for human failing. It had to. It was absorbed in a task soon to become a dilemma.

When Brinden had gone Fawn-Cochley said: "A strange chap, that. Did you notice the way he talked about his wife?"

"He talks like that about everything. He's clever too."

"Clever all right. Poor Helena." The old man sighed. "She's a handful but she's worth two of him."

"I'm not so sure," said Jervis, and the Major looked at him and said "Oh?" but Jervis smiled and busied himself with the hide which Asmani had cut up.

"They've had some words," the Major thought. "I wonder if anything *did* go on?"

He sat and watched Jervis working, and knowing the old man's eyes were on him, the pupil stayed absorbed in his task. The old man was thinking, perhaps he had something to say. When two people have been associated for some time in a common isolation, their intuitive powers usually sharpen so that one can begin to read the other, one feels the other's mood or apprehends his gloom or pleasure before deciding to voice some opinion or other. It is a kind of quiet, mutual grazing of each other's minds and spiritual privacies, seeing things which are hidden and silently ignoring them, or one may probe into the other until the half-understood warning is given that he has gone too far. Each comes to know when to leave the other alone, and he may know this by a look, a gleam in the eye, a hollowness in a cheek. All this is when the initial conversational exploration is over and the dispositions moulded by isolation are come upon, the tempers, the eccentricities, the hint of some private mania. Each gets through the light foliage which surrounds the darker core, the rocky centre where the animal and the angel have been engaged in silent remorseless struggle since the first bloodied movement of birth. Fawn-Cochley had been years alone and he had noticed Jervis walking through his foliage for weeks. He was well able to judge with what innocence these rambles were made. He knew that youth had little or no plan when it put its finger on an area of thorns, when a question was not the one to be asked. Jervis's company had taken away some of his suspicion of the world, Jeru could see that. Now, too, the old man saw his own age pointed to by the vigour of the younger man with whom he lived. It was as though Jervis's presence, his speed, his leaping up and down the veranda steps, those effortless and elastic liftings of a sack of maize meal or a fencing pole, had shown him that he had been old for a long time and had not known it. And it was very hard to accept. From his own experience he believed that there was a period in a man's life, a time of restless and unbeatable confidence when, given opportunity, a man can face anything in nature. He had always believed that of himself, but he saw now that for ten years he had been a querulous old man, tolerated by Jeru and the servants. This was a blow which took weeks to absorb and of which it was not possible to speak. It seemed only a few days ago since he had toiled up mountains in blazing heat, the memory of the big tusks he had seen in the elephant herds photographed on his mind, and he would follow them for days if necessary until he came on them. Pieces of ivory, only, but which had brought from him every effort of which his body and spirit was capable. In that loneliness he had been able to draw on all of himself, giving none away to others in talk or the anxiety to persuade some woman on to her back, moving always, hard as a board and sure that he could survive all heat, all baked and broken trails, and every claw of nature's resistance to its disturbers.

"You should write your life," acquaintances had told him as they looked appraisingly at the "old-timer," during a drink and a chat on a rare visit to the Guyu Club. But what was there to write? When he reflected he saw that he had enjoyed his life, a life full of experiences in a newly discovered world of jungle and deserts. He had always sought the most outlying portions of that world, places where an Indian trader now had a store and sold maize and trash to the savages. There was nothing he could write of that life. "I raised my heavy rifle as the great beast reared ——" When he looked back he could not see his life clearly as the rare privileged listeners could see it in his imagination. He had enjoyed it, and now it was nearly over and he could not see any point in it. So what about the world to come? He was afraid and he was not accustomed to fear. He had become more attached to Jervis but was wary of this affection he found growing there. It was like surrender of self-reliance, like weakness in the face of age.

"Jervis," he said, "I've got one or two things I want to say to you." He groped about for words. Jervis studied the lined, sun-darkened face of the old Major and noticed that the eyes in their wrinkled pouches were watching his own with what seemed to be a humorous speculation. He put down his knife and held his numbed and aching hand. Asmani went on working, humming a song about a baboon watching women working in the maize patch.

"How would you like to own this place?" the old man said.

"Buy it?" Jervis laughed and then looked at the old man, knowing already what was in his mind.

"No, not buy it. Look here, I haven't a soul left in the world belonging to me. When I kick the bucket I'll have to

leave it to somebody. What about you?" He lit a cigarette
after giving one to Jervis. "Some day you'll marry and
settle down. Why not here? You like it, don't you?"

Jervis said that he did not know what to say. The other
day, he was thinking, an old herdsman had spoken of this
land as "Ours once," not in any antagonistic way, but as
though it were a fact and as if the new way was to be accepted. This old man had been born on the side of a hill near
Sabuga. When Jervis told this to Helena Brinden over a cup
of tea at her house, she had sat up at once in her arm-chair
and said: "Nonsense. I've heard this before. Another herdsman tried that on one of Fawn-Cochley's pupils. This place
was a wilderness grazed by the Masai and they had no
parasites. Nomads own nothing except what they can get
with their spears. This place was a wilderness, and when the
Masai went we came in here and civilised it. If we hadn't,
the Masai would still be wiping out the maize eaters." She
had watched him and he knew that she wanted him to
understand at once the difference between nostalgic legend
and a truth. He knew that nothing could have prevented
the coming of the white men. Now it was a matter of finding
a way to live together, of deciding how to alter a culture
based on the spear and cattle, and the devouring merciless
death which in that culture had been the end.

"Don't you listen to this stuff," she told him. "We'll
hear a lot of it one of these days, so get the facts right and
teach your herdsmen the difference between superstition
and rinderpest vaccine." Yes, it was no use standing back
and being thoughtful. He had to get on with the job or
decide that Africa should never have been discovered.

Now he was being offered a farm, being given a responsibility in a strange experiment. Why stand back from this
great adventure which men would carry on despite everything? "If you want me to have it, Major," he said, "I'll

take it on. And I'll look after it well." He looked at Asmani's hands, thoughtful.

"That's good," Fawn-Cochley said. He was relieved. He had given in to his age and it gave a peculiar feeling of relief, almost happiness. He could see that, thinking about it there before him, Jervis was uncomfortable, so he rose and said: "I'll go into the details some other time. But here's my hand on it." They shook hands and Asmani watched them, and though he thought of many reasons for this unusual thing, he could not find one which would satisfy him.

"The Bwana Major like you very much, Bwana," he said when Fawn-Cochley had left the veranda, but Jervis misunderstood him and was short with him. They fell into silence again, only the sawing sound of their knives breaking the hot afternoon stillness.

Chapter XXI

THE Dutchman Brinden chose for his hunter was the slim one, Huiter, who had taken Jervis on the first hunt for the lion, following the zebra chase. He lived with an ailing brother on the edge of a farm belonging to an Englishman near Guyu. He had come into East Africa as a youth with his father in 1908, walking beside the ox-wagons, his rifle loaded always and at the trail. No one had written much of those tremendous feats of the few Dutch families who crossed the wide, brown rivers, the jungles and wild prairies which made the territories now known as the Orange Free State, Portuguese East Africa and Tanganyika, hunting their way into what they regarded as freedom. As long as Africa had new territory there was freedom to seek. The urban civilisation could not catch up with these few who wanted Africa as it had always been. They were pursuing a dream, a dream of herds of game and Africans to work for them, the sons of Ham as described by the bearded black-clothed deacons in the South. There was not much time left for them, and in their half-primitive way they felt it. They had no neuroses, only a few theories about black men and why they were there, and a deep desire for a bit of land in the bush with some game on it.

Huiter could build a dam, train a team of oxen, measure a field with his eye, and fire a shot in a mine. He had always been able to turn his hand to something but had never made much money. His father was old now and lived on his own piece of land with an almost African feeling for mealies which, when ground into flour, formed his main food. He liked to potter about in the sun, drying strips of meat for biltong. He could not shoot very well now, and his son would sometimes take him an antelope to cut up and dry in shares for them.

Huiter was glad to get Brinden's offer. He liked the escarpment which separated Brinden and Fawn-Cochley from the plains. When he saw those plains, extending, it seemed, to infinity, he became anxious to move on. They affected him strongly. They were "the bush" where no lines had been drawn yet, no roads marked, no towns for men and women to soften in. On the escarpment it would be quiet. He was glad, too, that they wanted *him* for the lion-hunt. They knew who could shoot.

He had an argument with his new employer on the day he turned up at the Brinden farm. He rode in, a pack mule beside him carrying his pots and pans and blankets. Brinden was sitting on the veranda steps reading a book. It was mid-day and hot, and Huiter was glad of the bottle of cold beer which the Englishman offered him. He sat down on a lower step and took off his warm slouch hat, revealing a mass of thick, yellow, curly hair. His thin, red-brown face was covered with light, golden stubble. Brinden thought he must be about thirty-six. He watched him drinking the beer and he found himself envying him, this seemingly free man who only did what he wanted to do, or would eat maize meal until he found a task to suit him. He kept no end up, subscribed to no conspiracy of place or position, and was satisfied with his old faded clothing. Brinden, as always in the presence of a South African Dutchman, unconsciously treated him as one nearer to Africa in some peculiar way, as one of a race who had been there for three hundred years. Nothing could make them European again. They could never go back there. They were here for good, and it did not worry them if they ate an African meal of a ball of posho spiked with meat or a six-course dinner from a table. They felt no hostility from Africa. They kicked Africa in its face if it turned on them. They were involved in no plan, only in a habit of generations.

"Well, I've got your tent ready and a good double-barrel five hundred," said Brinden when Huiter put down his glass.

"I got my own rifle, Mr. Brinden," Huiter said with a stubborn smile. "I shot lions with it too often to miss now. It's a ·256 and you can't beat it."

"I think you should use something heavier," Brinden urged.

"No, man. I tell you I'll cut grass for you with this ·256 if you like. It's the best damn rifle in the world. If I see this lion I'll put one right through his eye." Brinden knew he was not boasting. He was telling him quietly what he could do.

"All right," he said. "Have it your own way. When do you want to start?"

"Right now." The Dutchman stood up. "I got grub with me but if you have a few spuds, man, I'd be glad."

"There's a *kikapu* full of spuds and onions lying with the tent. You'll find it with the Wa'Ndarobo near where Mr. Browning was killed. Now what about your horse and mule? You can put them up at my cattle *boma*. It's not far from your tent."

"I'll leave the mule here, if you won't mind. He's a damn nuisance when it's dark."

Brinden and Huiter drove in the box-body along the ridge towards the forest. "Look at them," Brinden said, pointing to the zebra. "They won't go up higher where we shot their foals but they won't go down either." The Dutchman said nothing, only sneered at the zebra as they drove past the grazing herd. The zebra was no good unless you wanted rifle practice. He was a waste.

"There's one thing I'd like you to do, Huiter," said Brinden. "If you get wind of this lion, try and call Fawn-Cochley and me. We want to have a crack at this brute too." Huiter thought about that. He was being paid, so he said:

"All right, man. I'll do that. I think we'll get this lion. I'll search every square foot for him." He was not at ease in a car. There *were* Dutchmen who had cars but they were soft, said people like Huiter. A horse and a rifle, man, Christ, what more did you want?

"Listen, Huiter. If you help us to get this lion I'll give you ten quid as a present."

"I'll get you this lion, Mr. Brinden. You'll see, man."

After leaving the Dutchman at the camp, Brinden drove up to Fawn-Cochley's house, but Jeru told him that the two Bwanas were at the *menanda* dipping cattle, so he drove down to the dipping shed. When he drew close he could smell the sharp chemical of the dip, and the cattle, wet with it and glistening, steamed in the sun as the herdsmen drove them away. The dull thump and splash as each cow plunged into the long tank of dip, the bellowing of calves and the yellow, gritty clouds of dust reminded him of the farming he had so long neglected. He had won, but it had been a long battle, and now his wife was pregnant, a woman again. He braked the car. What would it all come to? Would it work out well, or would the battle begin again? He hated her as much as he loved her, probably more. Pride was the important thing, not love, for him. He had wanted a woman with softness in her and Helena wanted to be a man, and he admired her for her ability to work, but never forgave her for it. There were times when he thought that it was she, and not he, who was made and fitted for this existence on the frontier of an ancient barbarism. He was too fond of reading and of speculation. She read, too, but usually about the country in which she was now making her life. He always read away from it, into the regions of the question about why we were here, the ingenuities of men who had taken time off to ponder while the others, and he was supposed to be one of them, grew corn and raised cattle, paid men to use their hands and hammered the world into new and brief shapes. No, he did not belong to this kind of life. There were poets who gave him glimpses of annihilation, poets describing the slow, steady munching of ruin's teeth despite all toil, but they never answered their own questions. They told of Europe's despair.

Brinden, in his solidity, his cold calm, did not appear to reflect the continual agitation which possessed him, that eye within, always watching, and seeing the end of everything, the apparent inanity of all effort to give permanence to life. He never grew impatient when wild beasts killed his stock, never cursed when disease came into a herd, or struck a stupid African. His eyes sneered when he came across these things. He took action but with a readiness to deprecate the effort. He had a sense of humour but it made the Africans stare silently when he used it on them, for it was like a serpent, carrying in it its own death. He was charitable and impulsive in his generosity, and always ready to be let down, for that was only the world. On the surface, as far as his acquaintances in Guyu were concerned, he was a good fellow, though "deep" and unknowable. He had served three years on the Western Front, as a sergeant of infantry, and when he had first settled in the country and the ex-officers who had settled near him had put up their signboards—"Captain Soandso," "General Whatsthis," "Major Whosit"—he had had his own put up—"Sergeant Brinden." It lost him a lot of friends, for various reasons. He had worked hard. Many of the others who had settled near him soon went. Africa beat them. It was the kind of place which put its finger into a man's weakness more swiftly than all the bloody infantry attacks of the war. Brinden had plenty of money. His father had manufactured war equipment. It was interesting, he would reflect, that while he was better read and richer than the "ex-officer" types and their wives, who formed the majority of his settler neighbours, there was always a vague line separating him from them, and across which they shared their common gentility like a conspiracy, though they might drink with him all night in the Guyu Club. To have been an officer was the thing, not that there was anything derogatory about being a sergeant. But why should he have been a sergeant for three years of the war if he was really a gentleman? Not even Colonel Prince-Brown, the club secretary, could answer that one, and he was an expert on the classes: "Spot breeding anywhere, old boy." Now, after years, he was almost accepted as of the class, but they were never quite sure where they were with him. The British took the complications of their social life even into the deepest wilderness. For many it was all they had in the world.

He sat in his car and watched Jervis through the dust-clouds supervising the culling of young calves and castrating them while Fawn-Cochley attended to the dipping. It was a marvellous life in many ways, though bloody, dirty and hard. He thought he had had enough of it, but he went on with it, year after year. He knew, too, that eventually he would retire to the house again and Helena would take over the farming as before. It made him angry to know that, yet there was a certain pleasure in recognising its inevitability. He sighed. He wanted a drink. He had not been drunk for three weeks. Perhaps to-night. Or why not a trip into Guyu and a good booze-up at the club, or maybe Loltugi and a yarning in the mess over a bottle of Scotch. He idled with the possibilities while the acrid dust floated about him from the stamping cattle in the *boma*.

He gave Fawn-Cochley and Jervis a lift up to the house. They were hot and thirsty. The old man looked very old to-day, Brinden noticed. About time the old chap relaxed a bit. So that was age, looking as though you hadn't slept for a week.

"I left Huiter at his camp," he told Fawn-Cochley. "The Wa'Ndarobo are coming to him to-morrow. He's going to warn us if the lion turns up." The old man nodded. He was very tired. Jervis said nothing. He was sick of the subject of the lion. It would never be shot. His eyes were sore from the sun and the dust. He was weary after the struggling with the half-wild cattle and he had had an argument with one of the herdsmen about the counting of the cattle in his charge. He had accused him of losing a cow and at the third counting had found he was wrong. The herdsman, an elderly, shaven-headed man with black, wrinkled

7

skin, had laughed innocently and Jervis had lost his temper, just as Browning had prophesied, he reflected later. Then the old herdsman had taken a small buckhorn of snuff from his armpit and tapped some of it on to the back of his hand and offered Jervis some. Jervis had never tried it before. He let the old man sprinkle some of the blackish powder on to his wrist and had sniffed it up in one breath. It had turned him almost blind and the tears poured from his eyes, while the membrane of his nose felt as though it was being consumed by fire. He had sneezed as he had never sneezed in his life before, and it was nearly ten minutes before the great irritation in his nose, and the resulting bout of sneezing, passed away. The old herdsman was shocked, and Jervis had eyed him suspiciously and tried to control his temper. It might have been deliberate. But could a primitive tribesman possess such a deadly and quiet sense of humour? He could not say.

"It is strong stuff, Bwana," the herdsman had said, grave, too grave perhaps. "Yes, you bugger," Jervis had answered in English. "Go now. Thank you for the snuff."

"It is nothing, Bwana."

"You were a fool there," Fawn-Cochley had said. "Their snuff, my boy, is made of raw soda and raw tobacco with a dash of dried cow dung to give it a bouquet."

"Do you think he did it purposely?"

"Ah, you'll never know that." Fawn-Cochley hid his smile. "It takes a bit of doing to get inside their minds. I've never done it. I wonder if you will."

So Jervis was thinking about this. Pride grew like a weed in this sort of situation. Why could he not have laughed it off? Because already he was uncertain of his position with the Africans, already he was worrying about whether they were giving him enough respect. It must stop. But it was more perplexing than he had imagined it to be! It was hard to be open and trustful of them. When they greeted him and said "Jambo," they usually added "Bwana," master, but if one failed to add "Bwana" it worried him. Was it deliberate? Browning could have explained so much. It might have been the sun that was irritating him, or the height. "Up here, at these heights, we all go a bit queer, you know," Helena had told him. "We get very touchy." It was worth remembering.

"You're both very solemn to-day," Brinden remarked. "What's up?"

"I'm not solemn," the old man said. "I'm just tired. Have a whisky with us. It's nearly sundown."

Over the whisky Brinden told them that Anna Browning was going to England for six months.

"There's a chance for you there, Jervis," he added. "You could run the place while she's away. She wants a manager."

"No," the old man said, "I want him here." He looked at Jervis, who smiled his agreement.

"You two seem to get on fine," Brinden said. To Jervis he remarked: "Can't say that for the other pupils he's had, you know." The Major coughed unnecessarily loudly and Jervis changed the subject.

Chapter XXII

THE two Wa'Ndarobo were thin. They were almost naked, wearing only short, soft skins hanging over their loins. Each carried a long quiver of arrows, like tubes capped with buckhide. Their bows were at their feet as they squatted and watched the Dutchman eat his unusual food. They had never watched a white man eat before and they were greatly interested. This one was a white man of few words, all of them sharp and somehow ill-natured. With this one it was wise to be silent. Stuck in the ground before them by their pointed, iron butts were their peculiar spears. They swelled into a bulbous shape above the centre of the shaft and were bound with sinew. From this bulb ran the long detachable iron spearhead, its blade barbed so that it would cling in their prey's vitals. Each of the two hunters carried a leather poison-pot slung at his waist.

"To-morrow," Huiter said, his mouth full of hot stew, "we hunt. Down there." He pointed to the plains below them. The two savages nodded. "Have you ever killed a lion with those things?" He indicated their spears with his fork. The two hunters looked at each other and grinned with their big white teeth.

"No," said one, "we kill to eat. This time we hunt lion because the other white man has promised us blankets and salt and a cow hide." The Dutchman nodded. Always out for what they can get, he thought, they'll pinch my kit if I don't look out. Whole worlds separated this white man and those two forest dwellers who had come out for blankets and salt and cowhides. They had seen many white men but they did not want their world. The white men stank. If a white man and black were in the presence of a rhinoceros and it charged, it always went for the white man, for that sharp smell they had, a smell like the sap of certain plants, thin and acid. And in the bush they moved with noise, but it did not matter, for they killed from afar with those roaring rifles.

"This one eats as if he has starved for a whole moon," one said to the other.

"They all eat like that," his companion said. "Their bellies are never empty." They sat and watched Huiter, noting every movement, every feature of his person, his

nose, his fingers, his bootlaces, the way he handled his fork,
for seeing things was their life and their minds were like
cameras focused on this unusual man and his possessions
strewn about him.

In the morning, when the sun was still swimming on the
world's edge in rosy veils, golden rays like lances shooting
up into the grey sky, the white man and the two savages
walked down the rocky incline to the plains. A troop of
wart hogs, mother and young, trotted across their front, the
mother bustling with suspicion, her big snout and curled
yellow tusks turned towards the men. "I could drop her
right there," Huiter was thinking, anxious to kill. They
entered the plain. Long, yellow, rank grass, hillocks piled
with broken rock and silvery-leaved leleshwa bush. Clumps
of sansavera, its long green swords tipped with black spikes,
grew everywhere. In a time of thirst, a man could wet his
mouth with the bitter, abundant moisture contained in the
fleshy swords of the sansavera. The women beat the tendrils
on rocks until the pulp was gone, leaving them with a handful of long fibres for making cord or rope. The Wa'Ndarobo were at home here. They could find roots to
eat, queer berries to chew, moisture in the strangest
places.

They swished through the long grass, thousands of red
ticks clinging to them as they passed, thirsty for a meal of
blood in order to complete their cycle. The sun burned
down on them as it rose into the sky which arched from
horizon to horizon in a cloudless bowl, only the great sun
in its wide expanse like a gong of fire. The two Wa'Ndarobo
stared ahead, their eyes unwrinkled in the glare, while
Huiter, his slouch hat shading his face, looked out from
narrowed, screwed-up eyelids, sweat rolling on his cheekbones.

They cast right and left until midday, when Huiter shot

a zebra and the two hunters dragged the big, ballooning grey bowels behind them towards the forest. He shot a Thompson's gazelle and in the shade of a mimosa thorn they cooked the meat, letting it stand near the glowing coals on spits made of cedar splinters. They ate together, squatting on their heels, the Dutchman at home here in the silent, rolling wastes of the bush. Because the scant fat of the antelope congealed quickly in the throat when cool, he ate the meat straight from the coals, gulping and gasping as he chewed. It was good. He let them drink from his waterbottle, and knowingly they poured the water into their mouths without touching the neck of the bottle with their lips. Huiter nodded approvingly.

Huiter had eaten snake, zebra, toasted locusts, baked elephant's foot and tongue, ants and grubs, in his time.

"This one will go a long way if he has to," one of the black hunters said to the other. "He knows this thing and that thing."

They offered him tit-bits of grilled gut, tender and succulent. He ate them and then toasted the liver and they ate that too. They lay down in the shade, their bellies full of meat, and one of the Wa'Ndarobo twanged the ostrich-sinew string of his bow and sang a song about bees in a low minor key. Huiter dozed for a while, and when he awoke they moved on, the two hunters dragging the zebra's bowels, scenting the trail with them. They came to a *manyatta* made in the Masai style, long, low huts of clay and reeds surrounded by a pallisade of piled, dead, white thorns. Millions of flies swarmed from the thick floor of cattle dung within the thorn stockade. A woman with long pendulous dugs stood watching them, flies clustered at the corners of her eyes. Then a man came out of one of the huts and spat in greeting. "Soba," he said.

"Give us milk," said Huiter. "We thirst." He gave them

thick milk in a calabash and they ate it. "We are hunting a lion," Huiter told the man.

"Then you have come to the right place," he said. He grinned, his wolfish face shining with sunlight. He was of a tribe related once to the Great Masai, but fallen, though living like the Masai on blood defibrinated by a stick and mixed with milk. They lived in filth but they were free. No one had come to them yet, no missionary, no commissioner; they grazed from water to water. They had syphilis now and many women were barren.

"Tell me about this right place," said Huiter.

"There is one lion here cleverer than the other. He has killed a bull there." He pointed to a nearby hill with his chin.

"When?"

"*Juzi*," which was two days ago, some days ago but not *somani*, which was weeks ago, months ago, or *somaaaani*, long drawn out, which was a year ago, two years ago, a thousand years ago. Huiter began breaking *Juzi* down. It seemed that the lion had killed here four nights ago. Good. They sat down among the flies, Huiter waving his hands, and they talked.

"So it is wounded. It has something which hurts its neck?" Huiter coaxed him. "Who has said this thing?"

"One of the small boys saw it running in the grass and he said its neck is hurt. And when it killed here it wounded three cows before it could kill. Why should that be?"

"Yes, why?"

"Because it is hurt, and when a lion misses and wounds three standing cows, it is old or it is hurt. And this one is not old. He is as cunning as a crow." The man squirted a thin stream of spittle into the grey thirsty soil. One of his eyes was gone in ophthalmia.

"That is good," said Huiter. "I will remember you."

"That is good too," the man replied. "Have you got anything you can give me? Here we have nothing." Huiter found a piece of fencing wire in the pocket of his bush shirt. He gave it to the man. Then he took one of the knife-swivels from the ring in his belt and gave that too. The man put it in the long, expanded loop of his ear-lobe. He pointed to the sheath-knife on the white man's left hip. "Do you want to give me that?"

"No. You can't have that," said Huiter, shaking his head slowly. The man sighed and asked: "Have you many cattle?" Huiter said "No." "Then you are poor?" Again Huiter shook his head. For a long time they talked like that, for it was important to this man who lived cut off from the great tribes now that the world had changed and the Masai had gone from here. He lied about the lion for an hour, trying to please the white man, but Huiter was patient and broke each lie up into its seed of truth. The two Wa'Nda-robo sat quiet, watching this man, their eyes still, like those of birds of prey. They showed no sign as they listened to his lies, following the skein and hearing Huiter examine them and cast them away. It was the way of things to make a story.

"You bastard," said Huiter to himself in Afrikaans, when the man began to invent again. Aloud he said: "You are right about the wounded neck of the lion I am seeking. But you are lying about this and that. But I can hear these lies each time. What good is this lying?"

"If I help you to find this lion what will you give?" the man pressed him gently. It was fair to ask. Huiter thought it over in his slow mind, which was unaffected by education, unlettered, free to digest everything like this mind he was grappling with now.

"I won't give you anything," he said at length. "But if I shoot the lion then your cattle will be free from danger."

"There are other lions," the man said hopefully, though not with much enthusiasm. As he thought would happen the white man threw it away, waving his hand. "I am hunting this lion for another white man," said Huiter, his eyes scanning the African's proud, narrow face. "Perhaps he will give you something." He stood up. "It is enough," he said. "I will find the lion myself." "Bugger you," he added in English.

"I will help you," the man said. "I will show you the wounded cows so that you will believe in me. Then I will show you where the lion dragged the cow he killed. Will you believe in me then?"

"Then, yes," Huiter told him. "You bastard," he said in English. "Stinking one with the heart of stone," the man replied silently.

They toiled up the hill, clambering among the rocks from which the heat rose so that Huiter could feel it like hot air against his cheeks. The sun beat on him, baking his shirt, drenching his neck and loins with sweat. The white man and the black men could smell each other, hating what they smelled, each thinking the other worse because of skin or race or food or something which was inferior.

"——this bloody place," Huiter said aloud when they stood for a rest. The glare and the heat made a furnace of the earth. The bushes, the rocks and the trees stood as though knocked lifeless by the sun. One vulture wheeled high above them, waiting for a gleam of blood, for a death. "You too," said Huiter, looking up at the planing speck in the sky. "Everything." They climbed on. "If this bastard has told me a lie, then I'll smash his——skull," he brooded, savouring it. It helped. It kept him going. Yes, if he got to the top and found that this bloody nigger had told him a lie, a deliberate —— lie, then he'd—he'd break his —— neck with his bare hands. "Do you hear that?" he said to himself, staring at himself, staring at the blackish brown, sweating back of the man who was leading the way. A steinbuck, small and red, stood quivering before them on its tiny pointed hoofs. There was a dull twang and an arrow went through its neck. It fell over, like a toy.

"Good," said Huiter. "That was quick."

"It is my work," said the Ndarobo. They had both walked with arrows ready in their bowstrings.

"That is all they can do," said their guide disparagingly. "They have nothing. No cattle. Nothing." He had seen Huiter's eyes admiring the lithe brown men.

"They must eat. They are the same as you," panted Huiter as they climbed again. "They are outcasts," the man persisted. "*Wa'shenzi. Wa'junga.* Fools."

"All right," he said in English. "Then —— you." He was nearly blind with sweat and his eyes were smarting. He hated this African in front of him. It helped. He hated the proud ones. Like the bloody Zulus down in Suid Afrika, they had to be kept down or they would spit in your face. "—— everybody in the world," he thought. "Why should I be here climbing up this bloody hill for ten pounds a month while that —— *rooinek* and his English pals are sitting drinking cold tea up on the ridge?

"I wonder how that young Englishman would like this, dragging across the bloody bush, uphill and down for ten quid a month. But he's a pupil and one day he'll have his own place. He'll get rich like the rest of the English while we poor —— Boers drive the oxen and build the dams for him. For ten quid a —— month too." Christ, man, but it was hot. He tapped the shoulder of one of the Wa'-Ndarobo. He began to laugh, half malicious, half true amusement.

"Could you reach the house of the old Major? The Mad One whose land is near our camp. You know his cattle *boma* on the hill near my tent?" It took a long time. Yes, he knew the Mad One; but the house? Well, it was like this. Huiter explained through his teeth, controlling himself. Christ, man, but sometimes it was enough to drive you mad. Yes, slowly, the Ndarobo understood. White man wanted you to know a thing like the flash of lightning, to say "Yes, I know, I know," and men did this, even when they did not know, to please the speeding brain of the white man. This Ndarobo, though, was careful. He saw the white man's teeth and his sweating face and his staring, mad blue eyes, but he was dogged. Only when he had understood all did he say: "Yes, I will find that house to-night."

"Then call the young white man and tell him we are in the home of this lion we seek. Tell him to come as soon as it is dawn to-morrow. *Sa nashara keshu.* Understand? Bring him. Show him. Guide him. Now go. And make haste or I will see you get no salt, no blankets, nothing. Do you understand?"

When the Ndarobo had gone, Huiter laughed. He would find this lion all right, but he would see first that the young redneck did some walking with him, tasted this heat, really earned his sight of this lion, which he, Huiter, would kill. He rubbed his inflamed eyes and cursed aloud, and his guide watched him with that proud, nilotic sneer, which is not a sneer, but is the sign of contempt for all who are not of his group. It did not matter that they would die of syphilis and inanition, that they were slowly dying because the frame of their cruel, wonderful life was smashed. They were better than all other men. Huiter knew this in his shrewd, illiterate way and he glared at the guide and said: "What are you standing for? Tired? Are you a woman then, that you are tired?" He forged ahead, his energy bought from rage, and the heat rolled down like molten gold from the sun, all but crushing him. He could feel it on his neck like a pressure, a burning weight. His guide could not keep up with him and called out: "Do you know, then, where you are going?"

"Come on," Huiter scowled at him. "Come on. Get up here in front and let me see this place where the lion ate your meat." So the white man was angry.

"You are tired," the guide suggested in a lazy voice, his smile flashing in the glare. He walked past the standing white man.

"Not tired, you bastard," said Huiter in English, and then in a mixture of Ki'Swahili and Masai: "Only weary of the black man's tongue, his lying tongue." He squinted into the one good contemptuous eye of the guide. "Understand. You have lied to me. Now show me proof." This made the guide humble. "I shall show you the proof," he said, and went plunging on in long strides through the blazing heat while Huiter followed, his rifle across his shoulders and his hands resting on butt and muzzle.

"—— you," he thought again, his demented eyes on the dark-brown satin of the guide's naked back. He was nearly exhausted. His tongue was like a dry clapper in his mouth. He tried to spit. The flocculent thread of spittle defied him. Christ, what a life. He wanted to sit down, but he would not halt the guide. The guide would stand and look at him while he sat, he knew. They were in competition, silent now, Huiter breathing hard but quietening its anxious sound, forcing himself to inhale slowly through the nose.

"There isn't a single —— wog who can outwalk me," he thought through his bared teeth. "Not a single bare-arsed bastard that will see me beat. No, by God. Not one."

"Here's the place," said the guide. The relief showed in Huiter's eyes and the guide saw it and smiled.

"What makes you smile?" Huiter was pugnacious, menacing.

"I did not smile, Bwana," said the guide, his expression one of concern.

The smell was familiar. The smell of a recent death, musty, rotten, not as bad as the day after, but it hung in the bush and the hollows. There were the bones, still alive enough to shine in the sun, rags of meat on them, the ribs like a framework of a barrel, the head still covered with skin where the vultures and the hyenas had been careless or hurried. The skeleton was lying under some bush, and the ground about it was trodden and fouled by the scavengers.

"I have not lied to you." The guide sneered into a laugh. The remaining Ndarobo smiled too.

"He has spoken the truth, Bwana," he said, clicking his tongue.

"Ah —— you," said Huiter, turning away to inspect the ground.

A soft wind began to whistle in the empty bulbs of the thorn trees, a thin dreeing sound, eerie and melancholy. Huiter looked at the sun. It must be about four o'clock. Soon it would be cooler. He sat down. The pleasure was like something new, something he had never known, as are all the palliatives to exhaustion. He drank from his water-bottle. Then he told the Ndarobo to cast for sign of the lion. Bent and narrow-eyed, the black hunter went over the ground and then moved off along the side of the hill, his eyes on the ground, like a very old man. The guide sat some distance from Huiter and looked out across the vastness of the plain below them at the single hills which rose sharply in the flatness, at the thorn trees and the scattered boulders. He knew every yard of it. It was home, this scorched barren wilderness where no white man came to live.

"He wants a lion," Huiter thought. "Let him work for

one like me. Wants me to bring him when I have it ready. No, man. He can come down here and have a bloody good sweat like me and work for his lion." He grinned and rocked to and fro, his hands locked about his legs. Then he lay down in the shade of the bush above him and sang Suiker Bossi in a deep ruminative voice. Jervis would bring Brinden too. All the better. Let them have a taste of this bit of —— up-country down here.

Chapter XXIII

"BUT why d'you want to take Asmani?" the Major insisted. "You'll spoil that chap, you know. Why take *him*?"

"Well, I can trust him and he wants to go." Jervis could not explain exactly why he wanted Asmani. It was not enough to say he liked him.

"But d'you think he's any use if you meet a lion?"

"He can carry my ·256. I'm going to use the ·500. He's keen to come with me. We get on well together." Jervis almost lost patience and the old man heard that urgency in his voice and looked at him from his old but lively eyes.

"All right. Have it your own way," he said. "Once you get an idea you hang on like a bulldog." He puffed at his cigarette, watching Jervis running the cleaning rod through the two bright barrels of the ·500 express rifle. "D'you know that, son?"

"What, Major?" Jervis did not even look.

"You're a determined young bloke." Jervis laughed and glanced up at the old man. He said nothing, though, and Fawn-Cochley went on smoking his cigarette. They were at ease together completely now. "He's got over that woman," Fawn-Cochley liked to think. "He was a bit bowled over by her, but he's got over it now. I wonder if he'll find another on his next trip to Guyu. Must keep him busy. This woman thing is a real problem."

"I wish Brinden would turn up," said Jervis as he snapped the rifle shut and lifted its weight in his hands. How much more confident and easy he was in everything he said and did, the old man noticed. How he had grown, too. He had lost that "English" look of the newcomer. His eyes were wider, it seemed, the eyes of a man who was growing used to ranging them over long distances. "That Ndarobo should have got there by now, surely."

"Take your time, son," Fawn-Cochley told him. "You've plenty of time." It was long past dawn. "But I want to get off, now. That Dutchman'll shoot without waiting for us."

"Take it easy, son." He gave Jervis a cigarette. The chill of dawn had evaporated and the veranda was warming. Nyangi came with tea and boiled eggs.

"You've ruined this toto," said the old man, watching the small boy lay out the breakfast on two small tables. There was more warmth in Fawn-Cochley's voice now. There was less criticism. What he had just said was in a voice he might have used to a son he was attached to, it was almost whimsical.

"He's all right," said Jervis. "Lazy, though."

"Cut his pay," the Major urged. "Why don't you cut his pay?" They had argued about this. Jervis did not believe in cutting a man's pay. "You'll get over that," Fawn-Cochley would tell him. "It's a theory you'll get over."

"No. I'll sack him if he doesn't improve."

"You'll be sacking all your life." The Major spooned egg into his mouth, one clever eye watching the young man.

"No." Jervis was stubborn, though cheerful. "I'll find the best *watu* and keep them with me."

"Well, I won't argue with you," the old man mumbled through egg and buttered toast. "I'll admit they seem to like your methods, but I'm hanged if I know if I could be as patient. Still, you're experimenting. We'll see how it goes."

They heard Brinden's car in low gear ascending the hill to the house, and Jervis began to gobble his food, half rising from his chair. Oh, to be young again, just for this morning, the old man sighed with his mouth full. "Be careful now," he said for the fourth time since dawn. "Remember what I told you. If it's coming at you, take your time, slow, careful and put it right between the eyes, but *don't* get excited."

"All right, I'll remember." He did not want to think of a charging lion. It dried his mouth if he dwelled on that.

"I feel sure you'll get it this time."

"Why?" Jervis asked. "Why do you feel that, Major?"

"One Dutchman and two Wa'Ndarobo is a good combination. And I feel you'll get it this time." He had been worried since the Ndarobo had arrived, and Jervis had jumped to his feet, saying: "They've found it!" It would be Jervis's first lion and the old man wanted to be there, but he had not the will for the trudge through that scorching country down below. He was worried, but there was Brinden and the Dutchmen, yet it would be no ordinary lion if they came on the one they all wished to see dead.

Brinden was irritable, yet striving to be polite. He glowered while Jervis pottered about finding cartridges, water-bottle, odds and ends. Damn him. He tried to make conversation with Fawn-Cochley, who at length said:

"You're grumpy this morning, Brinden. What's up?"

"Nothing's up," Brinden snapped back. "Why should there be anything up, as you put it?"

"All right. Sorry." The old man ate some more toast,

watching Brinden tapping his foot on the veranda step and smoking his cigarette as if it would be his last.

"D'you know what the Italians have done to me?" Fawn-Cochley said in a new voice, a warm, angry voice. Brinden shook his head. "No," he said, "what have they done to you?" That bastard servant had *forced* him to get out of his warm bed. "It's the lion, Bwana!" The lion! To hell with the lion.

"You know I always got my sulphur by the sack from one of those Italian firms in Mombasa. I use a lot, you know. Well, I wrote for my usual order of eight sacks, and d'you know what they wrote back to me?"

"No."

"They said, very polite of course, that as Britain had seen fit to enforce sanctions against Italy over this Abyssinian war they could not see their way to fulfilling my order for sulphur. Now what d'you think about that, Brinden?"

"Quite right," said Brinden, wanting to hurt the old man, but half convinced he meant it. "Why should they give us sulphur when we try to spoil their war in Abyssinia? They've got as much right to a chunk of this god-forsaken country as we have."

"Easy on now, Brinden. You can't talk that way. My sheep are going to die unless I get sulphur. What the hell's a sheep got to do with the Abyssinian war? They've got the sulphur and I've got the money. So why write me a bloody stupid letter like that?"

"Ah, it's a bloody mess, that's all. Still, it'll be over soon. The Italians'll have Abyssinia and then we'll all have sulphur again. So why worry?"

The whole satanic mess of the world revolted him. The slogans, the everlasting promise of heaven on earth, the propaganda, the grey men up to their necks in politics and lies, all screaming in their bloody wastes of failure. What was the use of trying to explain it to the Prawn-Cocktail, who could not get his sulphur for his sheep?

"It's pretty serious," said the old man slowly, maddeningly, while he stirred his third cup of tea. Jervis came back, ready. Brinden's temper had eased a little. He felt sorry for the old man murmuring about his sulphur.

"Never mind, Major. It'll all come right some day. We won't give the Italians oil and they won't give us sulphur. Well, I say, bugger the lot of them, all the politicians and their clap-trap. They make me sick. Bye-bye!"

"Bye-bye," the Major said. "Keep your eye on my pupil if you strike that lion, eh?"

"Ah," Brinden snorted, "bye-bye." They got into the car. Asmani climbed in the back beside the Ndarobo. "Who's this bloke?" Brinden asked Jervis.

"He's one of my *watu*. He's a gun-bearer for to-day." Jervis could sense Brinden's mood. "Why?"

"Gun-bearer, eh? What d'you think we are—white hunters? Can't you carry your own gun?" He laughed to smooth the rudeness of his tone. "No, I prefer him," Jervis answered, irritated too.

"Ah, what the hell does it matter," Brinden cursed as he tried to put the gear in, grinding it. They sat beside each other, sulky, as they gathered speed.

The Ndarobo was still paralysed by the wonder of being in the car. His belly did not twitch now as when Brinden had jerked his thumb and said "Get in," but his nerves and his blood were a-tremble each time the white man changed gear. He showed none of this to Asmani, who was fondling the ·256 rifle on his knees.

"How does this thing go? What does it eat?" he asked Asmani, indicating the car.

"It goes. Is that not enough?" Asmani told him, gazing at him from supercilious eyes. There was no answer to that, and the Ndarobo sat crushed for the rest of the journey to Huiter's camp. Asmani, quarter-way on his perilous journey to knowledge, like all his brethren in ambition and hope, did not question the wonders of the West. They were there, like trees and grass and death. Just things. As yet there was no question. But one day he would have his load on his back. He might have to repair it. While he did not question, he was safe. But one day he would be invaded, with his white master become brother. Vaguely, but very vaguely, he sensed that and did not understand what he sensed. The Ndarobo's question had set him thinking. He would have enjoyed explaining how the car went. Perhaps he could find out. He fretted. The Ndarobo prayed to a god which a Galla camel-trader had told him about. A god called El Wak, but no response came from this god, so quietly he was sick on the floor of the car as it bumped over rocks and pig-holes. His face was grey, and Asmani chuckled with pride when he saw this savage roll his eyes and mutter something incomprehensible.

After two hours' walking across the shale, over rocks and flints, through the long yellow grass, Jervis was soaked in sweat. His rifle weighed him down and his eyes were dimmed with the sweat pouring from his forehead. Brinden plodded on in front, behind the light-footed, quiet Ndarobo. Asmani came last, carrying the other rifle. Overhead, the sun flared. Jervis could almost hear it roaring in its flame. The whole land about them was aching in the sun, subdued, dried out, blasted into a sort of dream. It was up to one of them to call for a rest, but neither spoke. They plodded on, their minds far away from here, taking thoughts as they raced in and thinking them, taking others which replaced them, in that monotony of the raised and falling feet, though their eyes were moving all the time, seeing, yet not conscious of seeing. Brinden had made up his mind that the young fellow should be the one to ask for a rest and eventually he was rewarded.

"What about a rest?"

"A rest?" Brinden stopped and appeared to consider it. "Yes. We can have ten minutes' rest if you like." Jervis sat down, irritable with his weakness. Brinden sat down beside him. They sighed as they put their rifles at their feet. The barrels were too hot to touch.

"Nice piece of country," Brinden offered.

"Lovely," said Jervis. "Like Devonshire in spring. Jesus!" He eased his helmet from his head and his sodden hair grew cool.

"I'll kill this bloody lion with my bare hands if I see it," Brinden threatened. His lips were dry and he licked them. "Yes, a lovely bit of country."

"I wonder if the Dutchman's shot it already."

"Don't be pessimistic. We've got miles to go yet from what this Ndarobo says. Bloody miles."

They did not reach the *manyatta* where the Dutchman had drunk his milk until well after mid-day. They were tired. Brinden was bad-tempered and Jervis was listless, leaving everything to the older man and the Ndarobo. He had never walked in such sun before. It had reached down inside him like a burning sword and had scarred him. His clothes were black with sweat and his tongue felt like a cinder. His head was aching from the prolonged, swaying glare of that distant horizon which had never drawn nearer. He longed to lie down. Brinden watched him as they stood near the *manyatta* while a small, naked boy carrying a bow and arrows approached them. He saw that Jervis was done and now he was willing to relax for a time. He recognised that uncaring stance, that careless, listless watching and the drawn expression of the face. He was done himself, but now he was generous.

"We'll sit here and eat something," he suggested. "You're tired, aren't you?"

"Tired? *Aren't you?*" Jervis's face was pale under its film of sweat.

"A bit."

"Well, I'm buggered and I admit it." It was the way he spoke that informed the older man he could be honest too.

"So am I. I don't mind telling you that it's a long time since I've done a walk like that." There was a bond there now. They lay down under a thorn tree and stretched. The small boy, his eyes huge from goitre, came and stared at them.

"Bring milk. Have you eggs?" Asmani bullied the boy, who nodded eagerly. "Bring. And bring fast," Asmani warned him. The boy ran, wanting to get back quickly to watch the white men, of whom he had heard much from the grown-ups but had never seen with his eyes.

"Do you know Helena has not been in to Guyu since she met you there?" Brinden said. Jervis had fallen into a reverie. He came out of it carefully.

"Oh," he said. "Hasn't she?" Was that carefree enough?

"No. And do you know why?"

"No." He could hear his heart move faster.

"Because people say she caused Browning's death." Jervis prevented his sigh of thankfulness. He exulted in the lying down, in Brinden's friendly voice, in freedom.

"It's bloody mean of them to say that. What else could she have done?"

"That's what I want to ask you. Could she have done anything? You were there. Well, tell me. Could she?"

"No, nothing." Jervis raised himself on one elbow. Brinden closed his eyes. "Look here, Brinden. It was over too fast. She couldn't do anything. I can swear to that."

"No need to swear. But you can always rely on people to make the worst out of somebody else's bad luck. We're all the same. We love to see each other in the dirt. We sympathise but we love it. We're like these wogs only hypocritical, smug."

Jervis was quiet. Brinden went on talking about how bloody mean everyone was, how they took pleasure in seeing people suffer, yet did all they could when called upon to alleviate it. That was his experience of life, he said. Jervis did not understand it. The world was a wonderful place and people were only people, but he had not found them as Brinden described them.

"They're swines. Just swines. All of them. All of us." Brinden enjoyed the words as he spoke them. "Give me a horse or a cow any time."

Jervis had fallen asleep when a young man of the tribe came and addressed Brinden. He carried a beautiful spear nearly ten feet long, its burnished blade nearly three feet of narrow razor. He told Brinden that they had seen the lion and twenty men of the tribe were surrounding it and soon would find it. He slapped the five fingers of his right hand four times against the palm of his hand. "It is this thin red man with the restless way who has done this," he went on. "If he had not come here we would have done nothing, for our head man lies under a tree all day drinking milk. Now we will kill the lion. You must come, you and this young one who sleeps in the shade."

"Is it very far?" Brinden asked him. The loads of copper wire and rings tinkled in the young man's ear when he shook his head.

"No," he lied, smiling. "It is only there. *Huku! Hukuuuu.*" He dragged the syllable, stretching out his chin and pointing with it, pointing to Africa, out there in that glowing yellow heat of scrub and thorns.

"How far?" Brinden watched his eyes suspiciously, searching for the flicker, but it did not come. If the man had carried a wet piece of sapling on his journey, changing it as each piece dried, he might have answered in his garbled effort to transfer that kind of time into this weird relationship of sun and wrist-watch which it was said white men used. But he had come straight to the *manyatta*, loping, his mind full of sun and fantasy, and so he lied, for the white man's eyes were dull with doubt.

"We will be there before sunset," he said, and sensitive he at once caught the shadow which crossed Brinden's face. "An hour before sunset," he added, smiling with innocence.

On and on Brinden pressed him with questions. Was he sure that they had truly seen the lion and were surrounding it? When? Could it not wait until morning? No. Everything was true. Brinden looked at his watch. It was nearly three o'clock. Christ, if it was only possible to find out one single thing exactly from these Stone Age men, just one, once only, so that a plan could be made. He did not want to sleep out, he had had enough of that in his time. So he went on with his questions, feeling his temper thinning, stretching, drying for the spark. It was unfair to try and pin one of these chaps down, one of the raw Wa'shenzi from the howling bush, but what was he to do? They did not understand one another yet, great ravines of measurement, time, myths, sentiments, separated them. They stared at each other across the wide gulf of a million dead cultures, the African young and anxious to please, the white man middle-aged and thoughtful. Finally, and as usual, Brinden agreed. "All right," he said, grim. "We'll come." He shook Jervis, who woke sodden with the sweat of sleep in a cruel climate. His mouth was coated with warm gum and his eyes were aching from the glare of the morning's march. He knew at once that the older man had made a plan and that this plan involved more marching in that smashing heat which rolled in slow convulsions out there, changing the bush into greenish greyish smoke.

"We're going on," said Brinden. "This chap says they've got the lion bushed. We'll have to go fast." He saw the other's glumness. "I don't know how far it is, but we'll get there an hour before sunset. We've got to. Feel like a lion?" His question was ironic. He got to his feet and slung his rifle, and Jervis had to do the same, dumb and apathetic.

They marched all afternoon, across plain, climbing to ridges and staggering down the other side, through acreages of shattered rock, a nightmare scenery closed for ever to the white man's world, inviolate, secure in its parched and cruel silence. They panted, listening to each other's breathing, Asmani at the rear, tireless, bright-eyed.

The sun had rolled, slow and merciless, to five o'clock by Brinden's watch. They were standing on a long narrow ridge, swaying in their pause, looking down on to yet another endless area of thorns, grey-yellow grass, rocks; dry, sad Africa, its horizons ever infinite, unreachable.

"Jesus," Brinden panted. "Miles and miles of —— Africa." He grinned with dry lips. He knew Jervis was nearly beaten, his young soft flesh all but cowed, but he knew it would pass, into the leather stage to come, so he was hard. "You'll have to step out faster, Jervis," he said. "You're tired, aren't you? I am too. But stick it out." Jervis said nothing, just looked at him from sweat-reddened eyes. He wanted to lie down, wanted to croak— "—— the lion. —— you too. What's the point anyway?" But he looked expressionless at Brinden, and Brinden smiled. "I know," he said. "You didn't know it was like this down here. Those are the highlands up there"—he jerked his head. "The White Highlands. This is different." Irony again. Ah, Jervis lifted one leaden leg and stepped forward, and once again the four men went forward, the Ndarobo taking up again that tireless, maddeningly mechanical and springy lope ahead of them.

"There they are," said Asmani. Jervis turned and saw Asmani's hard, dark eyes, wide open, unwrinkled, fixed on something far ahead and below them. He was pointing with his chin. Yes, men far off, like spots in the greyness. Only about two miles away. The lion must be there some-where, a pinhead in a prairie, and close up this lion would be a huge clawed threat, ready to kill. It seemed incredible. It seemed hardly worth the day's scorching ordeal.

"We'll get there when it's dark." Brinden was gloomy. "But let's hurry." Again the lifting of sore, leaden feet, the scuff of their boots on the shale and stones, and the never-changing pad-pad rhythm of the two Africans' feet.

"Soon," Jervis was telling himself, "you may be facing a lion. What will you do? How can you even lift this ton of rifle to your shoulder, let alone sight it and kill with it?" He had never known a day like this one before. He had been tired but not wrung almost to breaking point as to-day had done with him.

Brinden had learned what the body can do in excitement. He had gone into battle, broken under his mound of equip-ment, and been sucked up into danger, that danger which uses the body as though it were new. He was tired but he knew that the lion, if they found it, would call from him a new kind of energy once he was committed to his ancient role with the beast. In the retreat of 1918 he had stumbled asleep on his aching feet, turned and fired, not missing, and it was like remembering a dream, thinking of that time, the German tribes making their final effort to overrun the pastures of Europe.

"Here we are," Jervis heard Brinden's voice far off, neutral. He did not care where they were. He trudged on.

Then he saw Huiter waving to them. "There's Huiter," Brinden said. Jervis sighed and Brinden squeezed his arm. "You've done it," he said. "So have I. And may I never do it again, by Christ. We're really here."

Huiter was full of himself, and Brinden was soon very English with him, very curt, very short, subduing him, asking for facts.

"I've kept it all afternoon for you, man," Huiter told Jervis. "It's in there." He pointed his rifle barrel at some thick bush a few hundred yards away. "At least it went in there about two o'clock. It's late. What do you say we do, Mr. Brinden?"

"Say? Shoot it, I suppose. Unless it'll wait for morning."

The Dutchman took him seriously, saying: "No. It's got to be now, or start again to-morrow looking for it." Brinden's eyes scorned him and Jervis gave a dry, hollow chuckle. Brinden's curtness with Huiter had made Jervis ashamed and he said: "It's good of you to have kept it for us all afternoon."

The sun was near the horizon, still golden and wreathed with whitish flame, no hint yet of the slow, flowing crimson of another evening's death.

"How d'you feel, Jervis?"

"Feel? I feel all right."

"Well, come on," Brinden addressed both of them. "Let's kill this bloody nuisance while we've time."

"Right, man. We'll have to be quick." Huiter unconsciously became the expert, the master. "We'll drive it out, upwind. You and Mr. Brinden have first go at it if I can get it out. I'd say you stand over there and have a go at it as it crosses the open." For Jervis the bush containing the lion had become a screen hiding menace. In there was the lion, waiting, and the hairs on his neck prickled as he took two of the long, heavy cartridges from his pocket and let them slip into the opened breeches of the ·500 and slammed it shut.

"You back me up with that thing," Brinden told him. "But if it comes fast and you get your chance, just shoot and I'll be shooting too. You know the rule, don't you? First hit and it's your lion, wounded or dead. It's yours if you hit it first." Jervis was nodding his head, his eyes fixed on the bush, and he gripped the heavy rifle which so short a time ago had threatened to weigh him down on to his knees. Now he was quivering and tense, all exhaustion gone from him, making Brinden smile. "Let Asmani go with Huiter on the drive. He can carry the ·256 and join us if the lion breaks cover."

"I'd sooner have him here," Jervis replied.

"What does it matter? We've got the Ndarobo. But if you're particular about it——"

"No. It's all the same. Let him go with Huiter." He sent Asmani after Huiter and watched him run after the Dutchman. "Join us as soon as the lion comes out of the bush," he called after him, and Asmani assented: "Ndio, Bwana."

Chapter XXIV

THE lion knew it was trapped. The smell of men was everywhere. He lay still, his head on his paws, in the dark-green shadow of the thick undergrowth. He had fed well the night before and had been in a sated sleep under a hot crag when the voices of men had disturbed him. His first instinct was to slip away unobserved, but the pain of his wounded neck, deepened by his sudden movement from sleep, had caused him to growl, and he heard the voices of men rise as they yelled to each other. He then broke from cover, moving with his belly as close to the earth as possible, through the long grass, and as they saw him the men began to run and call to each other, their spears flashing in the sun. The lion was angry but he had not turned on his pursuers as he fled from cover to cover. He wanted to escape and sleep again in the delicious cool of shade, but the hunters pressed him all day until he went into deep cover in the thick bush running down from a high ridge. From here he did not move. He listened. Men were all about him, though some distance off. It was with difficulty that he moved his neck, and the smell of the wound drew tick birds who uttered their short, harsh screams as they fluttered about his head, hoping to enlarge the wound with their sharp beaks in search of maggots. But he snapped them away. This smell had offended a mate who roamed this barren country. She was not far off, the lion knew. If these men left him he would join her. Savagely, he tried to claw at his wound, but he desisted when the branches crackled.

He heard the sounds of the hunters, their voices still now, but a branch broke here, a small stone rolled there, and he half rose, the long blocks of muscle sliding under his firm yellow skin as he moved off without a sound. There was no smell or sound of men ahead, but behind him now the hunters were moving in a line. Keeping to the thick undergrowth, the lion continued his silent, fluid walk, and his big smouldering yellow eyes gazed ahead.

Asmani urinated on the soles of his feet and then tramped delicately and quietly in the flattened yellow grass. He lifted his right foot, exposing the sole, and there on its moist surface were some coarse yellow hairs. Huiter looked at them and then into Asmani's grinning face. They felt the grass. It was still warm. Huiter pressed over the safety catch of his Mauser ·256 and laid his right forefinger along the trigger-guard, ready to throw the rifle into his shoulder. He did not like this, this stalk through thick bush after a lion with a spear wound in its neck. On each side of them the line of spearmen moved forward, and Huiter and Asmani, crouching, moved too. Asmani held Jervis's ·256 in his left hand, in his right a spear given him by one of the tribesmen.

For ten minutes they pressed forward, following broken grass, a pad-mark, a sudden sharp ammoniac smell of cat in the unmoving heated air of the twining foliage and bush. The long, writhing tendrils of wait-a-bit thorn with its curving needle spines tore at their legs. They felt nothing of it. What was under their feet or behind them was forgotten. Only that which was before them engaged their eyes, their noses, their whole attention. The white man and the dark-brown man communicated by quick nervous signs or by their eyes. Huiter knew that not far ahead of them was the lion. He might creep on. He might suddenly turn and come through the grass in a rush. As they advanced, Huiter moved the butt of the rifle up to his shoulder, his left hand extending the rifle outwards from his body. If the lion charged his rifle would be in action in less than a second. Step by step they moved forward. Christ, man, but this lion was as smart as two men and a woman. Huiter saw some fresh green buffalo dung. Well, to hell with that for a joke. A buffalo in this kind of bush was more than he wanted to play with. The buffalo, in bush, was something more dangerous than a lion. He looked at Asmani, who bared his teeth in a big smile and whispered "*Jana*," as he pointed at the buffalo dung—"yesterday." Well, maybe, but he still did not like it. A wounded buffalo had once nearly killed Huiter in bush thinner than this, and it was the one creature he feared and respected to the point of extreme caution. They could hear tick birds shrieking ahead of them. Christ, man, not a rhino as well, for the tick birds usually sat on the rhino's back eating the big grape-like ticks, or digging a hole where a scratch had opened their host's hide. The first thing you knew about a rhino in this kind of bush was an explosion, a crashing, and a ton or so of enormous bulk charging, mad with fear and rage. By Christ, it was worth more than ten quid a month; to-day's *safari* was, all right. He shook the sweat from his nose.

"I'm glad I'm not in there," Brinden was saying in an undertone as they watched the bush into which Huiter and the Africans had disappeared.

"It's pretty dangerous, isn't it?"

"It certainly is. But Huiter knows what to do, but I'd sooner him than me."

They stood about five paces from each other, holding their rifles at the ready, safety catches off, ranging their eyes from cover to cover. Between the bush in which the lion was hidden and the next cover was about a hundred yards of broken plain, dead ground here and there laced with thorn at its edges. Jervis was making an effort not to tremble in his anticipation. "When it comes," he vowed to himself, "I'll sight perfectly, press, not pull, the trigger, and then I'll have it. If I don't take every care I'll miss it." He was haunted, too, by the fear that he would not see the lion, for Brinden had said: "You'll have to keep your eyes moving. A lion can fool you easily when he's got a bit of cover." But it could not break cover without crossing this open ground. The grass was high but not too high to blind the hunters.

"They're taking a long time," Jervis complained. He was feeling the strain.

"So would you if you were in there." The Ndarobo stood under a thorn tree some few paces away to their left. He was chewing a piece of favourite root but his hard bird eyes were moving from bush to grass and back again. He had smeared the barbed blade of his spear with the green-khaki poison paste and he was resting the spear lightly, but ready, on his right shoulder. The sun was near the horizon now, and the whitish dusty aura of fierce heat had faded from its edges, revealing a cooler blueness of sky. A faint breeze touched the faces of the two men. "How silent everything is," thought Jervis. There was a strangeness about sunset in Africa when the world was poised in a deadness, an absence of sound, an eerie stillness as the first red and bronze dust slowly enveloped the sun and filled the western sky. He was beginning to dream in that hush while the sun slowly fell to its struggle on the razor-sharp edge of the earth, when the Ndarobo pointed with his spear. The two rifles gleamed as they rose. Jervis saw a yellow shape move from the dark bush, heard yells as the Africans moved after it. Everything was speeding up, a cinematic series of brief pictures, the lion coming up out of a hollow, his sight wavering on to its shoulders—"Smash bones—never mind the fancy shots"— then the cracking explosion as he pressed one trigger, feeling the recoil of the heavy nitro-cellulose charge; the lion actually fell, rolled over, rose again, and his tail shot up— "A charge! Jesus! No"—it sped on. Brinden fired three times, the lion disappeared from view. "You hit it, Jervis," Brinden shouted. "It's lying down. Come on. But careful." Jervis loaded again, tried to button up his pocket, but was too excited, and he ran beside Brinden. Huiter came out of the bush with Asmani and the Africans moved in a cautious semi-circle across the plain about the dead ground into which the lion had vanished. "I hit it. I hit it." "Did I really hit it first?" he called to Brinden, who answered: "Yes. It's yours." "Then I'm an old-timer at last," Jervis exulted, all his nervousness gone.

"The light's bad. Aim low next time," Brinden called to him. "Go that end of the *donga* and back Huiter up. I'll cover this end. It's in there somewhere." The shallow *donga* was sprinkled with thin bush and rocks. As he moved nearer to Huiter, Jervis searched the *donga* with straining eyes, telling himself to be cool.

Huiter and Asmani walked into the *donga* while Jervis stood above them. He could see Brinden about fifty yards farther down, his rifle ready. The lion could not possibly escape. There was still plenty of light, softer and cooler light now, like the thin, cold, golden light of autumn in England, but the air and the earth still maintained their breathless oven heat.

There are moments of excitement when the expected is incredible in its arrival, when the mental picture of what will happen is altogether different from what takes place, as before the straining and then astonished eyes of Jervis. He was peering into the centre of the *donga*, his rifle held at the high port, its butt pressing into his right armpit. He saw only dead grass and jumbled rocks and thorns. The lion might appear anywhere in that long and tortuous depression. Huiter was calling to the spearmen to move in closer and disturb the bush, but they knew it was a wounded lion and they were not as interested in risking themselves in that trap of thorns and rock as Huiter had hoped. While he cursed them and waved his right arm, Jervis looked idly into the *donga* about twenty feet below him and in the grass saw the head of the lion, its eyes watching him. "God," he shouted, and backed away until the edge of the *donga* hid the lion. He almost ran away but checked himself and after backing and scrambling some yards began shouting to Huiter and pointing in the direction of the lion.

Huiter put a bullet into the grass towards which Jervis was waving his hand. It richocheted and went whining into the sky. He saw the lion's tail swish and then stand up. The lion gave one explosive growl, rose and charged.

Huiter had time only to work the bolt while he held the rifle to his shoulder, aim and fire once. The bullet struck the lion in its lower teeth, shattering them, but it did not stop the lion. It came on with all its speed. Jervis was as though nailed to the ground. There was no time to shoot. He saw Huiter's white face and glassy eye, Asmani crouching beside him and holding his spear in the position to stab. The lion was almost on them, Huiter's mouth was wide open, and then Asmani dropped his spear and leaped for the branches of a tree on his right. He was half-way in a sort of slow-motion movement when the lion, a few feet from Huiter now, turned slightly left and, reaching up with its great spiked pads, took Asmani from his leap and crushed him into the grass, growling, a convulsed mass of yellow power. Asmani was screaming. Huiter was cool. He took his time. He knelt down and aimed into the ear above the chewing, growling mouth which was biting Asmani's head off. When he fired the lion shuddered and dropped where he was standing, on top of Asmani's feebly moving body.

"Got him." Huiter spoke huskily. He was mortified by the failure of his first shot at the charging lion, not because it had contributed to the mauling of Asmani, but because it was something that had never happened to him before, and Jervis and Brinden had seen it. Jervis looked at the scene with a horrified, almost stupefied, expression on his face. He had caused Asmani's death and he hoped no one knew it.

"He's dead," Huiter told him after seeing Jervis's ashen face, and his unmoving, demented eyes watching what he could see of Asmani's bloodied body under that sprawled mass of the lion. After a pause, and just before Brinden arrived, he added: "It wasn't my doing. It was yours. You could have shot that lion but you backed away."

"I didn't," said Jervis hotly. "You missed yourself."

"You —— well did it. So there." Huiter was aggressive now, but there was satisfaction in his face as he spoke. It soothed him, it smoothed his hurt pride when Jervis said nothing more. "He's *your* nigger, and he's your stiff. You could have killed that bloody lion, man, but I saw you back away. Still, it's your first, isn't it? It's yours anyway. You hit it first, see?" He sniggered, and drew his long sharp knife. "Want his tailtip?" Jervis did not say anything. He was near weeping, with remorse and shame, and with the realisation that Asmani was dead and that he had killed him, lost him. But this Dutchman and he were alive.

Brinden came too late to hear any of this, but from his quiet and subdued manner Jervis could see that Brinden knew what had happened. They dragged Asmani out from under the dead lion. His head was a broken, bloody pulp of bone and tissue, the quickness that had been the reliable Asmani now invisible, gone in a few crunches of the big, sharp fangs. Brinden and Jervis carried the body away to some high rocks and placed it in among them, a feeble attempt to preserve it from hyenas, contrary to what Asmani would have wished, Jervis knew, but it did not matter now. The tribesmen sat in a group, watching, like big birds near a kill.

It was at this moment that the lioness appeared. No one saw her coming, not even Huiter, who was busily paring away the thick coarse-haired tip of the lion's tail to give to Jervis. The lioness came so fast that Huiter had only time to look up, frantic, scream, fall and then flail his arms under the weight of the beast. He tried to stab her with his knife, but she tore him apart and he was dead when Jervis's first heavy bullet smashed her jaw and Brinden raked her with solids one after the other. She took some time to die, thrashing about near the body she had avenged herself upon, her eyes full of hate, watching the men as she died, while they shot at her again and again. It was nearly dark. Jervis sat down, afraid he would faint. He covered his face with his hands and forgot where he was. The breeze whistled in the thorn trees and the sun was only a thin blade of gold in seas of red mist.

"Well, don't sit there moping," he heard Brinden saying in a matter-of-fact voice. "It's been a mess but we'd better clear some of it up." He had instructed the Africans to build fires. They were now piling heaps of thorns and dead wood about the area of the kill where Brinden had said they would stay that night. He took a flask of whisky from the pocket of his bush-shirt, drank from it and then nudged Jervis with it. "Here," he said, "this'll pull you together. Have some." His voice was sympathetic. "After all, it's as much his fault as mine," Jervis was telling himself, but he was not successful. If only Brinden would talk about it. It was like a conspiracy, this avoidance of the tragedy they had both shared in. He started to say how awful it was, but avoiding mention of his failure when he had seen the lion and retreated in fear. Perhaps Brinden did not know.

"Do you *want* to talk about it, Jervis?" Brinden interrupted coldly.

"Why not? It happened, didn't it?" said Jervis, in a weak voice.

"Oh, yes. It happened all right," Brinden said mockingly. "But the less said about to-day, the better. We shouldn't have been careless. That lioness was there all the time, and Huiter's dead."

"And Asmani too." Why would Brinden not discuss Asmani's death?

"There's not much to say about that either." Brinden lit a cigarette and squatted on his heels. "Listen, Jervis, they

were both killed in separate charges. Both lions are yours.
You hit each one first, so they're yours. That's the story.
The less said the better. Don't go round saying how dreadful it all was." So he knew everything. He must have seen
him back away from the lion. Oh, God, how frightful to
have done it after all the effort, all the fantasy he had
indulged in.

"Did you see what happened when the first lion was in
the——" but Brinden waved his hand angrily and said:
"Shut up, Jervis, for Christ's sake. Forget about it. We all did
badly to-day. We had no right to lose Huiter. Asmani asked
for it. He lost his nerve and ran and he was taken. That's
all." Ruminatively, as though only now remembering
something he should never have forgotten, he went on:
"The lioness always sticks by her mate, or nearly always.
The lion, being just a bloody male, runs off if you shoot his
mate, but not the lioness. She'll come for you every time.
But I never thought of this one having a female. I always
thought of him as a lone one. But I was wrong."

"So was I," said Jervis, wanting some of the guilt too.
Brinden spat into the grass and said: "I was never much
of a hunting man. I've shot the usual quota, but I'm not
proud of to-day's effort. Just keep our mouths shut about
the dirty bits. After all, it's the luck of the game, so why
whet people's appetites? They'll make enough out of it as
it is. So just don't go about giving descriptions of how exactly it all happened." Jervis could see Huiter's face and
hear that snigger. He tried to think of Asmani as he had
thought of Browning, but Asmani had meant more than
Browning. He had been a kind of raw gold among all the
poor ore. Huiter, he noticed, meant nothing. He was just
a good shot who had missed his most important aim and
was torn to pieces for it. It was cold-blooded, feeling that,
but it was true. Huiter died at his only real pleasure.

Asmani had had no faith in his spear, and had run. He had believed in the rifle which he was not allowed to learn. So he was dead. Something like that.

"No, it's no use thinking about it," he said, feeling calmer, but there was something between them both now. Their relationship had been changed. He could see Brinden thinking about it in the light of the fires. There was a palpitating yellow light over everything as the dry wood blazed and the thorns split and crackled. When Brinden shouted to nobody in particular among the Africans that the Wa'-Ndarobo must skin the lions at once, a man called back that they had run away.

"Run away," said Brinden bitterly. "Don't want any trouble. They think it's all their fault. Poor bastards. Well, never mind. It doesn't matter now."

They drank some more whisky and then Brinden said: "I forgot. There's a policeman in Guyu. We'll have to show him the bodies, I suppose. Or we'll only have to come down here again and show him them here. So we'll have them carried back in the morning."

After a couple of hours a boy brought them milk and a few cobs of roasted maize. When they had eaten they fell asleep beside their rifles, to the grunting of hyenas which prowled beyond the fires. Jervis dreamed the day over again and awoke in the starlight, bathed in a sweat of terror. He sat and smoked until dawn and then he shook Brinden.

They quarrelled and argued with the Africans for nearly two hours but they would not agree to carry the bodies. Finally, Brinden clashed the bolt of his rifle and pointed the muzzle at them and started to snarl orders and threats. This upset Jervis, for these adventurous goings on were not as he had imagined them to be. They were ugly, frightening. The thrill of them was born in memory later. The Africans reacted at once, became active, ran about for boughs with which they made stretchers and were like men relieved of a burden. No superstition, no taboo, was as powerful as the muzzle of the rifle and Brinden's threats. For some reason he was unable to grasp, Jervis felt disappointed. He had begun to pride himself on his reasoning powers with Africans.

The lion skins meant nothing to him. He had shot two lions and he did not care. The skins were like maps of a horrible territory. He saw the rotten wound in the lion's neck where the herdsman's spear had pierced it months ago. He was nauseated by the shattering power of the bullets he had fired. There had been no sport in it. It was a job, part of farming in Africa, and he had botched it and he could not forget it. He could not look at the remains of Huiter after the first glance at it in the morning light. It was all part of some dream.

It was long after mid-day when they had climbed the last mile of the ridge to the dead Dutchman's camp. They put the bodies in the car, laying them on a bed of leaves. They stank already, and to Jervis the horror of this was overpowering, but Brinden could see that he was becoming callous. The tribesmen began to shout for pay, and because they shouted Brinden went into a quiet fury and climbed from the car. He struck one of them on the jaw, felling him among the low thorn scrub. The others were silent after that, looking on with dazed black eyes. Then they looked at Brinden and were sheepish. They had never seen a man struck by a fist before. They saw blood on the white man's knuckles.

"Why not give them something?" Jervis urged him, and Brinden, watching the tribesmen, answered from the side of his mouth: "Keep quiet, for God's sake. D'you have to plead for them in front of them?" He addressed the stunned tribesmen, who seemed to have forgotten the spears in their hands. "Clear off," he said. "We've killed two lions for you and lost two men. You can send your headman to my house and I'll give him something. Now clear off. Quick." They drifted away, muttering and whispering, leaving their fallen member in the thorns. He might be dead. In any case he was not walking about. If he were not dead, then he would arise. But what could men do for him?

"You were rather hard on them, I think," said Jervis uncertainly, trying to hold Brinden's eye. But the older man lost his temper again and shouted: "For Christ's sake, son, stop moaning about the bloody *watu*, will you? You moan about them like a missionary. Now, stop it, will you?" He looked as if he had a lot more to say, and Jervis lost control too.

"They've come a bloody long way against their will. Why couldn't we give them a few bob for doing it? There's nothing terrible in that, is there?"

"Well, go and bloody well give them some. Go on. Why don't you go after them and tell them you're sorry I've been nasty to them? Go on."

They glared at each other and then Brinden began to laugh. "You're a funny kid," he said. "Bloody funny. You'll have to harden your heart a bit if you're going to live in this country. Don't you see, Jervis, that those blokes didn't give one damn that two men had been killed, despite the fact that we shot two lions for them?" He knew more about Africans than that, but he was not prepared to forgive them just now for being what they were, men in a different world, caught in a tragedy darker than his own. No. They were as hard as bloody stone and all they wanted was money. He laughed again, trying to soothe Jervis, trying to be friends, but he saw that the younger man thought him cruel. "All right. Sulk then," he said. He pressed the self-starter and edged the car over the rocks.

At Fawn-Cochley's house they found the two Wa'Nda-robo sitting near the veranda. They were not able to explain why they were there. They had come to tell the Bwana M'zee, the old one, what had happened. That was all they would say. Perhaps they were afraid that in some way they were to blame and that the old one should hear their story and believe them. They were trembling with fear as they answered Brinden's questions. Brinden and Jervis glanced at each other, and Brinden pursed his lips. "They've told the Prawn-Cocktail what happened," he said. "It was all my fault," Jervis said, hopeless, but Brinden said: "Shut up, will you, for Christ's sake. I won't ask you again. . . ." It's the country that makes us like this, went on and on like a gramophone record in Jervis's brain, the country. It's an hysterical country, unreal, a lie.

Fawn-Cochley was stern and taciturn when he came into the living-room. Then: "A nice mess you made of it," he said to Jervis, cutting like a whip. "A bloody nice settler you're going to be, aren't you?" Then he turned on Brinden. "And as for you," he rasped, "anyone'd think you came out yesterday. Is that the best you could do? To-day's mess?"

"What's this all about, Fawn-Cochley?" said Brinden icily, at the same time lighting a cigarette. "Who do you think you're talking to? Your bloody *watu*?"

"No. But I got the news, though," the old man's voice began to rise. "The Wa'Ndarobo came here and I got what happened out of them. They said *you*—" he stabbed a finger at Jervis. "They said *you* had the lion under your feet and you backed out."

"That's a bloody lie," Brinden shouted. "Since when are the Wa'Ndarobo able to tell *you* what happened? Are you going to believe *them* or *me*? Just let me know that, will you?" He was convincing. His sincerity and his righteous

anger impressed the old man, who adopted a humbler tone.
"Well," he said hesitantly, "why should they lie to me?
They only told me what happened and answered my ques-
tions. But what *did* happen?" He looked from Brinden to
Jervis.

"That's better," Brinden said with a touch of his usual
irony. "Much better. Thanks. Well, two lions charged and
two men were killed. The two lions were shot. It's happened
before, this kind of thing, and it'll happen again. Jervis hit
both of them first. The Wa'Ndarobo are a couple of ——
liars, and that's all about it. Do you want to confirm any
of that? Shall I bring the Wa'Ndarobo in?" He was
grimacing with his bitter rhetoric and Fawn-Cochley
looked at Jervis with a milder eye. "So you hit them both
first, did you?" he asked. "They didn't tell me that. Look
here, I'm sorry. I'm really sorry. I'm afraid I get worked
up rather easily. You must have had a bloody thin time of
it. I'm sorry." Dramatically, he offered each his hand and
they shook it, Jervis sombre, unable to meet the old man's
eyes, but he mistook this for something else and slapped the
young man's shoulder. He drew on his charity. "Look here,
Jervis," he said, "I'm sorry. Let's forget it. I know you
can't rely on the *watu's* version of anything. I should have
remembered that. But it sounded convincing enough then
when I'd had no news of you." Jervis's face turned red.
He excused himself and went to his room, promising
Fawn-Cochley that he would be back quickly. He did not
know how to behave himself in front of the old man,
now that Brinden and he had joined in their common
lie.

Brinden was in a huff with Fawn-Cochley until the old
man was depressed and contrite. The performance quite
shamed Jervis but he said nothing. They had a meal together while Wangi put petrol and water into the car.

Brinden had sketched a satisfactory story of how Huiter and Asmani had died.

"It'll be pure routine with the police," said Fawn-Cochley. "You won't get there until near midnight."

"Doesn't matter," Brinden replied. He tore a piece of chicken from the bone with his small teeth. "They're pretty high now and the sooner we get there the better."

When they were getting into the car the old man touched Jervis's arm and in a low voice, said: "Cheer up, Jervis. It's all in the day, you know. I'm sorry for what I said." That made it worse. Jervis said: "It's quite all right, really," and then sat hunched in his seat beside Brinden, pining to be out of the old man's sight.

Some miles out on the dark plain he said to Brinden: "God, I feel mean. And I don't think the old boy is quite convinced anyway. I feel horrible."

"Then don't," said Brinden cheerfully. "Don't. You know all about Africa now. Darkest Africa. You know about lions too. We all do a few dirty things in our time and this is one of them, but it's the only way. You're too sensitive, son. You'll have to harden up or go and take holy orders or something." They drove on for a while, Jervis thinking: "He's a decent chap, I must say." "Listen," said Brinden, "you funked that lion to-day. I don't blame you. I'd have funked it myself, I'm certain. I nearly jumped out of my skin when I saw how close to it you'd been. If you were a more experienced shot you'd have need to feel bad. But not this time. And it wasn't your fault that Asmani bloke was killed. The great shot himself, Huiter, missed it, and as you've seen, you don't often miss twice with a lion. So there you are."

It was better when put like that. "Let's keep it to ourselves," Brinden continued. He turned and smiled. "Light me a fag, will you?" They smoked. Jervis brightened. No,

it was not all that bad. Poor Asmani. He could not forget
that—yet. Brinden told him he would. "There are more
good *watu* beside him," he said. "And he asked for it. He
was no warrior, was he? There he was with his spear and
he let Huiter down. We all let each other down. There.
Now, for Christ's sake, let's forget it."

Chapter XXV

THE policeman was young but he had a lot of experience.
He was a tall, dark, sombre man who sucked a cold
pipe and listened to them. He was wearing a green silk
dressing-gown, and he came out to look at the remains of
the white man and the black man lying in the flood of the
car's headlights where his askaris had laid them.

"Hard lines, that," he said. "But you got the lions?"
He nodded, chewing his pipe. "Come in and I'll book it."
He wrote it all down carefully. He knew more about
criminals than about wild beasts. He got out on to the
plains once in a while to shoot a buck or two, and one day
he might try for something bigger, but he was in no hurry.
Not now, after inspecting the two bodies. He had something
else on his mind just now. The *Watu wa Mungu*, the Men of
God, a sect of religious fanatics who lived in the forest between Guyu and the Chombo Hills. They lived in a mania
of the Old Testament and the bloodiest of their tribal
rituals. They called themselves by biblical names and they
came out of hiding only to kill for the Lord. The District
Commissioner wondered if it would not be a job for troops
in the end.

Discreetly, the policeman told them something of the
Men of God. Had they come across it out their way? No?

Well, it was the first time anything of the kind had cropped up in this part of the world.

"It's all this mission stuff,"said Brinden. "How the hell can they understand all that murder in the Bible and at the same time stay quiet? It's all this forcing of religion on them."

The policeman was non-committal. But he showed them a long thin sword with a crude cross marked on its hilt. They had found this during a chase after the *Wayu wa Mungu* in the forest. "I shaved with it yesterday morning," he told them brightly. "I bet my sergeant I could and it was a nice smooth shave. Fancy getting sliced with that thing."

"It's this religion. They're not ready for it. We're not ready for it ourselves yet. What do *you* say?" Brinden wanted the policeman to show where he stood as an official, but the policeman gave him a thin smile and said : "I never think about religion at all." He had spent some years among the settlers. He knew their life.

"H'mm." Brinden got up. "Do you want us any more?"

"No, thanks. That's all, I think. I'll put the bodies in the mortuary and they'll be buried this afternoon. You'll come, I suppose."

"All right." They would have to come, Brinden supposed. It was only right that they should. But neither of them wished to come and the policeman knew this. He knew, too, that only by coming when they did not wish to did people hold the frail fabric of society together. At least that was what his experience of police work had taught him. When they had gone, he sat at his desk and began to translate the report of a speech by one of the *Watu wa Mungu*. One of his agents had brought it in. A goat's eye nailed to a tree, spilt goat's blood and signs of hasty departure, the agent said.

"We have no clan. No root. We are lost," it said. "We cannot reach the Christian God and we have lost our tribes. We must kill. We must wash in the blood of sacrifice. We must purify——" The policeman sighed. "Oh, God," he said aloud. "Politics have begun at last. Poor bloody Africa. In the muck along with the rest of us." He bent to his work again, seeing into the dark, bloody, twisted future of change via politics and hate.

"Well, that's that," Brinden said as they drove to the club for breakfast. "Everyone will want to know about the lions. Lay it on and forget the sad bits."

Chapter XXVI

"DRINKS all round," Colonel Slipwood snapped at the Goanese barman, and then turned again to Jervis and Brinden. He was one of those young-old men wearing khaki shorts and a blue shirt with a red silk scarf tucked in at the neck. He had a long, lined, red face and his iron-grey hair was close cropped almost to his scalp.

"I must say again, youngsters, it was a bloody good effort. Two lions like that." He snapped his fingers twice. Brinden went on praising Jervis. He had been drinking since sundown, and now it was past ten. He had praised Jervis all evening and as he grew drunk he repeated himself so often that the praise became a refrain, no longer possessing meaning, only slurred words. "Yes," he would say, "dropped them both with his first shots. Better shot than that poor bloody Dutchman. Dropped them both with his first shot."

Colonel Slipwood, a keen and lively-eyed man of an almost clinical cleanliness, gave Brinden a curious look and then poured soda into their whiskies. He smiled at Jervis and winked. "To your lions," he said. "Thanks," Jervis responded lamely. Then he said what was on his mind. "It seems wrong, somehow, to have a good time when two people were killed by those lions, doesn't it?"

Colonel Slipwood fixed wide blue eyes on his suspiciously. "Not at all," he said. "It might have been you and Brinden, eh?" He looked at Brinden. "He always talks like that," said Brinden. "Always looking at the skull behind things."

"Curious thing to say," said the Colonel, sniffing. "But he's a curious chap, you know, Jervis. Brinden's a curious chap, we all say here."

Brinden added more whisky to his drink and then drained the glass.

"More," he told the Goanese. "All round."

Soon Brinden was drunk. Colonel Slipwood had joined his party where Lord Prockling, an aged man with a weak, hoarse voice, was telling for the thousandth time of what the country was like when he had arrived in it just after Stanley had left. Some young men in the party were looking at each other, and one said "Jesus!" but the old lord did not hear. He was quite deaf.

"Look at that old man. He must be very old to look like that," Jervis said to Brinden, who, without turning to look at the withered lord, said: "That's the past. Like the Prawn-Cocktail. They're lost here now. They want everything as it was. Impossible." He belched and said: "Christ, this whisky's got cordite in it." He began to laugh. He rolled his reddened eyes and Jervis asked: "What's amusing you?"

"To-day," Brinden said. "To-day. Here you are moping about Huiter and your Asmani, and everybody's congratulating you. But you don't want it, do you?"

"Would you want it?" Jervis's eyes were cold, and Brinden saw them and frowned. He did not reply at once. "More," he said to the barman. "Would you?" It was important for Jervis to know now. Brinden's calculated pouring of the soda, his silence, was loaded with something.

"No, I wouldn't," said Brinden. "We made a bit of a mess yesterday. But plenty of people get killed by lions out here. The great thing is to have shot them and to get back to the bar and have a drink about it. See? Now take the gallant Colonel there. Know what he did in a pinch? He once found himself facing a charging lion, and both barrels were empty. So he flung his gun-bearer. A good pension—only mauled a bit. And here the Colonel is, as large as life. That's presence of mind. He's the kindest of men too, but everyone does a few dirty things in a pinch. I know of a case where a Kikuyu cook poisoned a whole family he had been working for for twenty years. He was bored with them and wanted a bit of leave and they refused it. So they all had to die." He burst out laughing, excusing himself. "You mustn't mind me," he said. "I have a curious sense of humour, I'm afraid. The country's still in a raw state, you see. Queer things happen. You mustn't take that little bit of hesitation on your part yesterday too seriously. I know a chap who actually ran away. He saw the bloody lion come at him and he just ran for it. It ate him—or most of him, anyway. The gun-bearer shot it. So don't mope about yesterday. Drink up." They drank their whisky. Brinden stared at the Goanese barman, his eyes dreamy. He hummed to himself.

"That was when you had to be a man," the old lord was wheezing. "You had to be a man, then." Jervis watched his listeners nod.

"Listen, Jervis," Brinden said in a low voice, "I like you. D'you know why?" Jervis shook his head. The whisky was sour in his throat. He suddenly felt alone in this club set in the wilderness, listening to the voices about him, talking about elephants, rinderpest, the Indian problem, the Abyssinian war.

"Because you're cautious," said Brinden, grinning affectionately. He slapped Jervis on the shoulder. "I know you could have gone a long way with Helena, and you didn't." Jervis felt stunned. They looked at each other and Brinden grinned again.

"What d'you mean?" Jervis said in a whisper.

"You needn't start that stuff." Brinden waved his hand. He smiled again. "I know all about it. I know Helena too. It was sensible of you to draw back when you saw what was coming. I wanted to tell you that."

"Thanks," said Jervis. His face was pale. How cold-blooded Brinden was. No rage, no shouting, only this quiet, drink-thickened voice, a little sad in tone, commending him.

"Thank *you*," Brinden corrected him, sardonic again now. "I wished for a while you would take her away from me, but I'm glad now you didn't." He hooked a finger at the barman: "More. Do you want to tell me anything about it?" he continued to Jervis.

"There's nothing to tell."

"Good, so cheer up now." He raised his glass, waiting until Jervis touched his own glass against it. "To Helena," he said. "A bitch if ever there was one, but a good sport too." He laughed with the rim of the glass in his mouth, some secret joke.

"I'm going to get stinko to-night," he said. He banged his glass down on the counter. "What about you?" Jervis thought about it and then said: "I don't care one way or the other." This loneliness. This older, hardened man with the wound scar on his forehead and the bitter, agile mind behind it. It was a special kind of day for Jervis, like maturity at last, tasting lonely too, and incomprehensible in the next double whisky, which seemed to cheer him. He talked animatedly, warming to Brinden. "That's better. That's better," said Brinden. "You've lost that corpse look at last."

They joined a party of men and women who were shouting and laughing at a table on the dimly-lit veranda. In the outer ring of shadow while he sought a chair, the giant widow, Doreen Withers-Hamden, seized him and kissed him. He tasted the thick lipstick like warm grease in his mouth. He gripped her hard and kissed back, his hands on her thick warm back, his chest pressed against the great breasts. She sighed. "Kiss and forget," she said. "You were so nasty to me that night with Helena. Remember?" He could smell the sweet gin on her breath. "I was tight," he said. People took no notice of them. They were roaring with laughter while a man told them a joke.

"Well, I'm tight now," she said, "and I forgive you." She was beautiful now, white even teeth, thick creamy neck, like a meal. "I'm drunk as a coot," Jervis thought. "Sit here by me," she said.

"The really lovely thing that happened to old Chellingly is this," the raconteur continued while Brinden poured more drinks. "He slaved his guts out on his cattle for years and he had an absolute mania about cattle diseases, ticks, and God knows what. He was always sending blood slides from his cattle in to the vet, week after week, and the vet would examine these bloody slides and always he sent back the same little slip of paper, *you* know, 'No parasites present' and old Chellingly just could not bear it any longer. He was sure that the vet was not examining the slides but was just writing 'No parasites present' and leaving it there. So he thought he'd catch the vet out one day. He pricked his finger and made a smear of his own blood on the slide and sent that in to the vet. He thought the usual 'No parasites present' would come back, and *then* he was going to raise hell and show the vet up to the powers that be in the Veterinary department. But, by God, the vet was one up in the end, because old Chellingly got a report back which said: 'This blood smear, that of a baboon in the last stages of senile decay, shows no parasites present,' and old Chellingly nearly went out of his mind with rage." While the crowd laughed with alcoholic delight at this last story, Mrs. Withers-Hamden put her hand on Jervis's leg and stroked it. He could hear her deep breathing while she appeared to be absorbed in the speaker's next story. Jervis watched the bronzed and red-skinned men relaxed after another equatorial day at six thousand feet above sea-level, and the women, many attractive, sitting among them. He felt himself one of these people now. His loneliness had gone. He locked his fingers on Mrs. Withers-Hamden's hand, restraining its ardour.

He woke up beside her huge, warm, naked body before dawn came in through the black windows of her bedroom. She stirred in her sleep, murmuring. He dressed without a sound, then drained the decanter of water, his head heavy with pain. He went out cautiously into the chilly darkness and walked to his hut at the end of the club's residential area. It had been warm and comfortable in her bed. Despite his headache he began to laugh to himself, coming warm from the arms of the giant widow. There was nothing left now in the world to discover, it seemed.

He found Brinden fully dressed reading a book by his bedside light. Brinden laughed. "A big night, I should say," he said. He went on chuckling. "Have a last drink. You look like something the cat brought in." He poured out a whisky for Jervis. "To the biggest little widow in darkest Africa," he said, laughing again. They drank.

Chapter XXVII

ABDUL HAFIZ was reading *Mein Kampf* when Jervis arrived at the store. He put the book down and said: "Good morning, sir." His smile was bright, glad. Jervis gave him his hand and he gripped and shook it, the first Englishman's hand he had ever shaken.

"You look pulled down, sir. Pale. Are you ill?" He was willing to do anything for this friend. It was a strange thing.

"Too much whisky, I'm afraid," said Jervis. "Give me a cold beer. A really cold beer. Listen, what do I call you?"

"You can call me Abdul if you like, sir."

"Right. Abdul it is. God, I feel terrible." "He hasn't changed, even yet," Abdul thought. "I wonder when he will." He poured the beer into a long glass. "Here you are, sir." Jervis drank. God, it was wonderful, so cold, so soothing. They talked idly of his life at Sabuga with the Major. "You look like an old hand now, as they say, sir." Abdul risked it, this intimacy. How terrible was the world they lived in, each race cut off by so much, each race preferring its isolation save for the few who needed the company and goodwill of all but could not have it. Shut in by their caste, their race, their skin. Abdul felt the rare longing again for friends outside his small, patient, Indian existence in the vastness of this African continent. Englishmen could be good-natured, but they always had a shield in their hands, ready. Not this one, though, but for how long before he found his shield? Only God could say. He knew that Jervis was going to inherit Major Fawn-Cochley's farm. All the Indians in Guyu knew. Tulsi Ram, the fat Hindu clerk in the bank, who kept the Indian traders informed as to the state of each Englishman's income, had had the news direct from his friend, Babuji, the clerk in the office of the lawyer to whom Major Fawn-Cochley had written for advice. Abdul said nothing of his gladness for Jervis's good luck, but he looked at the young man who he hoped would now be his customer and his friend for life.

"What are you reading, Abdul?" The Indian gave him the book. "Hitler, eh? Do you like Hitler?"

"He is a strong man, sir."

"And do you like strong men?" He riffled the pages— "The Jews—the negroes—the Slavs." The mass of raving words. It was so far away. The little disappointed man in the shabby raincoat was so far from this store, this wilderness of snared, bewildered savagery, but his book was here, his hate, his longing to annihilate.

"He will make war, sir. Don't you think so?"

"Don't know yet," said Jervis, morose over the book. "But I expect he will. He hasn't much time for you, you know, the Indians. Do you know that Abdul?" He looked up into the Indian's dark eyes and smiled, playful.

"Would you like some more beer, sir?" He did not like to face what Jervis had said. He wanted India to be free. In some way, a few Indians had told them, Hitler might help India to be free one day, but it was not possible to see how. He did not see Hitler as Jervis saw him, but he admired the power, the curtness, the sharp, cutting edge of some of Hitler's words. It was probably because Hitler made the British power uncomfortable that he admired him. Yes, he thought it must be that. It was regrettable, but he could not help liking it. On the other hand, he knew Hitler wanted a Germany of supermen. His admiration for Hitler was mixed with a nostalgic appreciation of Kemal Ataturk, who had modernised Turkey and was revitalising Islam in a new way. So how explain what he felt to this Englishman? He poured out more beer, wondering if he had disappointed Jervis by reading *Mein Kampf*. Jervis threw the book on the counter. "Hitler's insane," he said. "Don't be taken in by all these words, Abdul. He's a liar and a madman." Abdul nodded, making it solemn. The whites fought on for possession of the earth, for the right to teach it and farm it. The rest stirred about uneasily in the rubble of their dead culture. *Kya Kurenge?* There was nothing that could be done about it. He told Jervis that he had some new stock in, liquor of all kinds, tinned goods, cloth, watches, yeast, medicines, even snake serum which lasted for eighteen months and was good against the bite of puff adder or cobra. They walked round the shelves, Jervis envying Abdul his quiet life amongst these varied things from all parts of the earth. There were black cigarettes from French North Africa in dark-blue packets. He bought some. He bought sweets, whisky, a packet of darning needles. When he was going, Abdul reached under the counter and produced a bottle of champagne. He handed it to Jervis.

"Good lord, champagne! What next? You haven't got any caviar here too, have you? Your store's a regular Selfridges."

"That's for you, sir. To celebrate the lions." Abdul beamed now his gift was given, its surprise value appreciated.

"So you heard about the lions. How?" No Englishman would bother to tell an Indian storekeeper that another Englishman had shot a couple of lions.

"What you call the bush telegraph, sir. The news travels quickly here. A Somali horse-trader told me yesterday that you had shot lions."

"But I don't know any Somali horse-traders." Abdul rubbed his hands together, pleased with his effect. What a lot an Englishman had to learn when he was in Africa.

"Everything that happens travels from African to African, sir," he explained. "They know everything that goes on. Do you know your nickname, your African nickname?"

"No," said Jervis. His eyes showed that his curiosity was aroused, his vanity full of hope. "My nickname. Why? Have I got one? Do you know it?"

"Yes, sir."

"Well, bugger me," said Jervis. "How d'you find that out?"

"The Somali horse-trader described you as the Englishman who had shot the lions and said that Mr. Brinden was with you. He used your nickname."

"What is it?" asked Jervis, half-heartedly, hoping it would be "Lion Heart," or "The Strong One," or "The All Knowing."

"It is 'The Bird Face,' sir." Abdul did not know what dagger of disappointment he had plunged into Jervis's hopes.

"The Bird Face?" he repeated after Abdul, lines appearing in his forehead. He was upset, Abdul saw now. "Why 'The Bird Face'?"

"They say you have a face like a bird, sir."

"But do *you* think I have a face like a bird, Abdul?" "He is hurt," thought Abdul. "I have hurt him. He is vain and I have hurt him. Alas!"

"No, sir," he said, reaching out to the young man's wounded vanity, balm in his eyes. "But Africans see you like that." Jervis was feeling his nose. Yes, it *was* rather long and a bit hooked. Could it be his eyes? Could it possibly be that they were so sharp and keen that the Africans likened him to an eagle? Could it not be that? No, Abdul said gently that it was probably because Jervis's face was calm and grave, a bit like that bird that hooted all night.

"An owl?"

"That's it, sir."

It was a great blow to him. "The Bird Face."

"What do they call Mr. Brinden?" Jervis asked. He was somewhat consoled when Abdul said they called Brinden "The Scarred One," because of the wound scar on his forehead. No prowess there.

"And what do they call Major Fawn-Cochley?" Abdul was very hesitant. He allowed himself to be pressed, to be cajoled, before he would say. "They call him 'The Madman,' sir, but you won't tell the Major Sahib, will you, sir?"

"No," said Jervis, "I won't say anything." Bird Face. Yes, it was a heavy blow and not to be shared with anyone. He remembered the champagne and he thanked Abdul for it, telling him he would drink it with the Major and would toast Abdul, who was very gratified to hear it. They shook hands. "You know, you're the first Indian I've ever known, Abdul. Do you know that? Are they all like you?" Abdul did not know how to reply. No, they were not all like him, he knew. He had crept a little way out of his shell to meet this Englishman who had not yet learned to hate Indians, because many of them kept three sets of account books and slaved slowly and patiently for financial power in this new land. He knew that Englishmen said about Indians in Africa: "They live on the smell of an oil-rag," and could find no ground on which to meet them. It was a mess.

"All like me, sir? I don't know. There are many of us who have never spoken to an Englishman unless it is about business."

"What a bloody shame," said Jervis. "Silly, isn't it? Don't you think so?" They each felt their guilt, a guilt of a kind indescribable, rooted in nothing save two worlds, one alive and as ruthless as it was just, and as unjust as it was generous, the other darker in its ruins, clinging to a dead world yet wanting the wristlet watches of the materialistic West which its new leaders taught it to despise. Across these ruins and these guilts they shook hands again, Jervis saying: "How bloody stupid we all are, eh? Well, one day we'll all have more sense." One day, yes.

"Good-bye, sir," said Abdul. "Salaams to the Major Sahib."

"Good-bye, Abdul. I'll see you in about a month. Keep some beer cold for me."

"I wonder why we've met at all?" Abdul pondered while he watched Jervis walk under the pepper trees, red dust at his heels. "Something will happen and he'll change. Something that is his race's fault and my race's fault too. None are guiltless." He searched his memory for some quotation from Ghalib which would mirror this guilt, this prison of race, but he could find nothing at the moment. He liked the British, and somewhere in that fact was India's whole trouble, but men differed as to where exactly. It would take honesty from both races to find where the ulcer lay, so much deeper than politics, than frigid viceroy or half-baked Congressmen with their words, their rolling, drugging, meaningless words.

He stirred the coals in his father's hookah and woke the snoring old man. "Drink," he said. "Drink hookah, Father," and the old man began to smoke and Abdul looked on, contented.

Chapter XXVIII

THE rains came in grey, blinding sheets, turning the red dust to a liquid mud, like thick blood against the grass. It poured for days, hammering on the tin roof of the house, soaking the land, and Jervis sniffed its smell on the earth like wet iron, a strange, new, metallic smell. He had not seen tropical rain before. He watched it strike the earth, where it created a dancing, silver explosion of water and flowed in streams among the freshening grasses. The house grew damp and the leather headband of his helmet turned green in a day. The Africans danced naked in the first downpour, their bodies like wet eels, and they yelled in ecstasy as they stamped and whirled in the red mud near their huts.

After the long burning approach to the rains, when the whole world about the farm had appeared to be dying in dry pastel colours of grey and red bluish dusts, quivering in the blazing light, the earth drank up the rain until it was full. The water flowed from it, pouring down hillsides, tearing cattle-tracks away, changing them to shallow ravines, the gradual erosion of Africa's rich red skin, and the old Major watched it with gloomy eyes. "See that," he said to Jervis. "That's erosion. The only thing is terracing and Kikuyu grass. I'm sick of telling the bloody *watu*. You'll have to be firm with them. Firmer than I've been." He had seen each rain eating the stamped-out cattle tracks into ravines. Too many hoofs. Zebra. The whole balance of nature awry. Jervis would have to do something about it.

"God, my rheumatics again." The old man held his hips, excruciated on the third day of the rains. "I'm cracking up all right."

"No, you're not," said Jervis, not caring, taken up in the sight of the land deluged to the horizon and the scintillating steam rising from the grass, long beams of dull golden light cutting through it as the clouds moved in grey masses across the wet sun. It poured down for hours, drenching the whole world, which had seemed to sigh relief on the first teeming day. Now it lay, sated by the leaden sheets of rain which lashed it with a loud, hissing urgency.

"Plenty more to come," the Major said, glancing at the

sky. "Glad I don't grow wheat, anyway." They puffed at their damp, swollen cigarettes.

A note came for Jervis in the afternoon. It said:

> DEAR JERVY,
>   Louie is tight and asleep and I think the baby will come to-night. I *think* for sure. Could you be a true angel and take a canoe to Loltugi and get Dr. Punter. You'll need chains.
>
> HELENA

He showed it to the old man. "H'm," he said when he had read it. "Brinden's been all right lately. Probably got tired waiting for the baby and opened a bottle. Poor Helena. Well, what are you waiting for, son? Go on. A nice trip you'll have too. I don't mind saying I'm glad it's not me driving in that. You've never driven in real mud, have you?" Jervis admitted that he had not. "Well," said the old man, "there's no black cotton soil on the way, so you're lucky there. But you'll find this red stuff will test your driving enough, as it is."

It did. It took Jervis until near midnight to reach Loltugi. The car was stuck seven times. Once he had given up, that was on the fourth occasion when the car stuck and churned itself up to the axles in the thick molten chocolate of the road. It was dark. He was sodden and cold and defeated. He sat at the wheel and cursed. After half an hour's straining, pushing, packing branches and stones under the rear wheels, and still the car was stuck, he was about to give up, stupid with exhaustion and anger, when Wangi said: "Once more, Bwana," and this time the car lurched its way out of the mud. He shook Wangi's muddy hand. "Bloody good, Wangi," he shouted through the noise of the rain, "you're a strong man. Good," and so on. Three times again they stuck until Jervis began to enjoy it, and his determination to reach Loltugi deepened until it was cold and dogged. They drove through the dark forest with its black trees streaming, the road a river of yellow shining water in the headlights.

He found Dr. Punter as he had found him on their first meeting, lying asleep in the arm-chair, the ash-tray full of cigarette ends, and a book lying open on his lap.

"Hallo, Doc," he said, when the old man woke up. "Do you never sleep in a bed?"

"Not now. I'm too old for it," said the old doctor, yawning. "God, son, you look as if you swam here. Had a bad trip? Well, I've got just the thing for you. Brandy and hot water." He crossed the room and took a tin kettle from a rusty oil stove. "See. I was expecting you. Now, don't tell me you're going to drag me out to Brinden's place at this hour." Jervis said he was sorry but that was the case.

"A new life entering the world," said Dr. Punter, assuming a pious expression. "And in the bloody rains at midnight. Well, mix yourself the brandy and I'll get my tools." The brandy was good, like melting fire in his cold belly, and Jervis sat down to enjoy it, savouring it because he needed it. He had done it, had overcome that awful sea of mud, and now he must do it again. He poured out more brandy and drank it greedily, the hot steam of the fumes tickling his nose and throat. He wished he could have given a hot brandy to Wangi, but "never give spirits to the *watu*," the Major had said during a discourse on the slow ruination of Africa. "Spirits destroy them. They can't stand drink." Poor Wangi. He had another brandy—for poor Wangi. All too soon the doctor was ready.

Jervis turned the car in the greasy mud and they started back in the pouring dark rain, his eyes peering through the rain spattering on the windshield. When the sun came up the road steamed before them and the country glittered in a mantle of rain jewels. They were bogged down time after time. Wangi was plastered from his eyes to his toes in red mud where the churning wheels had sprayed him while he pushed.

Jervis sat with Brinden while the doctor worked in the bedroom. They heard no sound, but Brinden was restless and worried. "Why," he kept saying. "Why do we bring kids into this bloody world?"

"Habit," Jervis suggested.

"Here I am, nearly out of my mind. And why? All over a kid. I was pretty far gone yesterday. I admit it. I drank too much. It was decent of you to drive all that way in the rain, Jervis. I'm grateful to you. But I suppose Helena will never forgive me. God, I'm a fool."

"Tell me something, Brinden. Why does a man drink *too* much? What is the reason? What causes it?"

"I don't really know," said Brinden. "It's very nice when you're half shot. The world looks a lot better and you go on until you're completely shot. That's all. I do it when I've been thinking a bit. I started boozing about five years ago when I knew Helena was stronger than I was. More guts, more drive. I don't think I ever got over that."

"Is it very hard?" Jervis asked, his voice carrying sympathy to the older man, who looked at him with what seemed a pathetic gratitude, but almost immediately the hard mask of irony came back again.

"Hard? No. Not now. You grow a kind of shell eventually but you never quite forgive. At least I can't. Queer, isn't it? But this damn kid will make a difference. A kid is supposed to distract you both from your war. Most husbands and wives spend their lives at war, at least the ones I know seem to. Comradeship in hate, so to speak, which is poisoned love. The kid alters that, I'm told. I hope it does."

"I hope so too," said Jervis sincerely, sorry for them both in their prisons of personality. "I'm free," he thought. "I'll always stay free and never be like this fellow with his acid heart." But he must try and sleep with Doreen again, that mound of resilient, struggling flesh.

The doctor came out and told Brinden it was a girl.

"A girl." Suddenly Brinden's face lit up. He smiled. "A girl," he said, lost in a brief thought. "I never thought of that. Why, I'm glad. A little girl." He shook the doctor's hand. "How clever of Helena to have done us a girl." He was happy, Jervis could see.

"If she can keep you off that bottle, Brinden, I'd say it's a good thing. Not that I couldn't do with a nip myself right now."

They wished the little girl and its mother luck over their tots of neat whisky.

When Brinden saw his wife lying still and calm in the bed, pale and beautiful, like warm marble, he was moved. She was like a new woman.

"I'm a bastard, Helena," he said, looking at her.

"I'm a bitch," she said. This attempt at dialogue made him uncomfortable.

"That's right," he agreed. "Nice sort of conversation, isn't it?" She smiled and closed her eyes. The baby resembled a boiled red monkey with a shrunken face. Brinden was not very taken with it but said it was wonderful. He felt happy, even against his will. How weird was life, how mysterious its emotional forces. One knows nothing.

"Don't forget the dipping this morning," she said in her new soft voice.

"Oh, yes, the dipping," he remembered. Diseases waiting out there to kill the cattle.

"Aren't you going to kiss me?" she asked. He kissed her, feeling nothing for her, only a weak compassion, yet there was a slow kindling of some new contentment. "Probably acceptance at last," he thought. "But even so, it's something." The struggle ending, truce, age not so far off now.

After breakfast, Jervis left the doctor and Brinden. He drove slowly home across the grass, through the herds of fat zebra towards whom he felt no longer that antagonism, that longing to kill. He had killed bigger game and had seen men killed by their claws. After the rains he would drive these zebra again, but without that former lust to destroy. Next time it would be work. The zebra kicked up their heels and surged past the car in a long, grey, dazzling gallop, rain flying from their hoofs in a fine, powdery spray. The sun was bright on the new grass and he smelled again the bitter, metallic scent of the soaking soil. He was tired and happy. He looked at Wangi beside him and wished it was Asmani sitting there. Asmani of the lively bright eyes and impatient, straining mind, but gone to earth, torn up by the lion. So much had passed, in a year, the biggest year so far of his life. The year of the lion. *Myaka ya Simba*.

The old man was sitting on the veranda when he got back. "Hallo there, son. You've had a long trip, eh? How's Helena?"

"A girl."

"That's good. Makes the place quite domestic, doesn't it, hearing that. Quite civilised. It's as if the place was really settled at last now a baby's been born here. I was thinking about it just now. In a way I preferred the country the way it was, a man's country. But now it's another kind of country with a baby in it." He gave a long sigh. "How things change. I always disliked change, but having you here has made a lot of things different. And now this baby. It's a different Africa."

Jervis saw what he meant. He, too, liked the Africa of the old man's memory and he held on to it, but it was going, slowly, yet surely. The lions were out there but they would die. He had claimed two of them but there would be more to kill, and then, none. Schools and shops and buses, roads of asphalt to Sabuga, a long way away yet, but he saw what the old man meant.

"I wonder if the Italians will get stuck in that rain up there," said Fawn-Cochley. Away in the blue mists, softer now like thin smoky wool, Abyssinia lay awaiting its defeat. They looked at the horizon and the vague, dark blueness of hills hundreds of miles away under a grey sky.

"Your lion skins have come back. Twaruko brought them back from Guyu in the ox-wagon to-day."

Nyangi brought them. They were soft from the tanner's hand. He fingered the bullet holes. "This is the skin I want," said Jervis. He pointed to the ragged hole where the rotting wound had been. This was "the lion", the real lion who had killed Browning, clawed Charanga to his passive death, and then had slain the first African who had come beyond the strangeness into Jervis's affection.

"This one killed three men," he told the Major. "Strange, isn't it, just the skin all clean and neat now on the veranda." He felt the long claws: they were clean and polished now, the quiet relics of a stilled spirit.

"Yes, you got a good lion there," said the old man. "You can call yourself a settler now. D'you feel like a settler now?"

"Yes, I do," said Jervis. "I don't feel a stranger here any more. It's an interesting feeling." It was like age, perhaps, almost a mellowing.

"You'll see a different Africa from this one. I won't. And I'm glad. I've had the best of it." An Africa impossible to describe to the younger man. An Africa of innocence and fierceness, still there, but falling back before the new men and their machines. He looked down on to the great plains, wishing he was young again, not in this Africa, but in that other one now gone, of the red Masai with their flaring, arrogant nostrils and their lanky, lazy beauty, and of the land in which the ox-wagon could turn and plod to a hundred new horizons.

"You'll have a lot of problems in the future, son," he said. He lay back in the cane-chair, watching Jervis fold up the lion skin.

"*We* will," said Jervis, his eyebrows raised in question. "*We*." He did not like this mood of the old man's.

"No, *you* will, son. Not me. *You*."

THE END